Carnage from the Cursed Crown

The Kier and Levett Mystery Series
Book 5

Deb Marlowe

© Copyright 2024 by Deb Marlowe
Text by Deb Marlowe
Cover by Kim Killion

Dragonblade Publishing, Inc. is an imprint of Kathryn Le Veque Novels, Inc.
P.O. Box 23
Moreno Valley, CA 92556
ceo@dragonbladepublishing.com

Produced in the United States of America

First Edition August 2024
Print Edition

Reproduction of any kind except where it pertains to short quotes in relation to advertising or promotion is strictly prohibited.

All Rights Reserved.

The characters and events portrayed in this book are fictitious. Any similarity to real persons, living or dead, is purely coincidental and not intended by the author.

ARE YOU SIGNED UP FOR DRAGONBLADE'S BLOG?

You'll get the latest news and information on exclusive giveaways, exclusive excerpts, coming releases, sales, free books, cover reveals and more.

Check out our complete list of authors, too!

No spam, no junk. That's a promise!

Sign Up Here

www.dragonbladepublishing.com

⟫⟪

Dearest Reader;

Thank you for your support of a small press. At Dragonblade Publishing, we strive to bring you the highest quality Historical Romance from some of the best authors in the business. Without your support, there is no 'us', so we sincerely hope you adore these stories and find some new favorite authors along the way.

Happy Reading!

CEO, Dragonblade Publishing

ADDITIONAL DRAGONBLADE BOOKS BY
AUTHOR DEB MARLOWE

The Kier and Levett Mystery Series
A Killer in the Crystal Palace (Book 1)
Death from the Druid's Grove (Book 2)
Murder on the Mirrored Lake (Book 3)
Revenge in the Rogue's Hideaway (Book 4)
Carnage from the Cursed Crown (Book 5)

For all the readers who have worried over and cheered for Niall and Kara, I thank you a million times over for your passion.

Prologue

East Lothian, Scotland
1852

O*F ALL THE* arsinine *notions.*
He hunched against the cold wind as he crested the ridge, limping with each step. Hell and damnation, the horse had likely reached home by now. What business had the nag tossing him like that? Spooked by wind-swept branches? As if it was a high-strung thoroughbred instead of an overblown plow horse!

He sneered in disgust and kept up a continuous grumble as he headed downhill. Cripes, but his knee hurt more going down than up. He took the trail that led away from the house and out toward the dig site.

'Twas a ridiculous errand and a bedamned time to be sent on it, too. What person in his right mind sent such a message? And in the middle of the night?

Ah, but that one—he was a strange bird and no mistake. Everyone knew he was more than a bit off. Sending messages for meetings at midnight came low on the list of oddities he'd been accused of.

He shivered as he entered a copse. Here, even the scant light of the stars and the low moon was blocked out. Maybe the horse knew something he didn't? There was something in the air tonight. A taste of something more than the salt in the wind. Failure, perhaps. Betrayal. A hint of doom?

Bah! No. He banished such thoughts. He would not let it be so. It was just the lingering smoke in the air, still hanging about after yesterday evening's bonfires. And the air of change. How incredibly far his life had shifted in the few hours since those fires had been lit! But he was full of spite and anger and determination and he would not be bested.

He left the wood and moved through the ring of blackened circles and the art piece they surrounded. Going through the open spot in the ruins of the perimeter wall, he heaved a sigh, as he did nearly every day. The job had never held any interest for him, but he'd spent his days out here, digging, sifting, lifting as he was bidden.

No longer, though. *Everything* was going to change. And finally, at that thought, his spirits lifted. He'd be a different man soon. And the others would have to change and adjust as well, for he would be pursuing his own passions. He'd delivered the damned message—but it was the last request he'd be obliged to fulfill. Tomorrow was a new day. For them all. He'd take the next step toward an entirely new life.

He stopped near one of the sunken hut circles. "Ho! Are ye still here?"

An indistinct answering cry echoed. From the furthest hut? He moved toward it, sighing. There was no sign of a torch or lantern. Had the blasted man gone completely cracked?

"Where are ye?" He peered into the dark. "I gave your message to the man's serving woman. The old besom wouldn't even let me in the door. There's no use for you to wait about here tonight. She insisted 'twas the sort of news a man heard in the daylight, after a belly full of breakfast. He'll not even hear it until the morning."

The only response was the rush of the wind.

Had he imagined that answer to his call? Had it only been the sound of the sea? He cursed under his breath. It would be just like the man to not be here. And where would he be instead? He thought no one knew his secrets. Well, he was wrong. Likely he'd snuck away again, right to the place he shouldn't be going.

But no. There was the sound of shifting rock on the other side of the hut circle. And another. Damn it, this circle had the deepest depression of them all. The others were shallow, but this last one had sunk a good ten feet. Had the daft fool had an accident? Hurt himself?

He stepped closer and stumbled on something set near the rim.

"Holy shite!"

He wobbled like Cook's fancy jelly and nearly went over, but he managed to right himself. Fury coursed through him. What gobshite set this here? He might have fallen in, broken a leg or cracked his neck. He knew this place like the back of his hand. Whatever it was, it hadn't been here earlier today.

He bent down to feel the object and flinched at the whistle of air as something swept past—just where his head had just been.

He straightened. "What the—?"

His words and his air left him as the return swing of the wooden post hit him hard in the gut. Off balance again, he staggered, gasping for the breath that had left him in a *whoosh*. Stars burst in front of his eyes as the post swung again, striking him in the back of the head. The meaty *thunk* of it was all he heard as he tripped over the object at his feet and tumbled headfirst into the pit.

He didn't hear the snap in his spine, but he felt the flash of pain. He stared up at the night sky. It took only seconds for the darkness to swallow the stars—and he was gone.

Chapter One

Thirty hours earlier ...

Miss Kara Levett leaned forward in a futile effort to speed the carriage along. They moved along the coast road at a fast clip, but they were behind schedule. She fixed her gaze out the window, but not even the brilliant sunset over the sea could distract her from her impatience.

Across from her, her friend Gyda Winther cast a jaundiced eye over the landscape. "I think they must have granted Niall this title just to get him away from London and settled in the back of beyond."

Niall. Just hearing her betrothed's name ratcheted Kara's anxiety higher. She wished they'd arrived already. Nearly a month since she'd seen him. They had rarely been apart so long since the fateful day he'd snatched her from the Crystal Palace to prevent her from being accused of murder.

"King William gifted the title to Niall's grandmother long ago," she reminded Gyda. "I'm sure he chose the best extinct title the Crown had available to grant."

Kara hadn't known the secrets in Niall's past when they met. Almost no one had. She'd learned to know his kindness and warmth, his artistic soul, and the breadth and strength of both his mind and his forge artist's body. He'd stood by her as she fought to clear her name, and in each other they had eventually found... everything. They'd waded together through several adventures and bonded in heart and mind. She'd scarcely been able to believe her luck in finding, at last, a man who encouraged her to embrace her differences and lauded them instead of being threatened by them.

"I know you are nervous," Gyda said quietly. "But I don't think you should worry."

Kara could hardly believe the state of her own mind. She wasn't the sort who wallowed in worry. Even when the secrets of Niall's past were exposed, she hadn't flinched. So his mother had been the secret child of King George IV and his illegal bride, Maria Fitzherbert? Kara hadn't turned a hair. Knowing that secret—and hiding it—had helped shape Niall into the man she loved.

But this latest development? Niall's past had been exposed when a league of criminals tried to use them to damage the English government and the balance of power across Europe. The knowledge had been kept as quiet as possible, but men in the justice system and the Home Office had learned the truth—as had the royal family. Those esteemed personages had sent word of their approval of his efforts to defeat the League of Dissolution, along with encouragement for Niall to take up the title that had been granted to his grandmother and her heirs.

And that? The thought of a ducal title that would have most women spinning in rapture? It scared her in a way that villains and murderers had failed to do.

"Niall is not going to change," Gyda said, reaching across and pressing her hand.

"No," Kara agreed. "They are placing power, land, and people in his charge, and he will handle it all beautifully. He has no need to change. He is honorable, strong, and responsible. He's everything that a duke should be."

"You are all of those things, too, Kara."

"And that's the root of it," she said, allowing a tinge of the worry she felt to color her words. "They won't wish for me to be any of those things. I've been in Society, Gyda. My father was a baron. I've spent plenty of time in that world. Women there are ... not like me. They are expected to be quiet, loyal, pretty, and fertile. And nothing else."

Gyda grimaced. "Well, you are loyal and pretty. Two out of four isn't so bad, I suppose."

Kara laughed.

"Fertile?" Her friend raised a brow. "That has yet to be proven. But you'll never be quiet."

"I never did manage it. Nor could I fade into the background or keep my opinions to myself. I couldn't content myself with dressing fashionably and throwing dinner parties. I couldn't give up my art or my interest in science. I definitely could not leave the running of my family businesses to someone else, without a say in the planning of it all."

"Niall will never ask you to abandon any of that."

"I know! Do you know how much it's meant to me? His acceptance of all the things that Society despised—all the things that make me who I am? Gyda, this last year, it's the first time I've felt as if I could truly breathe. The utter relief and freedom I've found with him ..." Her eyes closed. "I broke free of all of that judgment and disapproval once. Now, I'll be forced to enter that world again. And though I hate the thought of taking on the burden of their scrutiny again, I will do it for him. But the thought that's killing me is knowing I'll be exposing Niall to the same."

"They will love Niall all while wondering why he doesn't take you in hand?"

"Exactly."

Gyda scoffed. "I predict he won't give a damn."

"That's because *you've* never given a damn. It's admirable. You inspire me. But Niall does care what others think of him, deep down. It's all part and parcel of growing up as he did. He'll already be facing speculation because of the way he's coming into the title. I hate to add to it." And Kara feared he might come to resent it.

"You are worrying too much," Gyda chided. "Don't borrow trouble. It will arrive on its own." She lifted a brow. "It always does."

"That's true enough." Perhaps she was right. Perhaps Kara should let her worry go and just enjoy the thought of seeing Niall again.

Frowning, Gyda leaned toward the window. "Did you say we'd be passing by Niall's land on the way?"

"Near to it, at the least. The acreage of his new estate shares a section of a border with Lord Balstone's. And surely we must be getting close to Balburn House by now."

"Well, I sincerely hope that those houses are not Niall's responsibility."

Kara moved to see what she meant. The road had veered inland, away from the cliff tops over the sea. It rode the top of a ridge at the moment. She could look down to see a row of stone tenant homes built into the hillside. The thatch was ragged, the stone crumbling in places. Shutters hung askew or lay on the ground. Grubby children chased each other in a dusty lane.

"Good heavens. Surely they are not Niall's? I know the title has been extinct, but the Crown appointed a land agent."

"Perhaps he pocketed the money meant for improvements?" Gyda speculated. "Or perhaps these are not Niall's lands, but the earl's?"

"It doesn't speak well of his management if they are," Kara said quietly.

"Tell me why again. Why did Niall agree to this project? Bronze sculpture is not exactly his usual art form."

Kara's mouth twisted in amusement. "Because he had no forge in Edinburgh? He came when he was summoned as a Scottish peer, after the general election. He met with the lord clerk register. He announced his vote for the sixteen Scottish representative peers. But, honestly, he became incredibly restless once all the formalities were done."

"They knew what they were doing, didn't they? Giving him a title that doesn't allow him to take a seat in the House of Lords in London?"

"Niall thinks they just want to watch him, to evaluate how he handles the title before they think of giving him any further power. They could, you know. All they would have to do is grant him a peerage in Great Britain."

"Sneaky devils."

"He is resigned. But he was also bored. We were to wait for the land agent to come up from London to turn over the keys and deeds to the estate, but he was delayed. Niall was positively fidgety until the Earl of Balstone approached him with the idea. Niall liked the man's passion for his archeological subject. He liked the idea of trying something new. And it would only require a studio for sculpting, instead of a forge, which was much more easily obtained."

"Easy—until it comes time to craft the molds and pour the metal," Gyda scoffed.

"Well, yes. And that is why he went with Balstone to his home to accomplish those last, important steps."

"While you waited in town for our arrival," Gyda said sympathetically.

"Well, we did miss you and Turner and Harold dreadfully. And Lord Stayme, too, of course."

"The old man sends his greetings, and I'm to tell you to hop back to London quickly." At Kara's worried look, Gyda shook her head. "Don't worry. He's happily up to his ears in some extremely sensitive search for a foreign agent. He'll be well occupied. But what of you?"

"I was happy to stay back to meet you."

"You must have been bored, especially after Mrs. Braddock left you as well."

"No, I was fine. I certainly would never have held Eleanor back from accepting such a promising commission. It was kind of her to come along as my companion and chaperone to begin with, and she did wait until Niall left for Balburn House before she departed for France." Kara shrugged. "I knew you all would be arriving shortly, so I took the chance to acquaint myself with some of the city's artistic community. Edinburgh is a fascinating city with much to see and plenty of people who are interested in history, art, and science." She grinned sheepishly. "And there was the other consideration that kept me in the city."

Gyda waited expectantly.

"The slight fact that I wasn't invited to accompany Niall to Balburn House."

Gyda laughed. "Well, you are invited now." She made a face. "Too bad we will be arriving late."

"I know," Kara fretted. Her foot tapped out her anxiety and impatience. "I know you cannot prevent something like a horse going lame, but the delay! I hate to start off an acquaintance with neighbors on a tardy foot."

"Perhaps your reputation precedes you and they will put it down to your unladylike ways."

"Thank you, Gyda. You are so reassuring." Kara couldn't help but grin.

"You are welcome." Her friend gestured. "Look. There it is, I think."

The road had begun to descend, but they were still high enough to spot the roofline in the distance.

"Good." Kara sighed in relief as she eyed the brilliant colors still painting a last strip of sky. "Niall said in his last letter that the ceremony is planned to take place once full dark arrives. We should just make it." She touched careful fingers to her hat and coiffure. "How do I look?"

She'd been saving this carriage dress and coat for a special occasion. The green wool was warm and brightened by bronze trimmings and furred cuffs. A fall of cream lace at her throat bore the same bronze trim. The skirts were graced with an elegant flounce. She wanted to make Niall proud when she met some of the people that would make up their social circle when they resided here, for at least part of the year.

"You are as bonny as heather, isn't that what they say up here?" Gyda tugged her own blue coat tighter. "That wind is biting. I hope they have whisky to warm our blood if they mean to make us mill around outside. That's one thing the Scots do well."

"I'm sure there will be something to warm us." They passed through a wood as they headed down and toward the house. Kara noticed it was tangled and overgrown. Perhaps the tenant cottages were not the only things needing attention?

"Well," Gyda said as the carriage turned into a long drive. She eyed the place as they made their way through a stone gate and past an ancient wall. "I would venture to guess that his lordship is not married."

"I don't know, one way or another. But what makes you say so?"

"Look at this place." Gyda was pressed close to the window. "It's lacking a woman's touch. So plain. Nary a trellis, vine, fountain, or pot to ease the eye. Not at all like you keep Bluefield Park."

It was austere, Kara agreed silently as the carriage rolled to a stop and they stepped down. There was no lawn or anything green within the stone perimeter of the wall. Only gravel. Several carriages were parked along the circle near the house, but there was no sign of life until a footman opened the door and a butler emerged to stand at stiff attention.

"Miss Levett?" he asked as she approached.

"I am she," she said with a smile. "And this is my friend, Miss

Winther."

"We expected you earlier," he said flatly. And yet the disapproval was clear.

Kara raised a brow. "We had difficulties with our hired horses. But I hope we are in time for the ceremony?"

He gave a short nod. "Just in time. They are ready to begin. If you will step inside?"

Gyda stepped close. "Odin's arse, but he looks like he should be nose down, trailing the scent of a fox through the brush. Those drooping eyes! Those sagging jowls! He's more like a hound than a butler."

"Shh." Kara gave her friend an admonishing look, but the servant did resemble a hunting hound, right down to the long ears. "Let's just go find Niall."

They swept in. Kara paused to admire the worn flagstone floor and the ancient carved paneling.

"Here you are, then. Miss Levett?" A middle-aged woman entered the entry hall from the left. The sound of a party surged in with her. But the laughter, conversation, and clink of glasses were cut off again when she closed the door.

"Yes," Kara began, but she didn't get a chance to say more.

"We expected your arrival earlier." The woman was dressed in a black gown, obviously expensive and dripping with jet-beaded fringe. Her hair was dark and piled high, and her tight expression made it appear as if her maid had been too vigorous with the pins.

Kara drew a breath and reached for patience. "Yes. Apologies. We had difficulties—"

"Never mind it now. You'll want to go upstairs and change. A pity. You'll miss the ceremony."

"Nonsense," Gyda declared. "The party is to take place outside, is it not?"

"The unveiling is," the woman answered shortly.

"Well, then. We are dressed and ready for the evening in the open air."

The woman's mouth pursed even tighter. "Very well. If you are content to attend in all of your road dirt."

Kara gave a little laugh. "I assure you, we did not tend to the lame horse ourselves. We are more than ready, Mrs....?"

The woman lifted her chin. "I am Mrs. Grier, sister to Lord Balstone. As my brother is unmarried, I act as his unofficial hostess and mistress of Balburn House." She sighed in resignation. "Come along, then. Everyone will be making their way outside. You can bring up the rear."

"Thank you," Kara said softly.

"Yes, your warm welcome has been a delight," Gyda told her, baring her teeth.

The woman appeared unaffected. "Bring my coat and gloves, Largray," she told the butler. She opened the door and actually clapped her hands at them. "Come, come."

"Yes, Kara, don't dawdle." Gyda grinned and tugged her forward. "Let us go and see Niall's latest creation."

That was all Kara needed to hear to soothe her ruffled feathers. Moving past Mrs. Grier and her pinched expression, she hurried in the direction of the party.

⋙⋘

NIALL KIER, THE newly minted Duke of Sedwick, stood still and silent in the dark. The preparations were done. The piece was mounted on its sturdy base. The plantings were arranged. He was happy with the final results. As he'd hoped, the figures looked natural, as if they belonged in this distinctive place.

It had been an intriguing change of pace, taking part in a project like this. He'd learned new skills, and, most importantly, he felt that he'd accomplished something special. Still, he was looking forward to getting back to his forge.

Or, more correctly, he was looking forward to building his new forge—on his new estate at Tallenford Priory. Smiling into the dark, he pulled in a deep breath of sea-touched air. His estate. His land. His people. He hadn't expected this flood of contentment at the idea, but he couldn't deny it, any more than he could hold back his feelings of satisfaction and vindication.

The land agent had arrived yesterday. Niall held all the deeds and paperwork now, as well as the keys. Tomorrow. Tomorrow he and Kara would go and inspect their new home.

He just had to get through the drama of this evening.

Balstone had insisted on it all. The ceremony. The audience. The flamboyant flair of the unveiling. The man enjoyed anything that enhanced interest in his archeological project—and his own reputation in the field. No doubt there would be a few journalists included in the crowd tonight.

Ah, and here they came. Niall spotted the flicker of candlelight in the trees.

"They come!" Balstone said from his position ahead of him. The man's excitement was nearly palpable.

"I see them." Niall fervently hoped Kara was in the procession making their way from the house. He'd expected her to arrive in time for an early dinner, but doubtless there had been a delay. He didn't bother worrying. The threats and repercussions he'd been apprehensive about after the exposure of his family history had never emerged. Also, she was traveling with his assistant, Gyda. Together, those two made as formidable a pair as he'd ever seen.

The parade of guests arrived in the clearing before the ruins of a stone perimeter wall. As they had practiced, several footmen—the only ones allowed to carry illumination, in the form of short candles—herded the group into a semicircle at the edge of the wood. There were a few murmurings and a bit of scuffling as they took their places, but the crowd remained mostly silent, as they'd been asked. As they settled, the footmen doused their candles.

A few excited whispers were heard. Moments passed. Velvet night embraced the space. The sea wind blew. The crash of the surf, not so far away, sounded abruptly louder.

And then Balstone opened his lantern, just enough to cast a small circle of light around him—and no further.

"Welcome! Friends, family, neighbors, and honored colleagues, I thank you for coming to the unveiling of an exciting new piece of art in my family's collection, a new tribute to the history of Balburn House, our family, and, indeed, our community and its rich history."

Someone applauded, but Lord Balstone was only getting started.

"Many of you know of my family's connection to the ancient people that once occupied these lands, and to the distinguished ruling class that led them. The Cursed Crown, an artifact believed to date from the late Bronze Age, has been passed down in our family for generations."

"Aye. Along with the trouble it brings," someone intoned, loud enough to be heard.

"Yes, yes. The nonsensical rumors and gossip about the curse will persist," Balstone said dismissively. "But we live in an age of science, of reason. The crown always fascinated my father. The history behind it inspired him, first in naming his children"—he paused for a second as a quiet wave of laughter rolled over the crowd—"and it also inspired him to sift through multitudes of papers and parish records as he tried to trace the lineage of the family as far back as he could discover, always hoping to reach the ancestor who wore the crown."

Balstone gestured, the movement encompassing the dark, open space around them. "My own studies took me down a different path. It began the fateful day when, as a young man, I wandered into this place. It was an overgrown mess then, but in the tangle I found something odd. Something old. It was the ruins of the perimeter wall that stands behind me. I followed the length of it, caught up in awe at the age and enormity of it—and from that day, I have dedicated myself to exploring this fascinating archeological site. From the clearing of the land, to the unearthing of the entire wall, to the discovery of ten hut circles inside and a midden heap just beyond, I have made a career, over the years, joyfully unearthing one discovery after the next. My father chased the glory of a kingly ancestor, but I have spent countless days discovering the trinkets and small treasures that paint a picture of our ancestors' simple daily lives. I've found immense satisfaction in learning about the tools they used, the weapons they made, and the modest baubles they wore. It was only recently that a new idea came to me. A different way to pay tribute to those who lived and died right here."

Raising his lantern, Balstone reached up and shuttered it. The darkness rushed in again, causing the crowd to begin to mutter. Then, in a perfect precision of timing, seven bonfires flared to life all at once.

The wood had been doused with accelerant to make the flames leap high almost at once. Arrayed in a circle around Niall's newest work of art, the fires burned high, sending light to reflect off the lines and curves of the bronze figures.

"I give you *A Bronze Age Family*," Balstone declared.

Niall had depicted an early British man and woman, standing in conversation, a child sitting at their feet. Balstone had extensive resources in his library and in his collection, and he'd pored over them with Niall in consultation. Niall had appreciated the input, and he felt comfortable with the representation he had created. The figure of the man wore a short tunic, a close-fitting hat, and a wide, decorated belt from which hung a sword and a shorter blade. His cape was fastened at the front with a decorative medallion that was a close copy of one that Lord Balstone had unearthed here. The woman wore long skirts and a cropped top. Her belt was wider and adorned with three metal plates, intricately carved and with raised points in the middle. The child wore a simple tunic belted with rope and played with a collection of shells. In the fluttering light, they seemed almost alive.

The crowd appeared to be riveted at the unveiling, but Niall was searching their number for a familiar face … *There.*

He was meant to stay in this spot and await his cue, but his heart leapt and his feet were moving the instant he caught a glimpse of Kara pushing her way to the front. He swept her into his arms, circling with her once then kissing her deeply, and silently rejoicing when she wholeheartedly returned his embrace. "Saints," he said, pulling back. "You are a sight for sore eyes." He raked his gaze along her smart ensemble and comely form. "If I am ever daft enough to try to stay away from you so long again, remind me of the sheer stupidity of such a notion."

"Next time I'll go along with you, or come after you sooner." She glanced over at Balstone's dour sister. "Invitation be damned."

Laughing, he kissed her again.

The sound of a clearing throat sounded close by. "Ahem," Gyda said, talking over Balstone's continuing speech. "I've arrived too, don't forget."

Niall broke the kiss and reached out for her, sweeping her into a shared embrace. "Aye," he said gruffly. "And I'm grateful for it."

A few titters sounded in the crowd and Niall looked up, then over his shoulder. Balstone was staring, his brows raised, and Niall realized he'd missed his cue.

"As I said, I am very grateful to Niall Kier, our new neighbor and the new Duke of Sedwick," Balstone repeated, raising his hands toward the crowd. "Come, let us hear from the artist!"

Laughter and encouragement rang out. Niall let go of both women with a rueful smile. Moving back into the ring of bonfires, he nodded his thanks for the applause and waited for it to die down.

"I wish to thank Lord Balstone for the opportunity to create this piece. It has been an adventure, to be sure. Most of my work is done in the forge, so I was grateful for the chance to stretch my wings a little and experiment with sculpting. I've learned new skills, always a welcome development, and I am very pleased with the end result and how it fits into its new home." He smiled at their host. "It was Balstone's passion for his subject that convinced me to take on this project. I admit, I previously had no knowledge of our distant ancestors or their way of life. I didn't even know enough to realize I could cultivate an interest, but Balstone is generous with his knowledge and expertise."

"I think you mean relentless," someone called out.

Niall grinned. "I think *you* mean enthusiastic," he replied. "And I will never fault a man for sharing his passions and interests. Indeed, I had no notion of how much we can learn from archeological pursuits like this one, both about our forebears and about ourselves. I find it a noble pursuit, to look back and contemplate how far we've come, to consider how and why and even where we go from here." He lifted his chin toward Balstone. "I thank you, sir, for the opportunity to learn about your work and the broader components of your field. I've found it so interesting that I hope to keep abreast of it all." He shrugged. "Perhaps someday I will have the chance to dabble in such discoveries myself, but until then …" He gave a little bow. "I will happily celebrate yours."

Straightening, he caught a strange expression on Balstone's face as he stared back at him. Niall blinked and wondered what he'd said wrong, for he thought he saw both fear and hostility cross the man's face.

It disappeared quickly, though, as the crowd moved forward to congratulate them both and the footmen began to circulate with trays of champagne. Stepping through the crowd, he reached for Kara and brought her in close to his side before turning to greet the surge of guests with a smile.

Chapter Two

KARA KEPT CLOSE as Niall was inundated with congratulations and questions. Everyone was extremely complimentary—and also very curious. His status as a new duke and the new owner of Tallenford Priory, as well as the night's celebrated artist, made him the object of everyone's interest. He fielded the attention with his usual ease and assurance, and he unfailingly introduced her as his betrothed or as his future duchess. Thankfully, the guests were all kind, and she encountered no repeat of the veiled hostility their hostess had shown.

"Your Grace!" someone called.

Kara exchanged a look with Gyda. Neither of them had adjusted to the formalities of Niall's new title.

"That's going to take some getting used to," Gyda whispered. "Champagne might help. I'm off to search out one of those footmen."

Kara nodded as her friend slipped away and the man who had hailed Niall arrived at his side.

"Well done, sir!" the man said, beaming. "Very well done, indeed." He was a ruggedly handsome, dark-haired gentleman, a little older than Niall, perhaps. He clapped her betrothed on the back. "I cannot count the number of times I've heard Balstone drone on about the people that lived in those huts back there, but you've made them come to life." He stared over at the bronze figures, shaking his head. "How real they look, especially in the firelight."

"Thank you." Niall clasped the man's shoulder in return. "Full credit to Balstone for dreaming up the firelit revelation. Please, allow me to present my fiancée, Miss Kara Levett. Kara, Mr. Dalwiddie and his wife will be our nearest neighbors. They own the land on the other side of the priory."

Kara brightened. "How lovely! I am very glad to meet you, Mr. Dalwiddie."

The gentleman gave her a bow and a grin. "My wife was thrilled to hear you would be here this evening. She's an English transplant as well." He gazed out over the surrounding crush. "She was right behind me a moment ago. Kate? Kate!"

"Coming!" A small woman slipped through the crowd to Mr. Dalwiddie's side. Dipping a curtsy to Niall, she looked eagerly between them. "A triumph, Your Grace. Your art is magnificent." She raised her brows in Kara's direction. "And this must be Miss Levett?"

"She is," Niall said with pride. "Miss Kara Levett, meet our soon-to-be neighbor, Mrs. Kathryn Dalwiddie."

The woman was short-statured and very thin, but there was a bloom of health in her cheeks and her grip was as firm as her smile was friendly as she took Kara's hand. "Oh, I am so happy to meet you at last. I've heard ever so much about you, and I know we will be fast friends."

"I'm sure we will be." The woman's friendly eagerness soothed Kara's nerves.

"Oh, but one vital thing I have not heard." Mrs. Dalwiddie watched her expectantly. "Do you ride?"

Kara blinked in surprise. "Oh. Yes. Of course."

Mr. Dalwiddie rolled his eyes. "Kate, engage the lady in a bit of small talk before you start grilling her about her experience with horses." His smile managed to convey both tolerance and pride. "My wife is a bit horse mad, Miss Levett. She's a bruising rider and loves the hunt."

"I was born in Leicestershire," Mrs. Dalwiddie confessed. "The hunt is in my blood."

"That area is home to the Quorn, is it not?" Kara asked.

"It is indeed." The lady looked thrilled that Kara was familiar with the topic.

"My Kate is a skilled trainer." Mr. Dalwiddie's pride was evident. "Her hunters are gaining quite a reputation."

"It takes a remarkably steady mount to be a good hunter, does it not?" Niall asked.

"Indeed," Mrs. Dalwiddie said. "The horse needs a calm disposition to tolerate the milling pack, the noise, the crowd of horses and riders. There are other requirements as well—"

"Which we will discuss some other time," her husband interrupted. He looked to Kara. "Perhaps when you join us for dinner one evening?"

"That sounds lovely. Thank you." Kara hesitated a moment. "Mr. Dalwiddie, you mentioned that your wife is a transplant." She looked to the other woman. "Has being English been an issue for you? Have you encountered much ... resistance? Since you moved here?" She couldn't help but glance over at Mrs. Grier.

Mrs. Dalwiddie's brows rose high. "Oh dear. Had a grapple with Elfred Grier already, have you?"

"Don't worry," her husband said in a reassuring tone. "Elfred is gruff with nearly everyone."

"But especially with me," his wife declared. "And not because of my English blood, but because she once fancied my husband for herself—or so I've been told by several local gossips."

Mr. Dalwiddie shook his head. "Oh, don't believe that old nonsense, Miss Levett. I've told Kate to ignore it. Dunstan, Elfred, and I all grew up together. She was older than us boys, but we three ranged all over the region as children, from sea to hills. I've always felt a brotherly fondness for her."

"I'm quite sure her feelings for you were not those of a sister," his wife said tartly. "But it does not matter now. She married elsewhere and you married me." She took her husband's arm and laid her head on his shoulder. "I'm quite sorry she was unfortunate in the loss of her husband, but I am not going anywhere."

"Nor I, my dear." Mr. Dalwiddie tucked his wife's hand in his arm and turned to Niall. "So, tell us what you think of the priory."

"I will let you know once I've seen it," Niall said easily.

"What?" The gentleman sounded as shocked as Kara felt. "You've been so close for weeks, and you still haven't seen it?"

"Well, I have been more than a bit occupied," Niall said, laughing. "And the estate agent just arrived yesterday with the deeds and the keys."

Kara softened as he smiled down at her.

"I decided to wait until Kara arrived to go over. We'll be spending a good part of all of our years there together. We should see it first together."

"Oh, Niall." Kara was deeply touched. "Thank you."

"How romantic," Mrs. Dalwiddie sighed. "Jacob, we need to remember to be more romantic."

"Yes, my dear. Let us start now and head over to get you a glass of champagne, shall we?"

"That sounds like a wonderful start." Mrs. Dalwiddie reached over to press Kara's hand. "I know you'll need a few days to settle in, but let's get together soon, shall we? I'll send an invitation." She grinned sheepishly. "And I will wait anxiously for a return summons, for I've been wanting to see the inside of the priory for ages!"

"You shall have it," Kara vowed. "As soon as we are able."

"What's this?" Lord Balstone approached. "You are not poaching my idea, Jacob, and trying to convince Sedwick to create something to liven up your old pile?"

"No indeed, Dunstan," Mr. Dalwiddie said with a laugh. "That glory is all yours. Very well thought out it was, too, old man." He looked again at the figures shown to such advantage in the firelight. "Livens up the site considerably. Now, if you will excuse us, I've promised my wife a glass of champagne."

The couple departed, and Lord Balstone bowed over Kara's hand as Niall introduced her. "I'm so glad you arrived in time, Miss Levett. It would have been a shame to miss this."

"I agree, sir. The pair of you have done a magnificent job."

Their host cast a wry glance after the Dalwiddies. "Angling for an invitation to the priory, were they? Everyone soon will be. None of the locals, nor even their parents, have seen the inside of the place. It's been a point of speculation for years, but, of course, the gossip has ramped up considerably since it was learned you were taking it over."

"We shall be sure to host an evening fête, once it is feasible," Niall said. "If only to satisfy everyone's curiosity."

His sarcasm was lost on Lord Balstone. Kara eyed the man, wondering why he seemed so twitchy and anxious, even after the unveiling had been so well received.

"Yes, yes. Good of you. It will be appreciated." The gentleman's eyes were darting around the crowd. "Have you spoken to any of the journalists yet?"

"I don't believe so." Niall paused. "At least, no one has presented themselves as such."

"Be careful what you say, is all I ask," Balstone pleaded. "I only wish for positive reactions to be reported."

"I have only positive things to say about our experience working together," Niall said mildly.

"Yes. Good." Balstone jerked his head to the right. "And be careful of my sister, too. Don't let her bully you over that land dispute."

Kara's grip on Niall's arm tightened as she felt him stiffen beside her.

"Dispute?" he asked.

"Oh, an old issue," Balstone said. "Something she's been plaguing the land agent about for ages. Something about a border disagreement. A bit of land that both estates lay claim to. She wants it for drainage purposes, or some such thing. I don't pay attention to those sorts of matters."

He didn't pay attention to many estate matters, if those tenant cottages and the tangled wood were any indication, Kara thought.

Niall shifted. "The agent never mentioned anything about it."

"He likely thought the matter settled. But Elfred will probably give it another go, now that you've taken over the land. It would be like her." Balstone straightened suddenly. "There. That is Holland, the editor of the *Edinburgh Archeological Review*. I'll introduce you."

He dragged the editor over, and Kara listened quietly while the men discussed the significant findings that had been uncovered at the site.

After a few minutes, the editor cleared his throat. "You know, Lord Balstone, I don't think my report can be considered complete without a look at the Cursed Crown."

Balstone frowned, but his answer was forestalled when his sister stepped close to the bronze figures and clapped her hands for attention. "The wind grows colder," she called out. "Those of you who wish to get out of it, take yourselves back to the parlor, where warm drinks and food will be made available."

"Ah." Mr. Holland rubbed his hands together. "And there is my chance. You will show me the crown, won't you, Balstone?"

"Of course," the man answered grimly. "It appears everyone is heading back. Let's join the rest of the party."

Kara held Niall back as the men moved off. "Very well done, Your Grace," she said with a grin. "You truly have created something special."

"Thank you, Your soon-to-be Grace." He looked over at the figures. "It was an interesting experience. I'm glad I did it." He returned her grin. "But I miss my forge. I hope there is a suitable spot for one at the priory."

"We'll make one, if there is not." She took both his hands, and for a moment, they stood gazing at each other, filling the air between them with warmth, anticipation, and promise for the future.

"Come, Sedwick!" Lord Balstone called.

Kara laughed. "They are a dictatorial pair, are they not? We had better follow," she said, pulling away and tugging him toward the house. "Honestly, I wouldn't mind a glimpse of that crown myself."

⇶⇷

NIALL HELD KARA'S hand as they moved inside. The majority of the guests had followed Balstone and Holland into the small parlor where the Cursed Crown was kept on display. It was shut away behind glass, but the lighting was arranged to show it to advantage. A great many people had squeezed into the room. They stood, shifting restlessly, straining to see the piece, and listening to Balstone talking at length about it.

Niall stood with Kara at the back, in the doorway to the parlor. She rose up on her toes, trying to see over the crowd. "I can scarcely catch a glimpse of it," she said on a sigh. "Are those truly emeralds and rubies?"

"I believe they are. We'll come for a look at it later, after the guests have gone," Niall promised. "It really is an interesting object, like nothing I've ever seen." The crown did indeed have a primitive feel to it. Fashioned of gold and made to look like a circle of branches and leaves, it bore ruby berries and emerald buds. He could easily picture it atop the brow of a Bronze Age warrior king like the one he'd fashioned for Balstone.

"Listen to him," someone said, close to Niall's ear. "Going on about tribal hierarchy when all they truly want to hear about is the curse."

Niall turned to find a tall blond man hovering behind him, eyeing the crowded room. "Finley," he said. "I wondered where you got to." He jerked his head toward the larger parlor across the entryway and, at the man's nod, pulled Kara over to the nearly empty room. Making the introductions, he clapped Finley on the back. "Mr. Edmund Finley is Balstone's assistant out at the dig," he told Kara. "He was a huge help when I was making the molds for the figures, and an even better one when I was wrestling them into their final places."

"How fortunate Niall was to have you, then, sir," said Kara. "What interesting work it must be, exploring the archeological site, helping with so many discoveries."

The man inclined his head. "Ah, but 'tis Dunstan who makes the discoveries. I just do the digging and the sifting, the clearing and the carrying."

"Still, I would venture you've learned much, being right at his side."

"I would, sure, did I not turn a deaf ear to him most days." When Kara looked surprised, Finley shrugged. "It's for my own sanity, miss. Lord Balstone does drone on, almost without ceasing."

Kara gave him an understanding nod, but then leaned in. "Surely you must be able to tell us about the curse, though?"

"Oh, aye."

"Is it real, do you think?" She glanced at Niall. "As a student of science, I tend to think such things are figments of people's imaginations. But as an artist? I sometimes wonder if there are not any number of things we think strange or unreal that we just don't yet understand."

"Oh, it's real enough. Folks around here have borne witness to it through the generations."

Kara brightened with interest. "How does it manifest? Accidents? Unexplained deaths?"

Finley chuckled. "Och, no, miss. It's not so bad as all of that. The curse does seem to settle differently on each successive head of the family. One might suffer a near-constant run of blighted crops. Another might see persistent bad luck with disease in the livestock. One was said to be unable to eat most anything without horrendous stomach pains and had to live on gruel and boiled ale. Dunstan's father himself, well, he had terrible bad luck with his wives. All three died early, not many years after they wed him."

"Good heavens. How terrible." Kara cast a sympathetic look back toward the small parlor. "And the current Lord Balstone?"

"Well, and they do say his lack of a wife can be laid at the curse's door, but in all honesty, I think he's been cursed by the burden of his devilish harpy of a sister."

Niall shifted and cleared his throat, and Finley had the grace to look ashamed. "Apologies, miss. It is true, I don't share in the interests of my … employers." He shrugged. "Ah, but it won't trouble them for long. I'll be moving on to pursue my own interests shortly."

Niall was surprised to hear it. "You'll be staying in the area, I hope?"

"Oh, aye." The man's whole expression brightened when he turned to Kara. "Have you ever played golf, miss? Sedwick has already told me he's not experienced the game, but I've promised to teach him."

"Golf?" Kara repeated. "No, I'm not familiar with it."

"Well, and you'll have to come and learn from me, as well."

"It's a local sport," Niall explained. "A game played with sticks—"

"Clubs," Finley corrected him.

"Clubs," Niall said with a nod of apology. "And small balls."

"Oh, and it's a grand sport, it is," Finley enthused. "It takes practice, a bit of muscle, a good eye and some coordination, but it is a great deal of fun. It gets you outside and into the good sea air. No two games are ever quite the same, you see. It changes with players, conditions, and equipment."

"In fact, Finley is developing his own equipment," Niall told her.

"Aye. A new sort of club." Finley grinned. "It is amazing how the smallest changes on the club can bring the most amazing variations in your shot. Adjust the angle of the club's face and you can see the differences in the lift and distance that the ball travels."

"Ah, so you are a scientist of a sort yourself," Kara said with a grin.

Finley looked surprised. "Aye. I never thought of it so, but aye." He looked as though he liked the idea. "The science of golf."

"And women play the game as well?" Kara asked.

"So they do. 'Tis said our own Mary, Queen of Scots, played with her courtiers. Fact is, some of the fishing villages down east have hosted women-only tournaments."

"Is that what you mean to do, Finley?" Niall asked. "Leave Balburn House and sell your new clubs to golf enthusiasts?"

"No, no." The man glanced around before he lowered his voice and spoke again. "I've got my eye on a fair bit of land out on the cliffs, not far outside the village."

"The village of Highfield?" Niall asked. He looked to Kara. "It's the closest village—closest to the priory, as well."

"Aye. That's it. The land has a decent house with it, too. I mean to have the place and set up my own course. People do travel down this way from Edinburgh for a holiday that includes a beach and a bit of golf. I'll turn the house into an inn and create a challenging course. I'll sell my special clubs, too, but what I mean to do is to offer a topnotch golf holiday."

"What a grand idea," Kara said.

"Your plan is front heavy with work," Niall began.

"I'm not afraid of work," Finley insisted.

"I know that firsthand," Niall said.

"And I've a bit of experience at running an inn." Finley lifted his head.

Niall nodded and spoke gently. "I meant to say that I think you'll do a grand job of it."

"Oh, yes," Kara agreed. "I wish you the greatest success, Mr. Finley."

"Thank you, miss. There is a wrinkle or two to iron out, but I shall make it happen. I hope you and the duke will be among the first to come to try it out, once my course is ready."

"I will look forward to it. I find it admirable that you have found a way to make your passion become your life's work."

"Well, I did have a bit of help," he said. Something over her shoulder caught his eye, and he straightened and took a step back. "Speaking of help, I'd best be heading out to make sure those bonfires have burned down." He nodded toward the other side of the room. "I see Mrs. Grier's son has returned. She'll be bringing him around to meet the party." Reaching for Kara's hand, he bent over it and spoke in lower tones again. "Now, you be sure not to let yourself get alone with Mr. William Grier, miss." Rising, he gave Niall a significant look, released Kara's hand, and slipped away.

Niall exchanged surprised glances with Kara and then shrugged at her questioning look. "I don't know," he said. "Balstone did mention he lives a bit of a fast life in London, but nothing worse than that." His fists tightened at the thought of her being treated with anything but respect. "But we'll take no chances."

He was prevented from continuing as Gyda made her way over to them, her eyes wide. "Who was that tall, chiseled specimen you were talking to?"

"Edmund Finley. Balstone's assistant out at the dig," he answered.

"Does the heavy work, does he?" she asked. "No wonder he has such shoulders."

"Not for much longer," Kara said. "Mr. Finley means to dedicate himself to golf."

Gyda blinked. "To what, now?"

"Golf. It's a bit of a local passion," Niall told her. "A game of hitting balls great distances, aiming for small holes. At least, that's how I understand it."

"Well, I'd play his game with him, if he would pose with a sword and one of my shields in exchange. With those cheekbones and that frown?" Gyda marveled. "Throw a fur over his shoulders and you'd have the makings of a Viking in the flesh." She lifted a shoulder. "In addition, I'm predisposed to like anyone willing to go toe to toe with our hostile hostess."

Niall raised a brow. "What did you see?"

"The pair of them were arguing in a back passage. I spotted them when I came up the servants' stairs. They were face to face and snarling like dogs."

"Gyda, have you been carousing with the servants again?" Kara asked, laughing.

"Tried to. It's the best way to gauge the temperament of a place—and to guarantee the best service." Gyda gave a shudder. "But if the staff here is any indication, this is not a comfortable house. Even the servants are embarrassed by the offerings at this party. Negus and shortbread? I hope no one else came hungry."

"There is champagne," Niall reminded her.

"Yes." Gyda lifted her glass. "And this is the last of it. You may laugh at me for being friendly with the footmen, but it does have advantages."

"Well, the shortbread is delicious," said Kara.

"But not very filling. If the cook hadn't fed me a bit of bread and jam, my stomach would be gnawing at my spine. No. It's no one's idea of hospitality, if you ask me. And if you put all of it together with that woman's frigid welcome, I rather think I'll return to Edinburgh tonight."

Kara made a face. "I believe our hired carriage has headed back already."

"It's no issue. I've had an offer for a ride."

"From whom?" asked Niall.

"From the wife of a member of Balstone's archeological club. The Brodies. Have you met them?"

"Briefly, I think."

"Oh dear. Should I return with her?" Kara asked Niall. "I have a feeling Mrs. Grier might not approve of my staying here without a female companion."

"Nonsense," he protested. "Mrs. Grier herself is more than adequate as a chaperone. And you and I are going to Tallenford Priory first thing in the morning." He glanced across the room at their hostess. "Mrs. Grier can be curt, to be sure, but Balstone is comfortable enough. Still, we will keep the remainder of our visit short."

"Depending on what you find at the priory," Gyda added. "If it's in as bad a condition as some of the structures we glimpsed, it may take some time to get it in shape. In any case, I am not taking the risk. I'll head back to the city and help Turner keep Harold entertained. The pair of you can send word about the state of the place and let us know when you are ready for us to come out." She downed the glass of champagne in her hand. "I'll go and ask for my bags to be brought back down, and I mean to meet that Viking before I go, too." Her eyes widened. "I'll go now, as a matter of fact, as your *curt* Mrs. Grier is approaching."

Gyda moved away just as a throat cleared behind Niall. With a glance at Kara, he turned to find their hostess standing there, her hand gripping a young man's arm.

"Duke," she said with a nod. "You've not yet had the chance to meet my son, as he has been away in the city. May I present Mr. William Grier? Will, this is His Grace, the Duke of Sedwick." She cast a sideways glance at Kara. "And Miss Kara Levett."

The young man gave Niall a bow and a nod, but he fastened his gaze on Kara. "Miss Levett, I have heard of you. You showcased your work at the Great Exhibition, did you not? I had the pleasure of being in London last summer and managed to snag a ticket."

"I did," she said pleasantly. "As did Niall."

"What a mad crush it was, wasn't it? I'm afraid I never got close enough to see your famous automaton." The boy had a wide, boxlike face and slashing black brows. Niall watched his large, dark eyes widen in anticipation. "But I did hear the gossip when you were accused of murder."

Kara froze.

The boy's mother's mouth dropped in shock. "Murder? Murder, did you say?"

"Don't worry, Mother. Miss Levett's name was cleared. The true perpetrator was caught."

"Still! Good heavens. But you, a woman, as an exhibitor? To place yourself in such a situation. To open yourself to such notoriety and shame …" Mrs. Grier trailed away and stared at Kara in disapproval.

"Oh, that's not the half of it," young Grier said almost gleefully. "Miss Levett was already notorious before the Exhibition." Despite his mother's closed expression, he continued. "Did you know you are hosting a great heiress, Mother? Miss Levett owns a great many businesses and manufactories. It made her quite the target when she was younger. She was the victim of a famous kidnapping."

"Kidnapped?" Mrs. Grier paled as she regarded Kara as if she were somehow … contaminated.

"Oh, no harm done," her son hurried on. "Miss Levett was saved. Though you became something of a target, did you not? A challenge to the lower orders. How many attempts were made to snatch you up again?"

Kara's chin lifted, but the color had drained from her face. Niall saw the hurt—and the worry—in her eyes. He fought the instinct to step in and extricate her. Kara was more than a match for this young ninny.

"Four," she answered distinctly. "But I evaded each one, because I was clever and canny and developed the skills I needed to do so. They were not so different from the lessons a young lady learns to help her in Society, you see. For example, a lady never knows when she will need to extricate herself from a rude conversation."

A direct hit. Niall acknowledged it with a lift of his glass. But the young fool did not know when to quit.

"It seems quite remarkable, then, that you would consent to exhibit at the Crystal Palace. You left yourself exposed to thousands of strangers."

"How foolish it seems," Mrs. Grier said with a shudder. "It all sounds most unsavory."

"The Great Exhibition was a triumph," Kara returned calmly. "It celebrated art, science, design, and opportunity from every corner of the world. I am proud to have had a part in it."

"Miss Levett was not the only woman exhibitor," Mr. Grier told his mother reassuringly. "Mrs. Caplin also had an exhibit, didn't she, Miss Levett?"

Kara gritted her teeth. "She did."

"And who is Mrs. Caplin? Certainly I've never heard of her," Mrs. Grier said.

"I'm surprised, Mother." Mr. Grier tilted his head. "She is quite famous. She's made a name for herself as a corset maker. At the Exhibition she had on display a large selection of different styles of corsets. For women of all ages, sorts, and sizes."

His mother gasped in horror. "No."

"Yes," her son said gleefully.

"I'm sure I don't know what young women are coming to."

Kara shot the young man a pitying glance. "Since you were so fortunate as to witness such a historic display of knowledge and culture, I do hope you took away more than the means to torment your mother." She glanced at the crowd still filing back into the larger parlor. "Now, if you will excuse me, I believe I'll go and have a look at the Cursed Crown."

Niall silently cheered.

Mrs. Grier's eyes narrowed as she watched Kara leave. "I do wish everyone would stop calling it by that name. It's just another artifact. There is no need to perpetuate this nonsense about a curse, but even my brother seems to encourage it." She nudged her son. "You and Sedwick should take the chance to get to know each other. You will both be men of importance and standing in the borough, once you become the new Lord Balstone."

Niall's head came up. "Ah, that's right. You would be your uncle's heir, would you not?"

"Our family title is not the sort that can be found in Scotland, the sort that allows a female to inherit," Mrs. Grier said with a sniff. "But it can be passed through the females, of course. Will is the last man of Balstone blood."

"And I will lead the family into a bright future," Will Grier said in a tired voice.

"Of course you will," his mother said, straightening her shoulders. "I, however, must go and remind that wretched footman that he is here to serve drinks, not to engage the guests in conversation."

As she left, her son shot Niall an amused glance. "Apologies for riling your fiancée. She was right, you know. I was just trying to tease my mother."

"You might have done that without setting her against Miss Levett."

"Oh, she's already against her," Mr. Grier said wryly. "I just jumped on her latest grievance."

"Perhaps she would have fewer grievances if she had the support of her son." Niall looked at him for a long moment. "A mother's care and concern can be a true gift—one not everyone is lucky enough to possess." He was thinking of the orphaned Harold and the way that

Kara had taken the boy in, how she carefully saw to his well-being and thoughtfully tried to expose him to new opportunities to learn, to new experiences, outlooks, and prospects.

Mr. Grier's expression turned sour. "Yes, well, care and concern are not always the same thing." He raised his glass in salute. "Good evening, Your Grace."

Niall let him go. Other guests were hovering, waiting for a chance to speak to him. He circulated for a while, answering questions and making small talk. He was happy for this chance to meet so many local residents and interested people from the city. He and Kara and their makeshift family would be spending significant time here, with luck and hopefully decent conditions at the priory. They would have to determine how it would work, splitting their time between here and Bluefield Park, but they would find their way.

After a while he began to search for Kara in earnest. He understood her desire to avoid the unpleasant Griers. The woman's nastiness, as much as her son's, had him rethinking his plan to stay at Balburn a few days longer. Kara had held real reservations about his taking up the ducal title, most of which revolved around the ridiculous fear that she was unsuitable to become a duchess. Pure hogwash, in his opinion, but he didn't want Mrs. Grier's antagonism to reinforce Kara's worries.

He couldn't find her mixing among the guests. Surely she was not still examining the crown? He crossed through the entryway to the smaller parlor. The door stood cracked open. Pushing it wider, he peered in.

Kara was not inside. But Balstone and his sister were, and they were obviously in the midst of a heated discussion.

"No," Mrs. Grier said flatly. She took a step away.

Her brother reached out to grab her arm and stop her. "You must, I tell you!" Balstone hissed. "Find a way!"

"It cannot be done. You will sooner squeeze blood from a stone."

"It must be done! Everything hinges upon it."

His sister's head went up. Her eyes glittered like ice. "No, Dunstan. Everything does not hinge upon it. There are far more important matters at foot. For once, your wishes and your dig and your precious reputation are going to have to come second. Do you hear me?"

Niall slowly withdrew and closed the door as the argument raged on. Perhaps Gyda had the right of it. The atmosphere of Balburn House had shifted somehow. Or perhaps he had just awakened out of his creative fog enough to notice the negative mood of the place. Either way, it was likely a good idea to keep their time here as short as possible.

Chapter Three

Kara set down her utensils and leaned back in her chair. "Oh, goodness. I should not have indulged so, but I believe tattie scones and sausages are my new breakfast favorites."

Niall agreed as he scooped griddled mushrooms onto his flat, triangular scone. "Do you think we could convince Cook to add them to the menus at Bluefield?" he asked before taking a huge bite.

"She will, if you ask it of her," Kara said wryly. Niall was extremely popular with all the staff at Bluefield. She pushed away from the table. "Why don't you finish up here while I go and fetch my coat?"

He nodded. "Kara," he said softly as she stood to go. "I asked the housekeeper to have our bags packed and ready to go this morning."

She paused. "Because of me?" she asked, her heart in her throat.

"No. Because of *them*," he said firmly. He shook his head. "Gyda was right. I don't know what it is, but the place feels different. As if something dark has settled over this house."

She sighed softly, both in relief and fondness. "Have I told you how much I adore your sensitive, superstitious side? I trust your instincts and, I confess, I am relieved. But what if the priory is uninhabitable?"

"Then we'll head back to the city tonight and start making arrangements." He broke into a wide grin. "But hurry and grab your wrap. I can't wait to get over there."

"Neither can I." Smiling, she ran out and up the stairs. She'd been assigned to a room in the family wing, far away from Niall in the guest wing. As she moved down the corridor, she passed the earl's suite. The door was open, and he stood inside a sitting room, a book in hand. Glancing up, he saw her and called out, "Miss Levett! How are you this morning?"

"Very well, sir. I hope you are?"

"Very well, indeed." He waved a hand. "Come, would you care to see some of my father's treasures?"

Kara hesitated. What she wanted was to get on the road to the priory, but she had no wish to be rude. Nodding, she stepped inside.

"Perhaps you heard me mention my father's interest in tracing our family lineage last night? He succeeded in following it all the way back to a warlord who fought many battles in the Borderlands." Balstone picked up a shining golden buckle, intricately carved. "That ancestor might have worn a piece like this." He indicated another two pieces that also lay on display on the shelf. "Or perhaps these shoulder clasps."

"They are very lovely."

The earl regarded her. "You seem impatient to get away. Do you and Sedwick have plans today?"

"We do, sir. We are heading over to Tallenford Priory. We are both eager to get our first look at it."

Balstone didn't look pleased. "Well, I suspect it will not be in too good a shape. It has sat empty so long." He waved a hand. "Go, then! I look forward to hearing what you have found at dinner tonight."

Kara hesitated. "I fear we mean to stay at the priory, sir. But I am glad I had the chance to thank you for your hospitality. Your unveiling was an unforgettable event."

"Staying?" The earl frowned. "At the priory? Well, that is a very bad idea, indeed!"

Kara had no idea how to respond.

"It is sure to be moldy and musty. No fit place for a young lady. I told Sedwick that you are both welcome to stay with us while he arranges for work to begin on the place. It surely won't be fit for residence for a long while."

"That is a very generous offer, my lord, but we mean to get started on the work right away."

"What? Yourselves?"

"I'm sure there are things we might do. And we have some staff meeting us there today."

Balstone glowered at her. "Well, then. I suppose I cannot change your mind."

"Thank you again, sir."

The earl nodded and turned away. Kara left as quickly as she could, surprised at his mood. She hurried to her room. Balstone's staff was efficient, or perhaps they were just as eager to see the back of them as their master was for them to stay. Her room was empty, with only her coat, gloves, and hat lying on the bed. Snatching them up, she started back downstairs, only to encounter Mrs. Grier on her way up.

The woman stopped on the landing. "Miss Levett," she said darkly.

Kara stared. The woman looked tired and worn. "Good morning, Mrs. Grier. Are you well?"

"Yes, yes," she said impatiently. "I'm fine."

"Hosting an event like last evening's can indeed be wearing. I hope you find time to rest and recover today." Pulling on her gloves, Kara turned to go.

"A moment, Miss Levett. What is this I hear of your going over to the priory with the duke?"

"Oh, yes. We plan to see it for the first time today. We are both excited."

"Alone?" Mrs. Grier frowned.

"Well, we'll be driving over alone, but—"

"Miss Levett!" the woman interrupted. "I don't know how young ladies behave in London, but here they observe the proprieties, if they wish to be well thought of."

"As I was saying, Niall and I will drive out, but we will not be alone at the estate. The land agent engaged a cook/housekeeper, and she is to bring along several young maids as well."

The woman lifted her sharp chin. It was as pointed as her words. "Servants do not make sufficient chaperones. They are meant to be engaged in their duties, not keeping their eyes on you."

Kara laughed. "Oh, it's not me they will be keeping their eyes on. Everywhere he goes, Niall proves a distraction to females. I frequently have to chase the maids at home back to work. Especially when he is creating something in his forge."

"Do not count on such a thing. Like the young ladies, the servants in our region know how to behave," Mrs. Grier said with a sniff.

"Do they?" Kara gave a nod to the floor below.

Following, Mrs. Grier looked down. At the back of the entry hall stood the dining room door. In the doorway stood a maid, idly flitting her duster along the frame while she stared avidly inside. Mrs. Grier slapped a hand on the stair rail. "Mona!" she called out harshly. "Stop gawking and get back to work."

The girl jumped and hurried away.

Kara merely shrugged. "We shall be more than adequately chaperoned."

"Still, appearances must be upheld. Without a proper companion—"

"Mrs. Grier," Kara said softly. "My father was a baron. My mother was a member of Queen Charlotte's court. I have been presented to Queen Victoria and come out into Society. I may not be the conventional sort, but I am still a lady. I know what is expected of me and *how to behave.*"

"But—"

Kara gave the woman no chance to continue. "Good day to you."

She stepped lightly down the stairs.

Niall met her in the hall, shrugging back into his coat as he left the dining room. "All ready to go?"

"More than ready." Kara turned back to look up the stairs. Largray, the tall, thin butler, had come up behind the woman on the landing. He watched them over her shoulder, with his heavily hooded eyes and dour expression. "Thank you for your ... hospitality, Mrs. Grier."

"You'll have to walk," the woman said in a nasty tone. "I'm afraid the carriage is gone. My son took it and returned to the city last night."

"Oh, no worries," Niall called up to her. "We were up early this morning and walked to the village to hire a cart." He paused. "I haven't seen his lordship this morning. I left him a note. Please give him my best and tell him I'm sorry I missed bidding him goodbye."

"Wait. What's that?" Mrs. Grier hurried down the stairs. "You didn't mean—? You are not taking your leave? You will be back this evening, I presume?"

"No, indeed. I am not one to outstay my welcome. Thank you for hosting me as I finished our project." He held out an arm to Kara as his tone grew gentle. "But now, it is time for us to go home."

Breathing deeply, Kara let go of her irritation with the woman. Her heart thumped with appreciation and anticipation as she took his arm and stepped out toward their future.

<hr />

HE SAT ATOP a humble cart, behind an unassuming horse, but as they climbed out of the valley, leaving Balburn House behind, Niall felt lighter and more at ease than he had in years. He had the world's most spectacular woman at his side, and the air held a mix of fir and brine. No matter what they found at the priory, this—*this*—was all he needed to feel at home.

"Sea air and forest loam," he said. "It's the best scent in the world."

"It is lovely," Kara agreed, but she looked pensive as the cart climbed the ridge. "Niall, does Tallenford Priory have tenants attached to the land?"

"A few. According to Kincaid, the land agent, many moved on when the family died out and the priory sat empty, but there are a few farming families left."

"Do you know if their holdings are well maintained? In good shape?"

"Ah, you saw the cottages on the hillside as you drove in."

"Yes. Gyda and I were both ... disturbed."

"As was I. I've seen others like them too, during my stay."

"They are Balstone's, then? Not attached to the priory?"

"They are Balstone's."

He glanced over to see her frowning.

"I don't know why I'm relieved," she said.

"Well, I was a bit uneasy at the thought of taking over such neglected people and places as well. It could be a tricky business."

"Yes. A delicate balance, adjusting conditions and expectations."

"Exactly. After seeing those cottages, I grilled Kincaid about what we might find among the priory's tenants, but he assured me that they were in much better condition. *Perfectly functional*, were the words he used."

She frowned again. "I'm sure we can improve upon that."

"I'm sure we can. We will do our best by the people entrusted to us." He shot her a grateful look. "I'm glad to have you by my side. You do an admirable job with your people and servants at Bluefield Park."

"Most of it is due to my mother. My father was so often focused on the businesses, many of the estate matters were left to her. She was so caring, Niall. So thoughtful. And yet she was also practical and pragmatic. Somehow, the combination allowed everyone to thrive." Her tone softened. "I wish you could have known her."

"She would be proud to see you carrying on her legacy. Now we will spread it here, as well."

They both grew quiet as they reached the section of the ridge near the careworn cottages. "At least if they were ours, we could help," she whispered. "Why doesn't Lord Balstone?"

Niall shook his head. "From what I could tell, he does not look beyond the archeological site. He leaves the estate management to his sister."

"From all the signs, she has no talent for it."

"From all the signs, they have not much coin for it."

Kara looked worried. "Is it so difficult, then? To eke out a good income here?"

"No, not from what I have learned. I seized the chance, over the last weeks, to talk to Dalwiddie, and others, too." Niall nodded toward the magnificent view of rolling hills retreating from the landward side of the ridge. "They say these are the fringes of the Lammermuir Hills. It's an ideal place for sheep farming. There is plenty of arable land on the flanks of the hills. I thought we'd try our hand at sheep, as long as we find enough acreage that isn't overgrown."

Her eyes widened. "That should be interesting. I don't know anything about sheep farming. I cannot wait to learn more about it."

Gratitude warmed him. "And that is just one of the many reasons I love you."

She laid her head on his shoulder, and they drove on in silence for a while until he spotted a thick, leaning sycamore. "Look there." He gave her a nudge. "That tree marks the border of the priory's land."

"Fourteen hundred acres," she breathed. "Surely we can do some good with all of that."

"We can. We will."

He made the turn that would take them to the house. They traveled along a secluded lane, covered with a canopy of trees thick with new leaves.

"I feel like I'm entering a fairy land," she whispered.

He understood. Anticipation grew as they rumbled on. At last, he caught a glimpse of sandstone through the trees ahead. "Kara, look," he said, nodding.

She squeezed his arm as they drew nearer. Gradually, the trees on the right side of the lane began to thin. A hedge line started, and then a stone wall marching behind it. When they came abreast of the wall, the last of the trees faded away from the road, and they could look down at the house.

"Oh! Stop! Right here," Kara said breathlessly.

Niall was glad to do it. Emotion overcame him.

"It's like a castle," she said, awed.

It wasn't a castle. Not truly. But the house was done in the Scottish Baronial style, slightly gothic, with small towers and false battlements lining the irregular outlines of both the house and garden.

"A walled garden!" Kara gasped. "And look, Niall! A colonnade!"

The stone nearly glowed in the morning sun, but the hodgepodge, historically inspired construction meant that there were plenty of shadows, peaks, and arches to draw the eye. It was unique. It was beautiful. And it was theirs.

"Oh, Niall? What do you think?"

He looked at Kara. For nearly the entirety of his life, he'd hidden his emotions, his thoughts, his very self, behind a mask. Until her. With her he was free to just ... be. And so he gave her a look that showed everything he felt in that moment. "I think we are home," he whispered.

She leaned into him, and the only thing to do was to bend down to kiss her. And kiss her some more—until the horse shifted restlessly.

He pulled away, laughing. "Fine, then. Let's go."

The lane took them past the house and above it, before sweeping into a great, descending curve that turned into a short drive. It deposited them in a graveled space before the arched main entrance. Niall jumped down to hitch the horse to a post. "The gravel is thin," he said, stamping a foot. "And the lawns need scything, but—" He stopped and chuckled as he saw Kara turning in a circle, taking it all in.

"Look at it!" She ran to the side of the house where the colonnade formed one wall of the sunken, enclosed garden. "It needs care and attention, but it could be magnificent!"

An image flashed in his mind. Kara, sitting there in the sun on a blanket, a picnic strewn about her. She laughed in delight as a child toddled up, offering a flower in a grubby fist.

Niall stood frozen, his mind's eye fixed on the hazy, delightful scene. It was so vivid it felt like a glimpse of their future, not just a dream. He could feel the sun on his shoulders, almost taste the heavy scent of blooms in the warm air. He felt full, filled with almost too much happiness to bear. Striding swiftly over to her, he swept her up in his arms and spun her about.

"Aye! Well, and here ye are—the pair of ye! Don't ye just make a sight?"

Niall stopped and set Kara down. Together they faced the arched doorway of the house. A woman stood there, flanked by the two miniature towers on either side. Short and plump, she wore a grin across her broad face. "Ye'll be the new duke, then," she said with a nod. "And his betrothed?" She dipped into a shallow curtsy as they approached. "I'm Mrs. Pollock, Your Grace. I was hired by Mr. Kincaid to be your cook-housekeeper." She ran a shrewd eye over Kara. "Although the gossip vine says ye've brought along a fancy English butler?"

"A pleasure, Mrs. Pollock," Niall said with a nod.

"How lovely it is to meet you, Mrs. Pollock," Kara said. "Yes. Turner is our butler and quite an indispensable member of our household."

The woman nodded. "To be honest, I'm that relieved to hear it. I'd far rather take charge of the kitchens and leave the running of the household to your man."

"Excellent," Niall said, relieved to be spared any domestic squabbles. "Tell me, Mrs. Pollock. Do you make tattie scones? We've only just discovered them."

She gave him an appreciative glance. "Only the best in East Lothian, sir." Pivoting, she raised a hand. "But come and meet the girls I've brought with me."

Niall smiled as three young women in caps and aprons filed out from inside.

"Here are Ailsa, Brigitte, and Catriona," Mrs. Pollock said smartly. "All are fine, upstanding girls and good workers."

"A, B, and C," Niall whispered to Kara, then grunted as she elbowed him.

"Good morning," he said to the maids.

They all dipped curtsies. Someone giggled.

"Enough tittering," Mrs. Pollock ordered them. "Back to work with ye."

The girls turned and marched back from whence they came, but Mrs. Pollock paused to glance over at the cart. "I brought a lad for the stables, as well, Your Grace. I'll have him take care of the horse and cart. Hired, I imagine?"

"Yes, indeed, but I've taken them for the week. We'll need to find a horse fair and see to the hiring of more."

The cook ran a knowing glance over the trunks in the back of the cart. "Overstayed yer welcome at Balburn House already, did ye?"

Niall laughed. "Not exactly worn out, but perhaps you'll have heard of the phrase 'Leave while the leaving is good'?"

Mrs. Pollock chuckled, but Kara bit her lip.

"Ah, dinna worry, my dear. I may ha' been in service in the city for the last ten years, but I was born and bred in these parts. Balburn House has always been known for its ... peculiarities." The cook grew serious. "I dinna hold with such inhospitality myself, Your Grace. I do not accept such unwelcoming or parsimonious ways in any household

I'm to be part of, ye understand. Guests are guests and should be treated as such. And servants are part of the household and deserve good food and solid lodgings if they are to be expected to put in a good day's work. And no dodgy docking of wages, either."

"I agree wholeheartedly with every one of those sentiments, Mrs. Pollock."

"Good. Just so we're clear." She turned to go back in the house.

Niall took up Kara's hands.

"You look happy," she whispered.

"I feel ... hopeful," he returned. "I think we can be safe and happy here."

Her expression softened and his heart shifted. He could scarcely believe how much he felt for this woman. The depth of his love for her had settled in his bones and become a part of him.

Behind them, a throat cleared. "Och, we'll need to get a woman in the house if the both of ye mean to stay," Mrs. Pollock said.

They laughed softly together, before Kara let go of him and, smiling, began to follow the cook. "Our friend Miss Winther will be arriving soon, within the next day or two, if we send word quickly," Kara told her. "She'll be coming along from Edinburgh along with Turner and my young ward."

"That's all well and good, but we'll fix up the room next to mine until she arrives." Mrs. Pollock lifted her chin. "I won't have snide talk about my lady, nor the morals of the household." She shrugged. "We've only got a couple of rooms aired out, scrubbed, and ready, in any case. Upstairs, it's just the ducal suite."

"I'll be happy to stay downstairs with you, Mrs. Pollock," Kara reassured her. "I've no wish for gossip to spread, either."

"Good, then. Come in, then, aye? I'll show ye the house."

Snatching Kara's hand back again, Niall breathed deeply as they followed the cook in. He stopped just inside the door to take it all in.

The floor was creamy marble, covered in the center with a thick carpet of turkey red. In the back left corner of the entry, rounded marble steps turned into a curved staircase.

Beside him, Kara gasped. He knew she was transfixed by the large painted panel along the stair wall. It was bedecked with a gorgeous landscape of a riverside village, complete with cliffs rising beyond and, farther on, a glimpse of the sea. It was lovely, but Niall's gaze was fixed on the sturdy wooden railing as he imagined a graceful design of iron in its place. Perhaps with unfurling leaves and—

"We did scrub and polish up the entry," Mrs. Pollock said with satisfaction. "We wished ye to feel good about the place on first stepping in."

"You've succeeded, Mrs. Pollock. Thank you."

"Now, don't ye wish to see the rest?"

"Indeed, we do," Niall said softly. "Every last inch."

Chapter Four

KARA SAT AT the scarred oak kitchen table late the next morning, making lists while Mrs. Pollock coddled eggs and fried ham for a delayed breakfast. The table was old, but spotless and shining, just like the rest of the kitchen.

"That does smell good, though I shouldn't be hungry at all," Kara declared. "We were offered drinks and a bite at nearly every croft and cottage we called at this morning. I thought it wise to accept something small whenever it was offered." She and Niall had set out early to visit the tenants left to the estate. They both wanted to be sure they were well cared for, as well as to inspect the empty places, with an eye to filling them when they could.

"Aye. 'Tis always best to offer and accept true hospitality," Mrs. Pollock said.

"It was a relief to find them in good shape. It means we can begin on the house right away." Kara paused, making a note. "We'll have to clear out the schoolroom and prepare one of the small bedrooms near to it. Harold will love the place once it's cleaned. All that light and space! He'll fill it with collections, projects, and experiments in no time." The kitchen and the ducal suite were gleaming, but the rest of the house needed a thorough cleaning and sorting.

"Aye. It seems daft to have filled the nursery with so many discards, when there are such attics just waiting." Mrs. Pollock was adding herbs and mushrooms to her eggs.

Privately, Kara quite sympathized with the previous owners—or anyone wanting to avoid attics. She gave a shudder.

The cook tilted her head while pouring a dab of cream into the coddling pots. "My own dear mother knew the lady who was the last of the family here. She had grown quite old and had shut up much of the priory, as her retainers were aging as well, and she just didn't use many of the rooms. They sometimes had my mother in to help with jobs that were too much for them. Perhaps they were just too feeble to climb the narrow stairs into the attics."

"You might be right. We'll need to hire a couple of footmen. Turner will see to that. We can move everything to another room for now, and let the footmen take them up to the attics later."

"There are plenty of other bedrooms we can use for the temporary storage," Mrs. Pollock agreed.

"We'll go through and list the discards as we move them, and survey all the other rooms as well. I should begin an inventory, as I don't think one was included among the papers that the land agent gave to Niall." Kara paused, thinking. "We will need to ready a room for Miss Winther. I'd like to give her a lovely spot of her own. Which of the bedrooms in the family wing would you recommend?"

"The blue room is spacious and quite near the duchess's rooms. The view overlooks—"

"Mrs. Pollock?" Niall's call interrupted her. He came in waving a piece of parchment. "Ah, Mrs. Pollock. Brigitte said that this was delivered last night?"

"Aye, Your Grace. Messenger came after ye'd both retired for the night. Ailsa and I were in here banking the fires and setting the bread to rise overnight when he pounded on the service door. Scairt the life out of both of us."

Ailsa, toasting bread, nodded. "It's true. My heart nearly jumped out of my chest. Your Grace," she added, giving a quick curtsy.

"And you are sure the message came from Balburn House?" Niall asked.

"So the lad said," Mrs. Pollock replied. "He mentioned it was about some trouble with the payment due to ye, sir. Well, I told him I wasna going to wake ye for such news as *that*. I told him I'd leave it for ye and ye'd see it this morning."

Kara watched as Niall frowned down at the note. "Is there something amiss?"

He held it out to her. Taking it, she looked it over. The paper was thick and ragged on one edge, and folded over once. She flipped it open.

> *Trouble meeting your fee, but have a solution.*
> *Meet me tonight at the hut circles.*
> *Midnight. Moon should be up.*
> —B

"You haven't been paid for *A Bronze Age Family*?"

"No. Balstone paid for the materials, though, so I wasn't troubled over it. I assumed he'd pay the rest when he could."

"So you didn't press him for it?"

"No. There was no need."

"And since you didn't, it hardly seems like the matter would necessitate a midnight meeting."

"That is my thought. And the other thing is, I've worked with Lord Balstone in his study over the last weeks. I've seen his stationery. It is much finer than this and embossed with his name and title."

Kara fingered the rough vellum. "Perhaps I'm wrong, but also, he doesn't seem the sort to sign off with something so casual as a single initial."

"No, he doesn't. At least, I haven't noticed him doing so in any of our correspondence."

Kara looked up. "But what is it that you suspect? That someone else sent this note and wanted you to think it was from Lord Balstone?"

He shrugged. "For what reason? It makes no sense." Shaking his head, he reached for a slice of toast. "I've got a list of things to do today that's as long as my arm. If Balstone truly wanted a meeting last night, I've missed it—and I don't really wish to spend time today going over there to inquire about it. It will wait."

Ailsa placed more toast in the rack. "Aye, sir. Best to wait. Ye'll not wish to be going over to Balburn House this morning. They will all still be in a frenzy."

Kara exchanged a puzzled look with Niall. "What frenzy, Ailsa?"

"Over the killin'. They are likely all atwitter and still waitin' on the police to arrive."

Kara straightened on her stool. Niall looked flummoxed.

With a bang, Mrs. Pollock dropped a lid over her simmering water bath. "What are ye going on about, girl?"

Ailsa hunched her shoulders defensively. "Well, ye did tell me and Catriona to stop gossipin' this morn, Mrs. Pollock, else ye'd know."

"And now I'm telling ye to explain yourself. What's this about a killing?"

The girl's eyes went wide. "A murder, it was! They found the body this mornin'. I heard it from Rabbie Keith when he delivered the eggs."

"A body?" Niall sounded shocked. "Not Lord Balstone?"

"No, Your Grace. 'Twas one of the servants."

"Which one?" Kara asked.

"I've no notion. Rabbie didn't know."

Mrs. Pollock shook her head. "It's naught but storytelling, I say. There's a good half-dozen of the staff over there that is far on in years. It will be one of them, died in their beds, I predict. Rabbie is just spreading gossip along with his eggs."

Ailsa looked mutinous.

Kara looked to Niall.

He was frowning at the note again. "I'm sure you are right, Mrs. Pollock." He looked up to meet Kara's gaze, and her thoughts must have shown on her face. "No," he said swiftly. "There is no call for us to go over there. The authorities will handle it."

"I don't even know how the authorities work in this region," she said thoughtfully. "Is there a police office in Highfield?" she asked.

"Oh, no," Ailsa told her. "We've only the one constable, Mr. Creel."

"Old Cabbage Creel is what they call him," Mrs. Pollock scoffed. "They'll likely have to send to Prestonpans. It's the nearest town with a police commission. And, in turn, they will have to send for the procurator fiscal. It's him who will be in charge. If it is a murder, that is, and not just a natural death."

"No doubt Lord Balstone knows exactly how to proceed," Niall said firmly. He moved to take a seat at the table, but paused behind Kara to kiss the back of her head. "We've had more than our fair share of such adventures," he murmured. "We are well out of this one."

Kara nodded and hoped he was right. But that note … She slipped it in her pocket, just in case.

<hr>

THE SUN HAD sunk low on the horizon when Niall handed his pitchfork to Jamie, the young stable lad. Stretching, he walked out of the long stone barn. Dalwiddie had been kind enough to sell him a load of hay and oats, and now the last of it was stored away. With a sigh, he eyed the lowering sun. He'd been hoping to finish in time to inspect some of the other outbuildings. He was impatient to find a spot for his forge, but that was something best done in the light of day.

He paused at the sound of a horse on the gravel drive. Who could that be? Dalwiddie, perhaps, come to check on the delivery? Niall called for Jamie and strode out, following the drive along the side of the house to the front.

A gentleman was dismounting as he rounded the corner. Jamie sped by to take up the horse as Niall called, "Good evening to you, sir."

"Good evening." The man was tall and dark and slightly younger than Niall, perhaps. His face wore an intelligent and assessing aspect as his eyes slid past Niall to take in the details of the house and its environs. "Could you please inform the Duke of Sedwick that he has a visitor? It's urgent that I see him straightaway."

"I am he, I am afraid," Niall said with a twitch of a grin. "How can I help you?"

That dark gaze snapped back. "Well. How awkward. My apologies."

"No apology necessary. I can scarcely blame you when I meet you covered in hay dust, Mr....?"

The man bowed. "I am Ian Darrow, Your Grace. Procurator fiscal for this region."

Niall sobered. "Oh. We'd heard there was a death at Balburn House, but if they have called you in, it must be serious."

The man's gaze sharpened. "How did you hear of it so quickly?"

"Servants' gossip." Niall lifted a shoulder. "I understand the news was delivered to our kitchen maid along with the morning's eggs."

"Amazing, how swiftly that network moves." Darrow shook his head. "I am sorry to intrude, but I hoped to speak to you and your betrothed. It should only take a few minutes."

"Of course. Please, come inside. I apologize for not being able to host you in style, but I'm afraid none of the receiving rooms have been uncovered yet. However, the housekeeper has a snug parlor that we might borrow."

"Any private place will suffice."

The gentleman paused as they entered the front door. He stood, taking in the entry hall, just had Niall had done. Niall waited a moment, then beckoned him down a passage on the right and through the green baize door that led downstairs. He paused to poke his head in the kitchen. "I beg your pardon, Mrs. Pollock, but we've a caller. May we use your little parlor for a while?"

The cook didn't look up from the pot she was stirring. "Help yourself, Your Grace. Ailsa will bring tea."

"Thank you. And will you send for Miss Levett—"

"I'm here!" Kara came running lightly down the servants' stairs. "Catriona caught sight of a visitor." She paused at the bottom to smile at Darrow. "Good evening."

"Miss Kara Levett, may I present Mr. Darrow? Mr. Darrow, my fiancée." Niall stopped farther down the passage and held open the door to the housekeeper's parlor, which Mrs. Pollock had taken for herself. "Shall we talk in here?"

The pair of them filed in, and Niall shut the door behind him. He went to hold a chair for Kara. "Mr. Darrow is the procurator fiscal," he told her.

Her smile faded. "Oh, I'm afraid your presence here means something unpleasant has occurred?"

"I'm afraid so."

Kara colored slightly. "Do forgive me, Mr. Darrow. You deserve a better greeting than that. Indeed, we are very happy to make your acquaintance."

"Ah, thank you. No worries, though. It's part of the job, in many cases." He eyed Kara a little more closely. "But not many are quick to realize it. So again, I thank you." He paused to take in the dust on her skirts and the smudge on her cheek before turning to run an eye over Niall's old plaid and comfortable linen shirt. "But then, the pair of you are unusual, are you not? I heard the priory would need work after sitting vacant for so long, but I didn't expect to find the new duke and his duchess-to-be doing it themselves."

Niall chuckled. "I'm afraid we are doomed to meet no one's expectations, but we hope people will adapt once they get to know us."

Darrow looked thoughtful. "Some will, some won't," he ventured. "There are those who cannot look past a title, even a small one like procurator fiscal." He shook his head. "In any case, I don't mean to keep you." He looked to Kara. "The duke said you'd heard of the unfortunate death at Balburn House?"

"We heard a servant had died, but nothing more."

Darrow pulled out a notebook and scribbled in it.

"Who was it who died?" asked Niall. "I was at Balburn House for nearly a month. I might have known them."

"Indeed, you did. In fact, from reports, the pair of you might have been the last to see the deceased."

Niall merely raised his brow, waiting.

Darrow watched him closely. "It is Mr. Edmund Finley who has been killed."

Kara gasped. "Mr. Finley? How dreadful." She frowned. "But he was Lord Balstone's assistant, not a mere servant."

Darrow shook his head. "I assure you, both his lordship and his sister quite considered the man a servant."

"You said he'd been killed. What happened to Mr. Finley?" asked Niall.

"It appears he was attacked. He suffered several hard blows and was pushed into the deepest of the hut circle depressions at the archeological site. He broke his neck in the fall."

Grief shadowed Kara's countenance. "I can scarcely believe it. He seemed such a lively, enterprising young man."

"What makes you say that?" Darrow said with surprise.

Kara blinked. "Well, it's just that he was so enthusiastic about his plans."

"You said we might have been the last to speak to Finley?" Niall frowned. "But our conversation with him took place at the party for the unveiling of my art piece. When he left us that evening, he was going out to check that the bonfires had safely burned down. Are you saying he was killed that night?"

"No. I brought the borough's coroner with me, and he believes that Finley was killed sometime last night."

"But then, how could we have been the last to speak with him?" Kara asked. "Surely someone must have seen him, spoken to him, at some time during the day yesterday?"

"It appears not. Nor was Finley missed by anyone at Balburn, as he had requested a few days off and received permission to take them."

"So no one knows where he was or went, after leaving the party two nights ago, until he was killed at the dig site last night?" Niall asked, thinking back.

"That does appear to be the case." Darrow looked at Kara. "You mentioned that he spoke to you about his plans, Miss Levett?"

"Yes. He seemed so happy and optimistic about his future."

"What exactly were his plans?" Expectant, Darrow held his pencil over his notebook.

"Oh. The golf course. The inn, as you must know."

"I'm afraid I don't. You are the first to mention any of this."

"I am?" Kara looked confused. "Mr. Finley had already spoken to Niall about his intentions. When he told me, I assumed it was something that everyone around him knew."

"It doesn't appear so."

"How odd."

"Could you tell me exactly what he said?"

Kara explained, and Niall thought back to that conversation with Finley. "You know," he said when she had finished, "now that I think about it, he did move closer and lower his tone when he spoke of his plans. It wasn't even necessary, as we were mostly alone in the larger parlor. Most of the guests were in the other parlor, listening to Lord Balstone talk about the Cursed Crown."

"Mrs. Grier was over on the other side of the room," Kara recalled. Her eyes rounded. "Oh, and Gyda said she saw Mr. Finley and Mrs. Grier arguing that night! Could it have been about his plans to leave Balburn?"

"Wait a moment. *Finley* was seen arguing with Mrs. Grier?" Darrow asked.

"Yes. The evening of the party."

"By whom, did you say?"

"Miss Gyda Winther. She's my forge assistant," Niall explained.

"Is she here? May I speak with her?"

"She's in Edinburgh right now, but she should be here within a day or two."

"I'll come back, if I may. I want to speak to everyone who attended that unveiling."

"Of course," Niall assured him. "You are welcome back at any time."

"Can you think of anything else Finley might have said that evening?"

"Only one thing ... He warned me not to be caught alone with Mrs. Grier's son," Kara said. "But I gathered that he meant the young man to be a threat to women, not a danger to Mr. Finley himself."

"Interesting." Nodding, Darrow made another note as the door opened and Ailsa came in with the tea tray.

"Just a quick cup, I thank you," the fiscal said as Kara offered to pour. He took the teacup from her and leaned back in his chair. "There has been some talk about the pair of you, you know," he said casually.

"There usually is," Kara said with a sigh.

"Oh, don't worry. I've heard nothing impertinent, let alone derogatory." He paused. "Mostly."

"I'm sure I have Mrs. Grier to thank for that qualification," Kara said, handing Niall his cup.

"I wouldn't worry about it. The woman hardly seems to have a kind word to say about anyone. But others are talking, too." Darrow raised a brow. "There was one topic that garnered my attention."

Niall sat back. "I assume you refer to our ... adventures?"

"If that's what you call them. You two do seem to have a proclivity for ... excitement. Specifically, cases of murder. And, as I understand it, you have a special relationship with Scotland Yard and certain members of the English government." He drained his cup and set it down. "The thing is, and I'll try to put this delicately—"

"Do not worry, Mr. Darrow. Kara and I have no plans—indeed, no wish at all—to interfere with your case. Not this one or any other of your enquiries. We are in East Lothian to establish ourselves here at Tallenford Priory." He gestured. "And as you have seen for yourself, we have plenty of work to keep ourselves occupied."

"I am relieved to hear it. Not that I mean to disparage your talents, for I hear they are formidable, but—"

"But this is not our purview. We understand, sir. We are new here and not likely to be of much help, nor are we looking for *excitement* or acclaim."

"Excellent." Darrow stood. "I should like to talk to your assistant when she arrives. Also, please contact me if you recall anything else that might be helpful."

"Of course." Kara moved toward the door. "Will you be staying at Balburn House while you investigate Mr. Finley's death?"

"No, indeed. I've taken a room at the Sheep's Head in the village."

"We'll send word once Gyda has arrived."

"Thank you."

They walked Darrow out and sent for his horse. Niall wrapped an arm around Kara's waist as they watched him ride out.

"You didn't mention the note summoning you to Balburn," she said quietly.

"No."

"Why not?"

"Because it has nothing to do with his investigation."

"Doesn't it?" She moved away and stared up at him. "Someone tried to arrange for you to be at the very spot where Finley was murdered, on the night he was murdered."

"Well, they failed, didn't they? I didn't go. I didn't get mixed up in whatever is swirling around Balburn, and I intend for it to stay that way." He reached for her hand. "I want to focus on this. On us, Kara. I confess, I like what I've learned about this community in the short time I've been here. Let's become a part of it. Make it a part of our world, the one we are creating together. But for this matter, whatever is happening over at Balburn, let's just keep to the fringe edges. Yes?"

Her gaze softened, but she still looked worried. "If that is what you wish, then yes."

"Thank you." He squeezed her hand. "Now, let's get back to work." He grinned. "We'll want to be ready for Harold's arrival."

Chapter Five

IN FACT, TURNER, Gyda, and young Harold arrived the next afternoon. Kara rushed out to greet them, embracing them each in turn, and gleefully watching their reactions to the priory.

Turner appeared both interested and satisfied—in the most understated way, of course. Gyda marveled over the exterior and heartily approved of the grand stairwell, while Harold ricocheted like a whirlwind from one thing to another, delighted with it all.

Kara, in turn, was delighted to find that the second carriage, full of luggage and certain items and comforts that Turner deemed necessary, also contained a brace of strapping footmen, hired from an agency in the city.

"Oh, bless that formidable foresight of yours, Turner," Kate breathed. "I have at least seven tasks I could set them to right now."

Turner beckoned the pair over. "Hamish and Hendry are cousins," he explained. "They were searching for a position together, and were willing to leave the city to find one."

"Welcome to Tallenford Priory," Niall said, inclining his head as the men both bowed.

"We are so happy to welcome you both to the household," said Kara.

Turner set them to unloading the carriage, and Kara called for Harold. "Come, let's show you your room and the schoolroom, then we'll take Turner to his set of rooms." She smiled at the man who had for years been her butler, friend, lab assistant, and occasional surrogate father. "The butler's office is very finely appointed, and I think you will approve of the wine cellar."

The rest of the day was spent in unpacking and exploring. In the late afternoon, they all sat down to a hearty dinner, save for Hamish and Hendry, who took the opportunity to see to their own rooms at the top of the house and would eat later. Everyone took their meal together in the kitchen, much to Turner's dismay.

"I'll see to restoring the dining room first thing," he said.

"I like eating in the kitchen," Harold declared.

"I daresay you do," Turner said with a tolerant nod. "But I suspect you'd be just as enchanted eating in the barn, were it permissible."

The boy's eyes widened. "Is it? Is it perm—permi—"

"Permissible," Kara supplied. "And it is not." She grinned at the boy. "At least, not on a regular basis."

"You have the space to picnic in the schoolroom every day," Niall said. "It's so large and bright in there."

The boy bounced in his chair, and Kara aimed a look first at Niall, then at Turner. "Stop giving him ideas, the pair of you."

"Turner began it," Niall said, taking a bite of mutton.

"Well, my rooms are splendid," Gyda declared. "I give my thanks to both of you. But I notice the duchess's suite is as yet untouched. Where do they fall on your long list, Kara?"

"Last, I should think. I am perfectly happy downstairs with Mrs. Pollock."

Turner made a sound of protest, but Mrs. Pollock nodded sagely. "Aye, 'tis best, I think. It's better to be thought odd than fast. I won't have a word spoken against our lady. If I vouch for her, then no one in East Lothian will dare doubt her virtue."

Kara arched a brow. "You see?"

Gyda rolled her eyes. "Virtues are overrated. Frankly, I was shocked you summoned us so quickly. I thought you'd planned to stay at Balburn House a bit longer, while you evaluated this place and started work on it."

"Our plans changed." Niall shrugged. "And it was all to the good, as we've been able to avoid being embroiled in ..." He paused and glanced at Harold. "In their incident."

Gyda looked at him, surprised. "Incident?"

Kara widened her eyes at Niall. She hadn't had a moment alone with their friend to catch her up.

Frowning, Gyda glanced back and forth between them. After a moment, her jaw dropped. "You don't mean ... Not the sort of *incident* you two seem to keep bumping into?"

"I'm afraid so," Kara said.

"What? Who?" Gyda demanded.

"Finley," Niall answered shortly.

Gyda gasped. "Not the Viking?"

Saddened again at the thought, Kara nodded.

"Viking?" They had caught Harold's attention. "Are there Vikings here?"

"No, dear," Kara said gently. "The Vikings are long gone. They are just part of history now."

"I've been learning all about Vikings," Harold said eagerly. "And Celts. And Picts. And Romans!"

Turner nodded, casting a look of approval at the boy. "Ever since you wrote, telling us of the work you were doing for Lord Balstone, the boy has been learning all he could about early British history."

"Well done, Harold," Kara said warmly.

"I even started building a Viking automaton. He's a bit bigger than the man I helped you with, for the horse clock. He has a sword!" Harold squirmed a little in his seat. "Can we work together on him?"

"Of course."

"Gyda, will you help with his shield?" the boy asked.

Gyda was holding her glass of wine and staring at it. Likely she was still absorbing the news of Mr. Finley's death.

"Gyda?"

"What? Oh, yes. I insist on helping with your shield," she told Harold. "I will show you some of my newest designs."

Harold was shifting in his chair now. "But where is the workshop here? I didn't see it."

"We haven't set one up yet," Kara told him. "It may be that we have to use one of the rooms in the house this time. If you will help me, we'll examine them all, and find one with the right size and situation."

Gyda set down her wine and let out a long breath. "But where is the forge? That's what I want to know." She looked pointedly at Niall.

He brightened at the question. "I have an idea for it, actually. I went out exploring this morning and found a small stone barn in a field out past the stable block. I suspect it held goats at one time. It has a wide door in front, slightly arched, but I was thinking we'd need to add another door at the back, or a large window at the least." Niall grinned at Kara. "Being able to open the two walls at the forge at Bluefield has quite spoiled me. The flexibility in light and temperature has won me over on the arrangement."

Mrs. Pollock hustled over with another platter of hot rolls. "Hearing you all talk of airiness and picnics has reminded me." She looked to Niall. "Did the land agent tell you about the Viewing House?"

Kara straightened. "The Viewing House?" She looked at Niall, too.

He frowned. "I don't think so?" He thought a moment. "Unless... He did mention a gazebo on a cliff, with a view."

"Aye, that's the one. It's like nothing ye've seen, I'll wager."

"It's on the river that forms a section of the boundary of the estate? To the west?" Niall asked.

"Aye. There's a good length of it that wends along a cliffside, where the burn has cut through the hills. There's a rock causeway across the water—though it makes a slippery and dangerous crossing. And there's a pretty view of the countryside. One of the old dukes admired the scene. He built a sort of summerhouse out there. It's a gazebo of carved stone. It can be left open to enjoy the view, but it also holds folding shutters to protect from the elements, should ye care to close them." She shook her head. "I havna seen it in years, but we used to take a boat out past it when I was young."

"It sounds lovely," Kara said.

"'Tis. I havna seen the view from the house, of course. But the interesting thing is—it doesn't sit on top of the cliff, but is set into the midst of it."

Kara tried to picture it.

"How was that accomplished?" Gyda asked.

"I've seen it," Catriona said tentatively. "From the water. There's a flat spot, an open space, in the face of the cliff. The Viewing House is built on it, right up to the edge."

"Fascinating," Niall murmured.

"How far is it from the house?" asked Kara.

"There used to be a trail out to it, starting past the walled garden," said Mrs. Pollock. "I don't know if it's been kept clear. Taking that, I'd guess it was close to a thirty-minute walk. The stroll was part of the charm, I gather. It was always a favorite spot for picnics and even small dinner parties."

Kara glanced at the clock over the long counter. "It's likely too late to take a look at it this evening."

"Aye. You can get to it a bit quicker, should ye follow the main road down to the bridge across the burn. There's a boathouse and a small pier down there. That's how the servants would haul the supplies out there—by boat."

"I am officially intrigued." Kara glanced between Niall and Gyda. "Perhaps, if the weather is fine, we can take a walk out there tomorrow?"

"*After* we check out the space for the forge," Gyda insisted.

"And after we send word to Mr. Darrow." Niall looked to his assistant. "The procurator fiscal wants a word with you. He's speaking to everyone who attended the unveiling at Balburn House."

"We cannot go tonight?" Harold asked, crestfallen.

"It will be dark by the time we made it out there."

"No view from the Viewing House, then," Kara added.

"My dear old mam said they made specially boxed china sets and tableware for the place, made easy to transport. They must be around here somewhere. Mayhap you and the girls could go and have a look for them?" suggested Mrs. Pollock.

"In the attics?" Harold looked to Kara for permission.

"Go right ahead, as long as you don't ask me to come along." Kara shuddered. Harold began chattering excitedly with the maids, but she was distracted by the sound of heavy footsteps on the servants' stairs in the passage. She looked up as Hendry came bounding into the kitchen.

"Excuse me, Your Grace, but I thought you'd want to know," he said breathlessly. "There's a delivery for you."

Kara's curiosity grew as Niall shot the footman a surprised look.

"I don't believe I was expecting anything. Were you, Kara?"

"Not I," she said, shaking her head. "Not yet."

"It's from Balburn House, sir," Hendry said. "Hamish and I heard the cart in the drive. We ran down to find the lads unloading a hopping great crate. They left it in the drive, right before the front door, and drove away. One of them said there's a note inside, to explain."

"Let's open it!" Harold jumped to his feet.

Kara could see Niall was nearly as curious as the boy. "Well, I suppose we were mostly finished with dinner, in any case. Thank you, Mrs. Pollock."

"It was delicious," Niall added.

"I've a cherry crumble keeping warm in the oven," the cook said. "Come back down for dessert after you've settled your curiosity."

"I'll help with the clearing, so Ailsa can go up, too," offered Turner. "I can see you are just as excited as the rest of them."

The maid's eyes lit up. "Oh, thank you, Mr. Turner!"

Everyone trooped upstairs and gathered around the enormous, unmarked crate.

"Here you are, Your Grace!" Hamish came running from the direction of the stables, holding a crowbar.

"What do you think it is, Niall?" asked Harold.

"I haven't the foggiest notion, lad. Stand back, now. There might be nails." Niall wrenched one side loose, then moved on to each of the others. After the last, Hamish and Hendry lifted the top off together.

They all stared down at the envelope resting on tightly packed straw.

Niall took it up and extracted a note. He read it out loud.

Sedwick,

We've a temporary lack of cash here, my sister tells me, which will mean a delay of payment to you. Along with my apologies, I send an artifact I acquired when a colleague's collection was sold off. It's a staff, believed to have belonged to a shaman or mystic. I feel I have learned enough of your taste to be sure it will appeal to you. Consider it a gift, to make up for the delay in payment.

In addition, I am sending along a bit of collateral, to show my good faith and to reassure you that I mean to make payment when I can—

"It's a crown!" Harold had been shoving straw aside and now revealed the top of the glass display case inside.

"Oh, heavens!" Kara gasped. "What has he gone and sent that for?"

"Is that it?" Ailsa gasped, shrinking away. "Is that the Cursed Crown?"

"That's it," Gyda confirmed. She looked to Niall. "He cannot mean for you to keep it? It's a famous family heirloom."

Niall glanced down at the note again.

> *Keep the crown safely for me, while I see to freeing up the coin I owe you. We'll exchange the crown for payment once I have it, but please keep the staff with my compliments.*
>
> —*Dunstan, Lord Balstone*

"That's all of it. And a key," he said, fishing it out of the folded paper and holding it up. He handed it to Kara. She took it and reached to pull Harold away as Niall and Hamish reached into the crate to lift out the display case.

"There we are," Niall said as it came free. "Carefully, now. Let's set it on the step."

Everyone gathered around again as the crown in its case was set on the stone, back from the edge. "There's a brass closure at the back," Niall said, reaching for the key again. After a moment, he unlatched it and opened the top glass panel on its hinges.

"Can I wear it?" asked Harold, practically bouncing on his toes.

"I'm sorry, Harold, but it is not a toy. I don't think any of us should wear it. I likely shouldn't even take it out at all."

"Just for a moment," Gyda urged. "I'd like to see it up close."

Reaching in, Niall lifted the crown out. The gold gleamed dully in the fading light. "It's dusty."

Ailsa took a step back. "I don't want to clean it."

"Well, now you know why it's dusty," Gyda said with a grin. She leaned in to inspect the piece.

"Balburn had his favorite relics sitting about his study," Niall said. "He handled them regularly. But he kept this locked away in the case, in that small parlor."

"He did speak of it with a certain tone that evening," Kara recalled. "As if he didn't care for it."

"I think perhaps he doesn't care for its notoriety, or for it to outshine his own discoveries," Niall ventured.

"Perhaps that's why he sent it as collateral, then. He wouldn't truly miss it."

Niall turned the crown in his hands. "It's beautiful workmanship, but it does feel as if it comes from another time, doesn't it?"

"Do you think the curse came with it?" asked Ailsa. She was hanging back, as if afraid to get too close.

"Absolutely not," Kara said firmly. "There is no such thing."

"Let's have a look at the other piece." Gyda had turned back to the crate and was digging through the straw as Niall replaced the crown and locked the case once more.

"Ah, here we are." Gyda lifted out a burlap-wrapped object, over two feet long and wide at one end. It was knotted closed with several lengths of rope. Niall cut them and took the bundle, carefully unwinding the burlap.

"*Cor*," Harold breathed as the last of it fell away.

It was old. Kara knew that, but not much more. The staff was of bronze, gone green in places with the patina of age. The shaft had been carved into a primitive sculpting of a man in robes. His long garments were etched with spirals, linked circles, and curved vines with eyes peeping from occasional leaves. Two stylized wolves knelt at his feet, and he wore a horned mask, the antlers elaborate and wide.

"Odin's arse," whispered Gyda.

"This one is dusty, too," noted Niall. "It's all through the wrappings."

"Another piece that was not one of Balstone's favorites?" Kara guessed. "But to give it as a gift?"

Harold's eyes were huge. Niall beckoned him closer and let him hold the thing. "Careful," he warned. "It belongs in a museum. I'll make enquiries the next time we are in Edinburgh."

"What shall we do with them, in the meantime?" asked Kara, eyeing the pair of artifacts dubiously. "Neither will fit in with the décor I'm planning."

"We can put them in the schoolroom," Harold said, brandishing the staff.

Niall shook his head. "No. Wrap it up again, will you, lad?" He gave Hamish and Hendry a nod. "You'd best put them in the sitting room in the ducal suite, for safekeeping." He glanced at the house. "Perhaps we'll move them to the study, once it's ready." He paused. "Although I hope we won't be keeping the crown for long." He glanced at Kara with a wide smile, his slanted eyes glowing with mirth. "I think Balstone's gambit has backfired. I was in no hurry for his payment before, but now I'd rather like to get that thing back to him, quickly."

Hamish and Hendry took up the display case by the wooden base and slowly maneuvered it into the house. Harold followed with the bundled staff, the maids behind him.

"Wash your hands when you are done," Kara called. "And then head back to the kitchen for your dessert."

The sun was setting. Brilliant reds and oranges lit the sky through the trees, but the shadows were growing near the house. Kara took Niall's arm and grinned at Gyda. "Well, here we all are. A new home. New roles. A new community. Another new adventure."

"And never a dull moment," Gyda said wryly. "Which is nothing new at all. Let's go eat crumble and fortify ourselves for whatever comes next."

Chapter Six

"Here you are." The next morning Kara had Harold and the footmen helping her to clear out the objects that had been stacked in the schoolroom. She handed Harold a box filled with several elaborate Baroque candlesticks. "Is it too heavy?" she asked as the boy hesitated.

"Of course not," Harold scoffed, eyeing the massive box of books Hamish was carrying with ease. "I can do it." But he paused, bent over a moment.

"Harold? Are you well, dear?"

He nodded. "Of course. Mrs. Pollock says I'm likely just gassy."

Kara bit back a laugh. "Would you care to rest a while? We can finish clearing this out without you."

"No." Harold straightened. "I can do it."

"Thank you, dear, but don't overdo it if you don't feel well. I do appreciate your help." Kara extended her thanks to the two footmen as well. "You are all so efficient. We are making quick work of this."

Harold puffed his chest at the praise, and Kara hid a grin. The boy appeared to be impressed with the pair of tall, strong footmen, and clearly hoped to emulate and impress them. Fortunately, the cousins were taking it in stride. They had all unpacked his things in the schoolroom, and Hamish and Hendry had been beyond patient as he showed them his favorite books, displayed the blade he had crafted for himself under Niall's supervision, and explained the various experiments he had packed up and brought with him.

They were relocating all the castoffs to the attics for now. Kara was organizing the loads down here and letting the others carry them up. She moved over to a stack of paintings leaning against a wall, sorting through them to find one small enough for Harold to easily manage.

"There you go," she told the boy when he arrived back, ready for the next load. "Hamish, can you reach that largest one, all the way in the back?"

She moved out of the footman's way, glancing at the painting before looking for another in Harold's size.

She was bent over, reaching, when it struck her—what she had seen. "Hamish! Hold a moment!" She spun around.

He peered questioningly around the frame of the large painting.

Kara stared. "Would you please set that down on the chair over there? I want to get a good look at it."

He obliged, and she stepped forward, frowning at the image. It looked to be a representation of a ceremony of sorts. Official-looking gentlemen were gathered around a set of beribboned gates set in stone pillars. Graceful stonework stretched out on either side. Several of the gentlemen wore sashes, and a crowd had gathered in the road before them.

Hamish stared as well, obviously attempting to understand what had caught her eye.

"You don't know where—" Kara stopped. "No, of course you would not, being from the city. Hamish, will you run downstairs and ask Mrs. Pollock to step up here? I know she's busy, but we won't keep her long. Tell her it is important."

"Yes, miss."

She was sending Harold upstairs with another box when the cook arrived. "Mrs. Pollock, thank you. You have some knowledge of local history. Can you tell me where this scene is? Is it somewhere nearby?"

The cook lit up when she turned and glimpsed the painting. "Oh, aye! Gracious me, but I haven't seen this in an age. You are right, miss. It is local. It's the occasion when they unveiled the new gates to the village in Highfield."

"New? Judging by the fashions, I'd guess this was painted at least fifty years ago."

"Well, that's still new to folks around here," Mrs. Pollock said, lifting a shoulder. "If ye drove here from the city, ye wouldna ha' seen them. They sit on the other side of the high street, on the road to North Berwick. It was to mark the turn of the century, ye ken, that they decided to replace the gates. Oh, the talk about it back then! I was only a girl, but I recall it. It's a sort of rivalry, through the coastal villages, for status. Folks here were proud of the braw new gates, but the others made snide remarks about wasting money and getting above ourselves."

"And you've seen this painting before?"

"Aye, well, a copy of it. There's one in the vicarage. I saw it many a time when I went to deliver my mam's preserves to Mr. Biddlesworth. Word is that there's another copy in the mayor's parlor, but I never set foot in that house, of course."

"Why would there be a copy of the painting here, in the priory?" asked Kara.

"Ah, well, that group standing at the gates, that's all the local gentry, isn't it? 'Twas they who donated the money for the construction of the new gates. See the tall gentleman with the gray stripe in his hair? That's the last Duke of Sedwick. He died just a few years after this. The woman at his side is his daughter. She was the last mistress here."

"Can you tell me about the other people in that group?"

"Well, here's the mayor. The previous one. Here's dear old Mr. Biddlesworth. That one's a Dalwiddie, but I can't say which one for sure."

"And this one?" Kara pointed to a tall blond gentleman standing to the left of the mayor.

"Oh, that's old Lord Balstone. Father to the current lord and to Mrs. Grier."

Kara stepped closer to look. "Is he, now?"

The cook eyed her curiously. "Is he why ye're asking? But why? He's been dead these last..." The cook's words trailed away. She stared at the figure and suddenly reached out to grip Kara's arm. "Saints alive! It's him! Or the spitting image of him, at the least."

Kara stared at her. "Who, Mrs. Pollock?" She'd certainly noticed the resemblance, but if the cook could second it...

"It's him!" Mrs. Pollock repeated. "I should have seen it before, but it's been years since I last saw this painting. He's very like the man who brought the message for the duke that first night ye were here."

"Wait. What's that?" Kara asked. That was not what she'd expected the cook to say. "Mrs. Pollock, this fellow, the old Lord Balstone, looks like the man who brought Niall that message?"

"Aye!" The cook frowned at her. "You never saw that messenger, miss. But that image reminded you of someone, too?"

Kara eyed the footman, who was watching them avidly. "Hamish, would you go out to the barn beyond the stables and ask the duke to come inside? Thank you."

Mrs. Pollock was not letting her off the hook. "Who did you think old Lord Balstone looked like, miss?" she asked again.

"He looks very like Mr. Finley," Kara said quietly. "The man who was murdered."

≫≫≪≪

NIALL WATCHED AS Gyda's trained eye took in every detail of the barn, from size, to slope of the roof, to the even stretch of the dirt floor.

"You are right," she said, eyes shining. "It needs another door. And it needs to be rid of the smell of goat piss. But the size! And the loft will be handy." She nodded. "There is plenty of room for us both. Perhaps we could even put in a crane, so I can hang a good-sized crucible. Just think, I could pour a dozen studs for my shields all at once."

"More efficient," Niall agreed. He stared about, seeing the setup in his mind's eye. "Yes. I think it will do very well."

"Your Grace!"

They both turned at the call to see Hamish coming through the meadow.

"Miss Levett asks you to return to the house," he said as he drew near. "She has something she needs to show you."

"Tell her we'll be right there, please." Niall moved to close the heavy doors and paused at a sudden ache in his gut.

Gyda was watching the footman retreat back to the house. "Before we go back, I have something to say."

He turned away from the closed door, his brow raised high in question.

"I understand that there is work to be done here. I am actually looking forward to helping put our stamp on the place. But Niall, you need to marry that girl. Soon."

He gave his friend and assistant a pained look as they set out, heading for the house. "I tried to convince her to push the wedding up when I was summoned to Holyrood. I wanted us to marry before we set out for Edinburgh, but she refused. She said it wouldn't be fair to those who expect an invitation."

"You know that's not it. She thinks you are going to change your mind."

"Ridiculous."

"You know it. I know it. But she is afraid you will realize she is not fit to be a duchess." Gyda made a rude noise. "That old battle-axe, the Grier woman, didn't help."

"I know." He sighed. "I'm hoping that Kara will be reassured when she is met with enthusiasm from some of the other women in the community."

"She needs reassurance from *you*, you great nitwit."

Niall shot her an incredulous look. "Kara knows how I feel about her."

"And yet she still needs to hear it."

"Kara is the most confident, accomplished—"

"Woman. She's a woman, Niall. She needs to hear it. She *deserves* to hear it."

"You really think so?"

"I know it. Now, talk about something else," she said as they cut through what must have once been the kitchen garden, to the servants' entrance at the back of the priory. "No one else needs to hear anything on the subject."

"I'll ask around for a good stonemason," Niall said obediently. "Dalwiddie might be able to recommend someone."

They passed through the mudroom and past the scullery, moving down the long passage through to the kitchens, servants' hall, and stairs.

"A moment, Your Grace," Mrs. Pollock called from where she stood, mixing something at the great oak table. "Miss Levett has need of ye. She's in my parlor."

"Thank you, Mrs. Pollock." He turned around and paused at another pain in his stomach.

Impatient, Gyda moved around him to open the door. "Kara," she called. "I think Niall has done it. The old goat barn will do nicely as a forge. We'll need another door, but the space is half again as big as the forge at Bluefield! There will be plenty of room for both of us and some new equipment, besides."

"Excellent." Kara smiled in greeting. "I am glad to hear it."

"Hamish said you needed to see us?" Niall asked.

"Yes. Or rather, I need you to see this." She gestured toward a large painting propped on the arms of a chair.

"Something you found upstairs?" Niall peered at it. "Oh, yes. I've seen these gates. They sit on the road into Highfield, on the other side of the village." He shrugged. "There are a little grander than necessary, I thought."

"Well, that's not a reason she would ask us to look at it. What of it?" asked Gyda. She stepped closer to the painting.

"Do you recognize anyone?" Kara asked.

"Oh! Yes. There! The Viking!" Frowning, Gyda took in the details. "Or not him, I suppose. But someone like him."

"Yes. Someone very like him," Kara agreed. She met Niall's gaze with a somber one of her own. "The former Lord Balstone, in fact."

Niall started. "That's Balstone's father?"

Kara nodded.

"And he looks remarkably like Balstone's assistant." Niall was quick to grasp the implications.

"Balstone's *dead* assistant," Gyda said pointedly. "But surely Kara is not the first to notice the resemblance?"

"Obviously not, but no one mentioned anything about it to me." He paused. "I suppose they wouldn't."

"That's not all," Kara said. "Mrs. Pollock recognized the similarity—"

"To Finley?" Niall asked.

"To the man who delivered that note the other night."

Niall blinked. "*Finley* delivered that note?"

"What note?" Gyda looked between them. "Have I missed something?"

"I didn't think so, until now," he answered, trying to grasp the idea that Finley delivered that suspicious message.

Kara met his gaze steadily. "Surely we must tell Darrow about the note now."

"Someone explain, please," demanded Gyda.

Niall cursed under his breath as Kara did so. "You are right," he said on a sigh when she'd finished. "I sent word to Darrow this morning, telling him Gyda had arrived. Now we'll have to tell him about the note. He said no one had seen Finley after the party, until he was found dead at the dig. But if Mrs. Pollock saw him the next night—it could not have been long before he died." He frowned. "It's damned annoying. I didn't want to get mixed up in this."

"Annoying?" Gyda repeated, incredulous. "A man delivers a message, beckoning you to a midnight rendezvous, where he ends up dead?" She looked Niall over. "Has it occurred to you that you are the same height and build as Finley? Perhaps *you* were the one that was meant to end up dead."

"Don't be ridiculous. I haven't been in the area long enough to make any enemies, let alone one that would wish me dead."

Gyda stilled. "Could it be Petra Scot?"

For a moment, Niall froze, gone numb with dread at the thought of the woman who had vowed to destroy him—and Kara, too. But common sense reasserted itself. "No, it's not possible. It is a small collection of communities along the coast, but a remarkably interconnected one. Our arrival is huge news, gossiped about in and amongst all the coastal villages. It's why Mrs. Pollock is so determined to protect Kara's reputation. If another new arrival was in the area, we would have heard about it. From multiple sources, likely."

"We didn't hear about Finley's possible connection to the old Lord Balstone," Kara pointed out.

"That's old gossip. Finley has been Balstone's assistant for several years. Although I'm sure if I hadn't spent most of my time in their company, someone might have whispered it to me."

Kara pondered that. After a moment, she looked at him, worried again. "Niall, what if you were not meant to be killed at that meeting, but perhaps set up as the killer?"

"Yes. Perhaps *because* you are new to the area and no one knows much about you," Gyda said thoughtfully.

Ire roiled suddenly along with the cramping in his gut. "Odin's *arse*," Niall swore, low and ardent. "Is it too much to ask?" he demanded. "Just *once*? Once, could the dregs and noxious drama of humanity just roll by us, leaving us unscathed?"

Both women jumped as he banged a hand down on a side table. He stalked out, slamming the door behind him and vaulting up the servants' stairs.

This was supposed to be a new start—a new beginning, among new people, without all the whispers and twitters of the last year's mayhem trailing behind them.

Damn it all. "Harold!" he bellowed from the front hall.

"Niall?" The boy's call echoed down the stairwell from above.

"Come on, lad! We're going for a walk!" He paced until the boy came racing down the stairs. "Let's go and see the view from the Viewing House."

KARA AND GYDA climbed the stairs a little later, debating whether they should set out after Niall and Harold now, or wait to give Niall's temper a chance to settle.

Above them, the green baize door opened and Catriona stuck her head through. "Mr. Darrow has arrived, miss. Where shall I put him?"

Kara stopped. "There really is nowhere appropriate. Leave him to me, Catriona." She looked back at Gyda. "Let's take him outside. It will be better to be private, and there are stone benches in the colonnade."

They found the fiscal in the entry hall. Kara apologized as she greeted him. "Would you mind speaking outside? We do seem to receive you in the oddest spots, but we are still seeing to the clearing out of bedrooms for everyone and haven't yet got to the parlors."

"No worries, Miss Levett," the fiscal answered agreeably as he held open the door. "In this job I've learned not to stand on ceremony." He eyed Gyda with appreciation. "Miss Winther, I presume."

Gyda nodded, face bright with interest. "Kara tells me you are the procurator fiscal, Mr. Darrow, but I confess, I have no idea what that means."

"It mostly means endless reports and an unfortunate amount of paper shuffling." He paused a moment, frowning toward the drive that curved through the wood and down to the house. But then he grinned as they turned toward the side of the house where the walled garden and colonnade stood. Sobering a little, he stood back to allow them to enter the colonnade before him. "In the case of a serious crime like the death of Mr. Edmund Finley, it means I am responsible for taking precognitions, directing the police in their enquiries, and for prosecution of the crime."

Kara and Gyda exchanged glances. "Precognitions?" asked Kara.

"Statements from witnesses or people connected to the case," he explained. "As I aim to do with you today, Miss Winther." He stopped next to a bench and held out a hand in invitation.

"How intriguing," Gyda said, taking a seat. "I shall write my friends and tell them I've given you my precognition. They will be puzzled and will likely suspect it is something a little scandalous."

Kara settled in beside her while Darrow leaned against the low wall and pulled out a notebook.

"And so it might be, depending on what you have to say." There was a definite twinkle in his eye.

"Alas, I never got to meet Mr. Finley, although I did admire him from across the room." Gyda's tone hardened. "I certainly hope you will discover who killed him, Mr. Darrow. Both Kara and Niall spoke highly of him, and that is enough to convince me he was a good man."

"Oh, I will find out what happened to him and why, never you doubt it. And on that subject, your friends mentioned that you saw him having words with Mrs. Grier the night of the unveiling."

"Words? He was scrapping with her, nose to nose. I admired that, too."

Darrow looked up and gave them both a wry glance. "Understood. But did you hear what they were arguing about?"

"No. They heard me as I came up the stairs and lowered their voices. Mrs. Grier stopped hissing at him long enough to shoot me a look of disdain."

"Why?"

"Because I was using the servants' stairs."

"Why?" he asked again, surprised.

"Because the underbutler told me he was opening the last bottles of champagne, and I went to be sure I got a share of it."

Darrow bit back a laugh.

"Mr. Finley did sound as if he was starting up again as I headed for the parlor, but I believe Mrs. Grier had had enough. The last thing I heard was her telling him it was over. *No more,* she said. *It's over and done with.*"

"And you have no idea what they were discussing?"

"None. It seems a good question to ask Mrs. Grier," Gyda said pointedly.

"In point of fact, I did mention the matter to her." Looking up, Darrow watched them both. "She denies arguing with Mr. Finley."

"Then she is lying," Gyda said flatly.

"It rather looks like she has something to hide," said Kara.

"It's the logical conclusion," Darrow agreed. "So why would she risk it?"

"That is for you to answer, Mr. Darrow." Gyda stood. "I sympathize, as it sounds as if you have a difficult job ahead of you, sir. As Kara has more to tell you regarding your enquiry, I suggest you walk out to the Viewing House while you talk. Mr. Darrow will undoubtedly wish to speak with Niall, and Kara, you can sweeten his temper before you bring him back."

"Where are you going?" asked Kara.

"I'm going to grab Hendry and make him help me clean out the rotting straw from that barn. It must be done before we begin setting up the forge. I have the feeling Niall will need somewhere to work off his frustrations." Gyda eyed Darrow. "And so will I."

"Thank you for your help, Miss Winther." Darrow inclined his head.

"Of course." Gyda pointed a finger at the man. "Don't let that woman get away with lying to you, no matter how rude she is." With a nod, she swung around and headed toward the house.

Admiration colored Darrow's expression as he watched her go. After a moment, he turned a curious eye to Kara. "You have something to tell me? Something about Finley's death?"

"I do. We do. Would you care to follow Gyda's suggestion and walk out with me to the river? Niall is out there now. I can explain along the way."

He hesitated. "Is it important, do you believe?"

"Yes. We've discovered our cook saw Finley on the night he was killed. Just hours beforehand." When he glanced at the house, she nodded. "Yes, of course you can speak with her, but I think you'll want to hear about it first."

"Very well, then."

"Thank you." She stood. "The trail begins beyond the back of the walled garden. Niall and the footmen had a look at it early this morning. It appears there has been some effort to keep the trail out to the Viewing House open, but no sort of regular maintenance." She looked with approval at his boots. "The trail is recognizable, but overgrown."

"Lead the way."

She did, taking him through the walled garden and out the door at the back. The wood came up close to the wall, but the start of the trail was obvious, if covered in grasses and weeds that reached well past her ankles. She was grateful for her own sturdy half-boots, but still, she kept to the trail of trampled growth that Niall and Harold had left behind.

Darrow looked to the sky. "We are heading east, I think?"

"I believe we are. Niall mentioned the trail meanders back toward Lord Balstone's land."

The fiscal nodded. "You said you and the staff were concentrating on cleaning out bedrooms in the house. Has the duke hired any gardeners yet? Or perhaps a gamekeeper?"

"Not yet," she answered, puzzled at the question.

Darrow looked serious. "I thought I caught a glimpse of someone in the wood, on the hillside above the lane that leads to the house. You must be careful, Miss Levett." He looked around. "These lands have been largely empty for years. There might be those who have taken advantage of that. They might be lurking, still."

"Poachers, do you mean?"

"That's the most likely explanation. You should be careful. Don't attempt a trek like this alone. There's no use tempting fate."

"Thank you for the warning. I'll have the staff keep their eyes peeled. But we'll be hiring new people soon. More staff for the house, as well as gardeners, grooms, coachmen, and the like. We won't be so isolated."

"Good," he replied. "Now, what was it that I must hear?"

She talked as they walked, starting with the painting and their discovery of Finley's resemblance to the old Lord Balstone.

"Oh, yes. It appears it was widely known that Finley was the old lord's by-blow."

"Was he, indeed? I thought it was possible he could turn out to be a cousin or some far-flung family member."

"No, no. The previous Lord Balstone had a well-gossiped-about fling with a shopgirl from Edinburgh, not long after his third wife died.

There was talk of it up and down the coast. There were rumors of a child, too. But the old man died without confirming it, and no one knew for sure until Finley showed up in these parts, looking for answers about his father. There was no denying the kinship, according to the gossips. Finley decided to stay, and Dunstan Balstone hired the man to assist him at the archeological site. The people around here all thought it generous of him, to give his natural half-brother the job."

"I feel certain his sister didn't agree," Kara ventured.

"Finley arrived during the time that Mrs. Grier was living in London with her husband. Admittedly, when Mr. Grier died and she returned home, she was reportedly very unhappy to find Finley at Balstone and continued to resent his presence."

"He's been at Balstone for years, I understand," Kara said. "That is a long time for resentment to fester."

"That was my thought also." Darrow halted. "Watch, just here, where you step. There are loose rocks in the path, and they are hard to see."

"Thank you," she said, stepping carefully.

"Of course. Now, what is this about your cook seeing Finley?"

"Well, when we unearthed the painting, Niall and I recognized the figure of the old Lord Balstone and his resemblance to Finley. But Mrs. Pollock recognized his resemblance to the man who delivered a note to the priory on the first night we stayed here."

"The same night Finley was killed."

"It appears so. He arrived quite late. Mrs. Pollock took the note, but refused to deliver it to Niall until the morning."

"And Finley left after delivering it?"

"So she says, although I gather he wasn't happy with her reluctance."

"What did the note say?"

The path had begun to follow a rising curve of a hill on the right side. Kara paused in its shadow to pull the note from her pocket and hand it over.

Darrow took it, walking slowly on as he read it and turned it over several times, examining it closely. "And you and Sedwick think it did indeed come from Balstone?"

"Niall has his doubts. He might have followed up on it the next morning, but we heard of the death at Balstone and thought it was not a good time to ask. But we didn't know at the time that Finley was the servant who died, nor that he'd been the one to deliver the message."

"I will want to talk to Balstone, but there are several disturbing implications to this."

"I know." Kara sighed. "Niall knows. He's not happy about it."

"In what way?"

"You were careful to warn us off becoming involved in your investigation, Mr. Darrow, but believe me, the warning was not necessary. Niall has no wish to get tangled up in this. He has a new title, a new start here." Kara paused. Looking up into the sun-dappled canopy of trees, she drew a deep breath. "Niall has long had to hide parts of himself away, largely because of family secrets."

"Yes. I did hear about his newly exposed bloodlines. There will be no hiding something like that now, not when he's been made a duke."

"True. It was a burden lifted from him when he no longer had to keep such secrets, but he's still a little raw, I believe. He wants to leave all the gossip behind and focus on restoring the priory and becoming a part of the community here. *Not* a part of another murder enquiry."

"That makes sense. This morning I would have appreciated his reticence. But this note? It changes things."

"I know." Kara's gut twisted a little with worry.

"It does look as if someone tried to drag him into the matter, in one way or another."

"I know," she repeated. "I'm no happier about it than he is. Nothing good can come of that note."

They both paused as the wooded trail ended. They found themselves at the edge of a riverbank. The shore was wide just here, and made up of silt and rocks. To the right was the rock causeway that angled across the water. It slowed the passage of the water, causing the river behind it to widen, gone shallow and lazy. The shore in that direction narrowed accordingly, with the spreading river on one side and growing cliffs, tall and craggy, on the other.

"There it is," Kara said, catching her breath. "The Viewing House. How beautiful it is."

She started along the narrowed shore, stepping carefully. The cliffs jutted out into the river ahead, and a path showed, clearly cut into the cliff face from the shore. It meandered a bit before it climbed up to reach the structure perched there. Octagonal, boasting an oxidized copper roof and stout cornered columns, the Viewing House was stunning. It stood open to the air, and Kara could see Niall standing at the stone-fenced edge, staring out over the gorgeous vista.

"Niall!" she called, waving.

He saw her and waved back.

"Come, Mr. Darrow! Let's go and see the view!"

The fiscal had stopped to gaze across the river. He turned to answer her and stopped, looking up at the cliff top. "Is there a path all the way to the top? I thought I saw someone up there."

"I don't know, but we'll soon find out. Look, Niall has started down to meet us." She raised a hand to her brow and scanned ahead. "I don't see Harold. Maybe he has climbed to the top."

"I do hope he's careful." Darrow was looking from the ragged cliffs to the chunks of shale and siltstone lying in the shallow waters of the river.

"Kara! Mr. Darrow!" Niall's shout drifted toward them. Kara picked up her pace. His tone did sound lighter. Perhaps the beauty of the view had soothed his nerves.

He wasn't smiling when she reached him, but he squeezed her hand in reassurance.

"Where's Harold?" she asked.

"Looking for rocks to add to his collection. He went down the path to the shore on the other side." Niall called out a greeting as Darrow approached. "Did you get a chance to speak to Gyda?" he asked after the pleasantries were exchanged.

"I did. But now I find I must talk with you again, Your Grace. And your cook as well, I hear."

"Yes. I hope it turns out to be nothing." Niall gestured. "But come, you've walked all the way out here—you might as well come up and see the view."

The two men started toward the path up the cliff. Kara, trailing, paused to drink in the peace of the scene, the soft sound of the water and the sun dancing on the river's surface. Something sparkled at the water's edge, and she hurried over to find a smooth rock, likely of milky quartz. Perfect for Harold's collection. She took it up and hurried off after the men. She was still a good way behind them when she saw Darrow stop. He looked up just as she heard it, too—a crashing sound from above.

A large chunk of stone was tumbling down the cliff face. It hit an outcropping above the men, bounced, and headed right for them.

Darrow gave a shout and pushed Niall hard.

Kara gasped. Niall stumbled forward. Darrow jumped back. The fiscal tripped and fell, tried to scramble away. The rock crashed into the shore right next to him, but then it rolled, crushing Darrow's leg beneath it as its momentum carried it toward the river.

The fiscal's shout of pain and anger echoed across the water, shattering the peace and spurring Kara forward.

Chapter Seven

"No. No laudanum," Darrow rasped.

"You are not going to wish to be awake while I set that leg," the surgeon warned.

Niall didn't even know the man's name. He was just happy to discover that the village of Highfield did indeed boast a surgeon. Jamie, the stable lad, had known where to find him.

After the accident, Niall had sent Harold hurtling back to the priory to fetch the footmen and send word for a doctor. Hamish and Hendry had wisely brought an old door with them to carry Darrow back upon. The fiscal had passed out when they moved him onto it, but he was awake now, and insistent.

"Not yet." Darrow panted through the pain, glaring at the surgeon and at Mrs. Pollock, who bustled in with a great pot of hot water. "Everyone out. I have to speak to Sedwick. Alone."

Mrs. Pollock hustled out. The surgeon objected, but Darrow insisted. "I'll take the laudanum after I've had my say."

The man went, grumbling, but Kara folded her arms and leaned against the bedpost. "I'm staying."

"Fine," Darrow grunted. He gritted his teeth a moment, then glared at Niall. "Before they knock me out, we must settle some things." His brow lowered even further. "Even after he sets my leg, I'll be forced to stay here for days, even weeks."

"You are welcome to stay for as long as you need, of course," Niall told him.

"We will gladly do anything to help get you recovered and back on your feet," added Kara.

"Yes, yes. Thank you. It will be too damned long."

Niall waited while the fiscal fixed his gaze on him, looking him over.

"You will have to be my eyes and ears. My legs, too, damn it all. The enquiry won't wait."

"Tell me whom you report to in Edinburgh, and I'll send word—"

"No. I cannot fail at this. The sharks will circle in the water if I do. I can do this. But first, I'll need you to go to my room at the Sheep's Head."

"I'll send for your things."

"No. You. You go," Darrow insisted. "Someone has already been through my room there and searched through my things. I know it wasn't you. I trust you to do it now. Fetch my notes. They are sealed in a wax folder and affixed to the underside of the shelf of the washstand." He let loose a long, shuddering sigh. "Don't get me wrong, Sedwick. I'm still in charge of this enquiry. But you are going to have to assist me."

Surprised, Niall shook his head. "We'll send for someone from the city. The lord advocate will wish—"

"The lord advocate wants this solved quickly. And quietly, if possible. It doesn't look good, having even a hint that a peer is suspected of murder. You have the skills needed to help me wrap this up." Darrow glanced at Kara. "Both of you. I've been briefed on some of your exploits."

Niall objected again. "We've no wish to push in or get involved."

"You are involved," Darrow answered flatly. "That note was meant to embroil you in this mess. You know it."

"But—"

"Someone is watching this house," Darrow said. "I caught a glimpse of him on the hillside above the lane leading to the drive. I went to have a look. He ran away, but it wasn't just a poacher. He'd been hunkered down in a spot where he could see the house, note who has been coming and going—and he'd been there for at least a day or so. And this—" He grimaced as he gestured toward his leg. "I saw someone on the cliff top as we approached. They were there before we arrived. They couldn't have expected us. This was meant for you."

Kara gave a moan.

"Damn it," Niall swore. "Damn it all to hell."

"Who?" asked Kara. "Why?"

"I don't know. There's something beneath the surface here. Finley was young. He's connected to that family. Balstone is jumpy. His sister is lying. I have no idea what your connection to all of this is—"

"There's no connection," Niall growled. "I created that damned sculpture for them. That is it."

"Look, I don't believe you are mixed up in whatever nefarious thing is going on."

"Well, thank you for that, at least," Niall huffed.

"But it is in your interests to find out what the hell is going on. So help me do it, damn it." Darrow laid his head back. "Now, give me the damned laudanum. It hurts like hell. Let's get this over with." He met Niall's gaze again. "Go and get my file. When I wake up, we'll start strategizing."

Kara was already at the door, summoning the surgeon. With a curt nod at the man in the bed, Niall turned and eased out past her.

He heard her follow as he stalked down the stairs.

"I'll go and change," she said. "Ask Jamie to ready the cart before you head up the hill to find that watcher's spot."

He stopped on the curve of the stair and looked back at her. "How did you—? Never mind." He shook his head and stared up at her above him. "I should never have taken that damned commission. I'm so sorry."

"Niall! None of this is your fault. You are right—we deserve a rest from this sort of... adventure." Her expression hardened. "But if Darrow is correct and they are targeting you? I won't stand for it."

"Finley was a good man." Niall sighed. "He deserves justice."

"And we deserve a bit of peace. But if we have to catch a killer in order to get it, then so be it."

Reaching up, he cupped her jaw. "Even in the midst of a damned mess like this, I know how lucky I am."

"As do I. Now, go and see what is to be seen up there while I get ready. I mean to make this a quick investigation. We have a lot to do."

He resisted the little push she gave him. "We do," he agreed. "But the first thing I want to start planning is a wedding." He lowered his voice to a whisper. "It's time, Kara. I don't want to wait any longer." He pulled her down, gave her a fierce kiss, then set off for the damned hillside.

"I'm sorry I was delayed," Kara said later. "I stopped in the kitchens and asked Mrs. Pollock to start baking. I need her to put together a collection of sweet breads and pastries."

She met Niall's questioning gaze with a serious one of her own as the cart made the turn onto the main coastal road. "We need an excuse to stop over at Balburn House. We can offer food to a house in mourning, and it's something we can offer both Lord Balstone and his servants—so we can get a chance to talk to as many as we can." She shrugged. "We need to know more about Finley."

"I hope Darrow has some useful information in his files."

"I assume Finley lived at Balburn?" Kara asked.

"Yes—" Niall stopped short. "At least, I think he did. It was my initial response, but now that you ask, I realize it was an assumption. Certainly he was at the dig every morning I was there, but thinking back, I never caught a glimpse of him at the house."

"So, he likely kept below stairs or avoided the house altogether, if Mrs. Grier was so disagreeable toward him."

They sat in silence a moment as the cart rolled on.

"She's my first candidate," Kara stated. "For the murder. And it's not only just because she is so bad tempered."

"She's on my list, too. We know she lied to Darrow. You know I would never believe that Gyda did not see that argument the night of the unveiling."

"And Darrow said she resented having Finley at Balburn House. Perhaps she didn't like the reminder of her father's peccadillos?"

"She does appear to be strait-laced." Niall paused. "Although Balstone did hint several times that her son has been in and out of trouble."

"What sort of trouble?"

"Oh, it was all innuendo, but it sounded like the usual antics that wealthy young men get up to. Gambling. Chasing women."

Kara thought of the tight-lipped woman who had greeted her so frostily. "No. She wouldn't like that, would she?"

"We should look into the son, too. What was his attitude toward his born-on-the-wrong-side-of-the-blanket uncle?"

She sighed. "We are starting from scratch on this one, aren't we?"

"We'll find our way."

Kara stared out at the sea as they left the wood behind. She couldn't keep the worry from building inside her. "Niall, what is going on? Why is someone watching us? Why would someone here try to hurt you?"

He reached out to squeeze her hand. "I honestly do not have the foggiest idea. At first, I thought Darrow's notion that someone meant that rock fall for me was nonsense. It makes far more sense that someone would wish to harm him—the investigator. But he was right about someone watching the house. I saw the spot. None of it makes any sense."

"You didn't have any disagreements with anyone while you were working on the statues?"

"No. Not a one. I'm completely befuddled."

"Well, we are going to have to keep our eyes open, and our minds as well. As much as I dislike Mrs. Grier, I cannot ignore the fact that there may be other suspects." She eyed him carefully. "And we must go softly as we poke around. I refuse to do anything to jeopardize our welcome here."

His gaze softened. "I am not worried about that. Not in any way."

"Mrs. Grier—"

"Is just an unhappy, disagreeable woman. It's well known. People here take what she says with a grain of salt. We've no need to worry over her."

"Unless she's a murderer."

"Well, yes."

"First things first. Let's get that file."

When they arrived at the village, they first left the horse and cart at the livery where they'd hired them. Afterward, they walked down the main street. There were a few others strolling the pavements. To a one, they all stopped and stared. A few bonnets tilted together as ladies whispered to one another. Kara tried to take it in stride.

"We are new and noteworthy, that is all," Niall said reassuringly.

He might have been right. A few faces looked friendly enough. But several looked flat and assessing. One woman hustled her daughter across the street, as if she had no wish to pass and be forced to acknowledge them.

Kara clenched her jaw and kept a smile on her face as they crossed a small bridge over a babbling brook. At the edge of it sat the courtyard of the Sheep's Head Inn and Tavern. Several tables were set up around it, but they were empty at this time of day. Potted plants adorned the flagstones, and a growth of ivy covered one corner of the inn. It looked warm and welcoming and made Kara recall Gyda's remarks on the stark aspect of Balburn House.

"And a good afternoon to ye."

Kara blinked as Niall held the door for her and she left the sunshine for the dim interior. A man approached from the taproom, smiling. She blinked again at the sight of him. He was huge. Niall boasted a large, muscular build, but this man stood even taller, with wide shoulders and an impressive girth.

"Good afternoon. I'm Sedwick," Niall began.

"Are ye, then?" the man asked with delight. "Ye're most welcome here at the Sheep's Head, Yer Grace. I am Norris, the proprietor."

"A pleasure, sir. May I present my betrothed, Miss Levett?"

"Ah, Miss Levett, ye are even bonnier than I heard. I'm pleased as punch to have ye both here. My wife has stepped out. She'll be that disappointed to ha' missed ye." He sent a questioning look between them. "We've all been wonderin' how ye found the priory? To yer likin', I hope?"

"The priory is magnificent," Niall answered. "It needs a bit of care, but we are looking forward to providing it."

The innkeeper looked pleased at this answer.

"I'm sorry to have missed your wife," Kara added. "Perhaps I will return with our friend, Miss Winther, so we can both make her acquaintance."

"Ah, so ye've a lady friend staying on with ye? 'Tis glad I am to hear it."

Kara understood what he hadn't said. She gathered there had been some talk about her staying at the priory, and she blessed Mrs. Pollock's notion to protect her reputation.

"Can I offer you a luncheon in our private parlor, then?" Norris asked.

"Thank you, but we cannot stay so long," Niall said with regret. "But I would like a private word."

Norris looked understandably curious as he showed them to a room at the back of the inn. The fire in the hearth was not lit, but the room was well furnished and as warm and welcoming as the outside of the place. Niall quickly explained about Darrow's accident. Kara was surprised to see the dismay on the innkeeper's broad face. "Oh, never say it! The fiscal suffering such a fate in our parts?" He snorted. "The folk in North Berwick will have something to say about it, I'm sure. They are already making the most of the gossip over poor Mr. Finley's death."

"Yes, we've heard there is a bit of rivalry among the coastal villages." Niall grinned. "We will do our best to be a credit to Highfield."

"Of course, and so ye are." The big man shook his head sorrowfully. "But two dark events so close together? The gossip will travel faster than the wind."

"The thing is, Mr. Darrow will not be able to be moved for a time," Niall explained. "We've come to fetch his things."

"'Tis good of ye to put him up, Yer Grace."

"Of course. We are happy to do all that we can to make him comfortable."

"I heard ye hired Mrs. Pollock for yer kitchens." Norris nodded his approval. "Her mam was a fine cook, indeed. One of the best in these parts. Though her daughter has been away to the city these past years, she'll not have forgotten our ways. You'll be well fed, and I'm sure she'll know all the right dishes to tempt an invalid." He paused. "There's the thing, though. There's a woman in the taproom. She came early this morning to see the fiscal. She's been waiting all this time. I'll have to tell her it's been in vain."

"Perhaps we should tell her," suggested Kara. "She might have a message for Mr. Darrow that we could pass on."

"Ah, that she might. If ye'd like, ye can find her in the near corner.

I'll go and fetch the key to Darrow's room and meet ye there."

"Who do you suppose she is?" Kara whispered as they left the parlor. "And does she wish to tell Darrow something about Finley?"

"What else?" Niall asked with a shrug. "But there is only one way to find out."

But when they entered the taproom, they found it empty.

"I s'pose she grew tired of waiting," Mr. Norris guessed when he arrived. He cocked his head, listening. "Ah, there's the sound of a coach arrivin'. Do the pair of ye need me to help ye gather the fiscal's belongings, or …"

"No, no. You see to your business," Niall told him. "We'll fetch Mr. Darrow's belongings and return the key when we've done."

With an air of relief, Norris headed for the front of the inn while Kara followed Niall up the stairs. He checked the number on the key and counted off rooms. They headed for the back of the building and found the correct room tucked into an alcove. Kara nearly bumped into him when Niall stopped abruptly several steps away.

A woman stood there, her ear pressed to the door. "Oh!" She stepped back, flushing a little at being caught. She peered at them, then flushed in surprise. "Your Grace!" She dipped a curtsy.

Kara watched Niall frown in question. The woman was dressed in brown wool with a smart hat on her head. "Miss Simmons?" he hesitantly asked.

"Indeed, sir." She looked pleased to be recognized. "Have you come looking for the fiscal as well?"

"No, not exactly," Niall answered. "Miss Simmons is lady's maid to Mrs. Grier at Balburn House," he said to Kara.

"Oh!" Kara stepped forward. "How nice to meet you, Miss Simmons."

The woman eyed Kara with curiosity, then dropped into another curtsy. When she rose, she wore a sour look on her face. "I am the *former* lady's maid to Mrs. Grier," she corrected them. "I return to

London this evening. I had hoped to speak with the procurator fiscal before I left."

"We've come to collect his things," Kara told her. "Mr. Darrow has had an unfortunate accident. He will be staying at the priory with us."

"An accident?" The young woman looked suddenly nervous. "What sort of accident?"

Kara watched her closely. "The kind that might have killed him."

"I think I must go."

Kara stepped into her path. "Why don't you step into Mr. Darrow's room with us for a moment? If you have something you wished for the fiscal to know, we can convey it."

Miss Simmons hesitated.

"I only met Mr. Finley once, but he seemed an engaging person with much to look forward to. Niall enjoyed his company," Kara said, gesturing. "We did not think him the sort of person who should be targeted by a killer."

"No. He was not," Miss Simmons said quietly. She seemed caught by indecision.

"If you know something that could help catch his murderer, then you can be sure we will relay it to the fiscal and not repeat it anywhere else. No one will know you spoke to us."

Miss Simmons drew a deep breath. With a nod, she squared her shoulders.

Niall unlocked the door. Kara gestured for the young woman to precede her. Miss Simmons entered. She moved to the center of the small room and turned to face them. "Mr. Finley was kind to me. He could see I was unhappy at Balburn House and he would tease me, tell me little jokes to rally my spirits." She dropped her head. "He was kind to everyone, all the servants, even though they are a crotchety lot."

"I'm sorry you were unhappy in your position," Kara offered. "I am sure Mrs. Grier must be sorry to see you go."

"Then she should have paid me what I was owed," the young woman said, lifting her chin. "Moving to this backwater, where there is little enough use for my skills, was one thing. But to delay payment of my wages for weeks, going into months?" She shook her head. "No. I am accomplished at my work. I can easily obtain a position in London where my skills will not go unnoticed nor uncompensated."

"I am sure you will. A good lady's maid is as valuable as gold," Kara agreed.

Miss Simmons bit her lip. "I don't want to be thought of as disloyal," she said quietly. "But I could not leave for London without telling the man charged with investigating Mr. Finley's death that he should speak to Mrs. Grier again, more closely."

"Why?" Niall asked bluntly. "We will be sure to tell him, but he will ask the same question."

The maid drew a deep breath. "Because my former mistress had been meeting Mr. Finley in secret."

Kara exchanged glances with Niall. "How did you discover it?" she asked the young woman.

Miss Simmons tossed her head. "A lady's maid knows many things. It's hard for any lady to hide a secret from her maid. We are privy to the most private, intimate details." She paused. "Which is why I hesitated to speak. My loyalty should be absolute." She gave a forlorn shrug. "But this goes too far."

"What does?" asked Niall.

"My mistress is a creature of habit. She rises at the same time. Takes the same breakfast every day. She works the same hours in the estate office and keeps all the records there, with the door locked when she is not inside."

"Mrs. Grier acts as estate manager for Balstone, as the earl is too involved with his archeological pursuits to keep up with it all," Niall reminded Kara.

"Yes," Miss Simmons confirmed. "She is in charge of all the business regarding the house and the land. Once a month, Mr. Dunn, from the Royal Bank of Scotland, comes to the house. He shares a brandy and a few minutes of conversation with the earl, then he and Mrs. Grier retreat to the office and work behind closed doors. There is much speculation among the servants about what goes on in there. Many believe that Mrs. Grier has mortgaged the estate, but no one knows for sure. But the gentleman comes on the same day each month, spends several hours, then he returns to the city." Her brows rose. "There is always comment about that, as well. Why does he not spend the night before setting out again?" She gave a snort. "I say it's likely because he's experienced the woman's notion of hospitality and knows to avoid it. In any case, Mrs. Grier's routine goes on. She retires at the same time most evenings. Only a party or an event like the unveiling of your statue, sir, can move her from her pattern. Each night I help her into her night rail and brush her hair a hundred strokes before I braid it. Afterward, she climbs into bed with her personal journal to make a few notes about the day before she puts out her lamp. It's always the same. Which means it is memorable when something changes."

"And something changed recently?" Kara asked.

"It did. The first time was last month. I came downstairs one afternoon with a bit of sewing to do and found the servants all abuzz. It seemed Mr. Dunn had arrived, well ahead of his usual date. At least, his horse was in the stable. The lads reported his arrival. And yet he had not been to the house."

"Perhaps he went out to the dig site to speak to Balstone," Niall suggested.

"That was my thought, exactly, but the master came back for his supper with no notion that the banker had called. Mrs. Grier seemed not to know of his presence until Mr. Dunn came to the door, just before dinner was to be served. He went into the parlor with the earl and his sister. The door was closed. The conversation was carried on quietly, with no chance for the butler, Mr. Largray, to eavesdrop. Though not for lack of trying." She snorted again. "The banker did stay for dinner, but all three of them appeared quiet and subdued. Afterward, Mr. Dunn rode away, even though it was late and had come on to rain. Mrs. Grier went to the office and carried several ledgers up to her bedroom—something she'd never done before."

"The servants never discovered where the banker had been before he came to the house?" Kara asked.

"Or whom he met with?" added Niall.

"No. And that evening, Mrs. Grier changed into her bedclothes, but she wore a wrapper and kept her hair up. She sat at her vanity with those ledgers and sent me off to bed. The next morning, both her slippers and the hems of her night rail and wrapper were wet. She'd been outside, surely, sometime during the night."

"But you cannot know she went to meet Finley," said Niall.

"Not that time. But Mr. Dunn returned a week later, and still before the date of his usual visit. He stayed but an hour, no more. And later that night, when I went to turn down the mistress's bed, I found a wallet tucked between her pillows. The leather sort that holds papers. Or banknotes. I did not open it, but I did not have to, to know that it was full of *something*." She crossed her arms. "That night, Mrs. Grier repeated her early dismissal, before I could take down her hair. I knew she would likely sneak out again that night. And I felt … *indignant*. I was owed nearly a month of wages by that time—and I wasn't the only one. If she had a wallet full of money, I wanted to know what she was going to do with it, if it wasn't meant to pay the servants."

"You followed her?" asked Kara.

"I did. She waited until past midnight, then she crept out of the house and followed the path to the stable yard. She met Finley there, in the shadows outside the tack room. He slept in a room above it."

Kara shot a look at Niall. Now they knew that Finley did indeed live on the estate.

"I had to move slowly and quietly. By the time I got close enough to hear them, they were in the midst of a great row. The mistress was *furious*. She was demanding something, and he was denying her. 'Do you think me a fool?' she said. 'I must have them. What do you think I've been bargaining for?'"

"He didn't give in?" Niall guessed.

"No, indeed. I'd never heard Mr. Finley speak so. He was defiant. Almost insolent. I think it shocked Mrs. Grier. When she finally understood that he was not going to give in, she threw the wallet at him. 'Do not even think of coming back again,' she warned him. 'If you do, I shall make sure you regret it.' She stormed off, then, back to the house. I had to duck behind the shrubbery so as not to get caught. But Mr. Finley seemed not to be bothered in the least. He took up the wallet and stepped inside the stables. He must have had one of the mules saddled and ready, for he went riding out almost before she could have reached the house."

Her tale dwindled, and the three of them held silent for a moment in the fiscal's empty room.

"Did you tell anyone of this?" Niall sounded grim.

"No. This is the first time I have spoken of it." She shrugged. "As I said, Finley was kind. And my mistress was not. I did not wish to stir up any curiosity about him, and there was already plenty of resentment about her. I just kept it to myself. Until now."

"Did you see them together again?" Kara asked.

"No. Nor did I need to, to know that they were *enemies*," Miss Simmons insisted. "And the man investigating needs to know."

"You are quite right," Kara reassured her. "And we will be sure to tell Mr. Darrow everything you said. We'll tell him in private, and no one needs to know."

"Thank you." Miss Simmons let out a long breath. "Now I can return to London with a clear conscience."

Niall held out a coin to the woman. Kara caught the flash of gold.

"When you are settled in a new position or household, send Mr. Darrow your direction, if you please. It may be possible he will need to call on you for a formal statement." At her frightened look, he gentled his tone. "It will likely only be necessary if he has a solid case against her and enough to see her prosecuted for a crime, in which case, you will be in no danger."

The maid closed her eyes for a moment, but gave a nod. "Please tell Mr. Darrow to be careful." She shot a glance at Kara. "You watch your back as well, Miss Levett. The mistress has taken a dislike to you."

Kara forbore from remarking that the feeling was mutual, but Miss Simmons clearly did not expect a reply. Tucking the coin away, she bade them farewell and swept from the room.

Her skirts had barely twitched around the corner when Niall was at the washstand, bending down to pull Darrow's file from its hiding place.

Kara stared. "Shall we read it now? Or get it back to the priory?"

"We've been in here a while already. Norris might be wondering at it."

"You're right." She opened the wardrobe and found a portmanteau. Moving through the room, she swept all of the fiscal's clothes and sundries into it. "Ready," she said when she had done.

Niall was rifling through a drawer in a bedside table. "This must be Darrow's, too." He tossed her a French novel.

"What of the file?" she asked, opening the case again. "Do you want it in here?"

Niall paused, then shook his head. "It's not so thick." He tucked the file into his waistcoat. "I think I'll keep it close."

"Then we are done." She met his gaze. "Let's head back. I'm anxious to see how Darrow is doing."

He held out an arm. "He'll likely be asleep, but I feel the same."

"So, we are thinking that the man from the Royal Bank of Scotland visited Finley on that first out-of-routine day?" she said, keeping her voice low as they moved toward the stairs.

"We are. Who else, considering what followed?"

"But what could he have consulted Finley over? Some news? But it must have been something concrete—Miss Simmons's story makes it clear Mrs. Grier expected something to be handed over to her. What could it have been?"

Niall stopped at the top of the stairs. "My own experience is coloring my perception of that story. I keep thinking of what *I* kept concealed, tucked away safely in a bank for so many years."

Kara's mouth dropped. Niall had hidden away the proof of his mother's legitimacy. The items and papers that had proved his connection to the royal bloodline. "You think Finley had a marriage certificate? Something that proved his mother was more than a mistress? A wife?"

"It's one explanation."

She frowned. "But it was Mrs. Grier who met with Finley. It was she who was seen arguing with him on more than one occasion—and only her. Wouldn't both Balstone and she have *both* been up in arms if Finley claimed to be a true born son, and not a by-blow?"

Niall shrugged. "Perhaps Balstone allowed her to handle the matter, just as he expects her to handle everything else." He started slowly down the stairs, thinking. "Or perhaps Balstone didn't care. But think, Kara. If Finley came out as a true Balstone, he would become the earl's heir presumptive, wouldn't he? Cutting Mrs. Grier's son out of the succession for the family title?"

Kara pulled to a stop on the landing. "Oh, heavens. Yes." She frowned. "But hold a moment—Finley has been working at Balburn House for years. Why would he not have shown such proof right away, when he first showed up? Or at least when Mrs. Grier moved back and made known her resentment of his presence?"

"I don't know." Niall lifted a shoulder. "Perhaps the proof was newly discovered."

She made a face. "That could be true. But if you are right and Finley had proof of such a thing, Mrs. Grier couldn't really hope to hide it. Someone, somewhere, would have known. Mr. Dunn, from the bank, would have known, if that was the news he brought—and shared with them all." She raised a brow at him. "You know firsthand now how closely these things are looked at—by the home secretary, the Committee of Privilege, the College of Arms. The truth would be bound to come out. She must have known she couldn't hide such a thing forever." She shook her head. "I'm more inclined to think it was something specific and damaging to her ... or perhaps to her son."

"You could be right."

"We should speak with Mr. Dunn."

"Darrow's accident complicates things. The banker would not be compelled to talk to *us*. Perhaps Darrow can summon him to the priory."

Frustration burned in Kara's chest. She wanted this solved, as quickly and as thoroughly as possible. Niall had lived under a cloud for so long, the thought of this hanging over him, of his being in danger for some unknown connection to this murder—it made her want to scream.

"There's something else," Niall said slowly.

She turned to him, expectant, ready to latch on to anything that would move this along.

"Finley rode out as soon as his exchange with Mrs. Grier was over. Clearly he was smart enough not to keep his secret—or that wallet of money or papers—close. So, where would he have hidden them? If we could find where or with whom he left them ..."

"Yes," Kara breathed. "But who would know?" She brightened. "Miss Simmons said he was popular amongst the servants at Balburn House. And Mrs. Pollock must surely have those baked goods ready to deliver."

They started down once more. Niall looked to the case clock as they descended to the entryway. "It's likely too late to get back to the priory and then on to Balburn, but first thing in the morning …"

"First thing," Kara said firmly.

Chapter Eight

"YOU SHOULD MOVE me into another bedroom," Darrow rasped. "There's no need to put me up in the ducal bedchamber."

"Nonsense. You are our guest. And there's no other bedroom fit for habitation right now." Niall picked up the file they had brought back. "There is nothing in here about Finley's plans to leave Balburn House. Nothing about his wish to establish a venue for golf holidays."

"That's because no one mentioned it or seemed at all familiar with the idea," Darrow said roughly. "He seems to have spoken of it to no one but the pair of you." The fiscal looked worn and more than a bit haggard from the pain of his injury, but he had slept through the night and awakened clear of mind, refusing more laudanum. Instead he had demanded strong coffee and a meeting with Niall and Kara.

"No one at all?" Kara asked, surprised. She held out a hand, and Niall passed her the file. "Not even the other servants at Balburn?"

"Why would he keep his plans so secret?" asked Niall.

"I have not been able to determine why." Darrow nodded toward the file. "His fellow servants all seemed to like the man. But they also all seemed reluctant to speak of him."

"Afraid of Mrs. Grier, I suspect," said Niall.

"Well, one of them changed her mind," Kara told the fiscal. "We found Miss Simmons at the Sheep's Head, waiting for a word with you. She's left her position."

"Simmons?" Darrow frowned, then realization dawned. "Mrs. Grier's dresser? I barely spoke with her. She was called away to brush shoes clean, or some such inane chore."

"It appears Mrs. Grier had good reason to keep you from her maid. More than she knew." Niall related all that the woman had told them.

The news brightened Darrow significantly. "At last, a real lead in this case. A legitimate brother would replace a nephew as heir, would he not? Would the nephew kill to keep his spot in line for the title?"

"Would his mother?" asked Kara.

"I need paper and pen," Darrow declared. "I'll have someone from the lord advocate's office speak to this banker, Dunn."

"That will take time," Kara said. She stopped, looking at a note in the file. "Someone ransacked Finley's room in the stables?"

"Yes. Sometime before his body was discovered. When he was found, the butler went to search his room and found it in shambles."

"Someone was looking for the items Mrs. Grier wanted," Kara guessed.

"But did they find them?" wondered Niall.

"My guess would be that they did not," Darrow said. "Mrs. Grier definitely appeared to be unsettled when I was in the house, asking questions. She did not display the demeanor of a woman who has tied up all the loose ends that might come back to haunt her."

"Who found Finley at the site that morning?" Niall asked. "Balstone?"

Darrow nodded.

"And how did you find his demeanor?"

"Sorrowful," Darrow said slowly. "But also a little ... jumpy. And annoyed at the effect that Finley's loss would have on his work."

"That sounds about what I might have expected," Niall said.

"Balstone didn't know about Finley's plans to leave his employ?" Kara asked.

"He didn't mention it," said Darrow. "No one did."

"So, Balstone and his sister were unsettled by Finley's death," Kara said. "Who appeared most distraught over it?"

"The servants are all genuinely mourning him. But one of the stable lads appeared inconsolable." Darrow shook his head. "Damned laudanum. The fog keeps drifting in and out." He nodded toward the file. "His name should be in there."

Kara rifled through it. "Tom Harden," she said. Looking up, she met Niall's gaze. "We'll be sure to talk to him when we are at Balburn House this morning."

Darrow looked alarmed. "I don't want anyone realizing you are helping me with this enquiry," he objected. "Let the perpetrator think they have delayed progress." He gestured toward his splinted leg. "Your work will be more effective that way."

"Not to worry," Niall assured him with pride. "Kara has arranged a cover for us."

His betrothed smiled at the fiscal's questioning gaze. "What could be more natural and neighborly than to bring a selection of baked goods to a house in mourning?"

Darrow sat back.

"We will talk to all of the servants," Niall began.

"But perhaps Tom Harden will have an inkling where Finley might have hidden something important," Kara finished.

"DRIVE ME AROUND to the kitchen entrance at the back?" Kara asked as the cart rolled toward Balburn House. "I'll take the tray in to the servants. You will be better received at the front door, with the platter for the family. Then we'll both deliver the tray to the stables?"

Niall agreed, although it was with a twinge of irritation that he confirmed her assessment. Norris's comment yesterday proved that there had been some talk about Kara's presence at the priory. He would have to make sure to arrange introductions with other locals as quickly as possible. Once they met Kara, they could not fail to love her. And he needed Gyda to overcome her general disdain of people and let her presence be known as well.

He insisted on carrying the laden tray for her, to the servants' entrance. A footman answered, and Niall saw the young man's hesitation and suspicion turn to pleasure as he eyed the multitude of baked goods.

"Clootie dumplings," he said with appreciation as Kara explained and he took up the tray.

"And Mrs. Pollock's cheese pastries will make you weep," Kara told him with a grin. "If you will present me to your cook and housekeeper, I would like to extend all of our household's sympathies for your loss." She gave Niall a nod and a smile and followed the servant into the depths of the house.

Obligingly, Niall drove around to the front of the house, where he happily annoyed Largray, the hoity butler, by asking him to carry the even larger platter inside.

Mrs. Grier came to investigate the commotion as Largray followed him inside, lamenting that he had no notion as to where to place the tray. Niall was reminded of Gyda's insistence that the butler looked like a hound when the man turned heavy eyes and a drooping countenance on him.

"Miss Levett asked our cook to prepare a selection of her finest pastries for you," Niall explained to the frowning woman. "To show our sincere sympathy for your loss, and because you will likely have police and other authorities, as well as visitors, coming and going."

"All of this fuss," Mrs. Grier said on a sigh. "Very well. I suppose Miss Levett has more experience of this sort of thing." She gestured at Largray, still fuming and holding the heavy platter. "Place it in the dining room, on the sideboard, for now. You can serve them at tea."

The butler moved off, and Mrs. Grier turned to Niall, folding her hands primly in front of her. "Well, this is fortuitous, I think. I have been meaning to call upon you, Duke. I gather my brother mentioned the parcel of land at our borders that has been in dispute? Won't you step into the estate office so that we might discuss it?" She turned, taking his acquiescence for granted, and moved off down a passageway.

After a moment, Niall followed. She led him into a small room and moved to sit behind the desk there, watching him expectantly.

Niall took his time, lingering in the doorway and examining her inner sanctum. It was tidy and only dimly lit with a small window. Bookshelves lined the wall behind her, containing ledgers and volumes on agriculture, farming methods, and house management. Her desk was empty and spotless. A map cabinet, stacked with shallow drawers, sat in one corner. He recognized it as a larger version of the one in her brother's study. The observation made him mentally compare the two places of work. Balstone's was richly appointed and slightly cluttered with displays of his discoveries, copies of the latest archeological journals, and the earl's own endless notes and drawings. It was a visual representation of his enthusiasm. Comparatively, this room was utilitarian and barren. Joyless.

Like the woman before him.

She gestured, and Niall took a seat. "Frankly, Mrs. Grier, I thought the land agent had settled this matter of a border dispute."

"Oh, yes. He settled it to his satisfaction," she said bitterly. "But I thought you might reconsider the issue." Sitting back, she released a sigh. "I understand my brother has sent you the Cursed Crown as collateral against the debt he owes you."

"Yes. Frankly, the gesture made me uncomfortable. I am content to wait until Balstone can pay my fee, without such gestures."

"Balstone will do as Balstone likes. It has ever been so. I tried to tell him that we could ill afford such luxury as a sculpture—and an unveiling party, besides. But my brother only cares for his pet project, and for attracting visitors and scholars to view it." She gave him a frank look. "You must have seen that Balburn is having difficulty supporting itself. My farm manager says that if we had that parcel of land to create adequate drainage, we could make a tidy profit planting the field on our side."

Niall glanced at the cabinet. "Do you have a map of the proposed spot?"

"Of course." She rose and crossed over, drawing a large map out of the top drawer and placing it atop the cabinet.

"Can we have a light, so that I might see it better?"

He rather thought she rolled her eyes, but she lit a lamp and brought it over. Bending over, he realized she'd brought out a map of all the Balstone acres.

"This is the area." She pointed toward a spot south and west of the archeological dig.

Niall had spent several days out at the dig site, at Balstone's insistence. The earl had been adamant that he understand the ancients he was meant to represent. In consequence, Niall had become familiar with the site and the land around it, as they had searched to determine the right spot to place his statues. "That bit of land is not even cultivated," he said in surprise. "It's still all forested."

"Due to lack of drainage, I gather," she said wryly.

Niall doubted she was right, but he didn't mean to argue the point with her. "Mrs. Grier, I know you are aware of the unusual circumstances in which I have come into the dukedom."

"Yes." She managed to sound even more disapproving.

"Well, then. Perhaps you can appreciate the sort of scrutiny I now find myself under. The powers that be are watching to make sure I am up to the task of handling such responsibility. I cannot think they will look kindly upon my selling off a parcel of my granted land first thing."

"A few acres," she said quickly. "Hardly a parcel. Surely no one would notice."

"I fear you underestimate the official interest in my adjustments to our new life."

She swallowed. "You have been our guest. A friend to my brother. You must understand how I am obliged to exploit every avenue of potential revenue."

Niall thought of the run-down tenant cottages and of the servant's unpaid wages. And then he eyed the obviously expensive mourning gown and jewelry she wore—and recalled all the others he'd seen her in. And he considered her son, kicking his heels up in London. "I do understand," he said quietly. "And I would like to help, if I can."

But more than that, he wanted to catch a murderer.

"I will consider it," he said slowly.

Her relief was obvious.

"But I will speak to the land agent before I make a decision."

Just as noticeably, her frustration returned.

He stood. "Now, if you will excuse me, I have more deliveries to make." He left, feeling her seething stare burning into his back, and knowing how much worse it might be, should she understand what they knew and suspected.

Chapter Nine

MRS. GRIER'S COOK, at first slightly affronted with the presentation of another professional's pastries, thawed once Kara expressed her appreciation of Mr. Finley's kindness and humor—and once she tasted Mrs. Pollock's clootie dumplings.

"You are right about Finley. A kinder soul never lived in such a big, handsome man," Cook said with a sigh. "And you may tell your Mrs. Pollock that her clooties are nearly as good as my old grandmam's." She poured a bit of cream over her plate and took another bite. "If you will, extend my invitation for her to visit my kitchen when she has time on a day off. We can exchange stories and dishes."

"I shall certainly pass the message along," Kara assured her.

The housekeeper appeared to be busy elsewhere, but the rest of the servants relaxed once Kara had passed Cook's muster. They all spoke quite easily of Finley, but no one had any useful information, no matter how delicately Kara asked.

"No, the poor man had no family to speak of," Cook said with a significant cast of her eyes upward. "His mam died just a few weeks after birthing him. He was raised by an aunt, who kept an inn in Edinburgh, but she passed too, several years back."

There was a sudden racket as chairs were pushed back and all the servants stood at attention. Kara looked back to see Niall in the doorway.

"Your Grace." A chorus of greetings followed a wave of bows and curtsies.

"Good morning, everyone. Forgive the interruption. I've just come to see if my intended is ready to go."

"Of course." Kara stood as well.

"We'd like to thank you for the gesture, sir," Cook said. "You and your lady. 'Tis kind of you, miss, and so I will tell anyone who asks."

"Thank you," Kara said quietly, knowing the value of everything the woman's statement implied.

"We do understand the loss you have all suffered," Niall added. "Our best to you all."

With farewells all around, Kara followed him out of the kitchen and up the stairs.

"My reception was a good deal frostier than yours," he said, leaning in to speak quietly in her ear. "Let's hope we meet with a better welcome in the stables."

When they pulled the little cart into the yard before the main stable block, a groom came running, his expression aghast. "Your Grace, my apologies! Had I known, I would have brought back your rig myself. We thought you only meant to stay for a moment's time."

"Rest easy," Niall said, holding up a hand. "So did we, and that's exactly what I told the boy who came out when I arrived. We are on our way back to the priory, but first we've come to make a delivery to you lads."

"Oh!" The man's eyes grew round when Niall climbed down and pulled the tray from the back of the cart. "You mean to … But this is for us?"

"Indeed. Our cook has made a valiant effort, and we have made deliveries to the family and to the house servants, but this batch is meant for all of you. We thought you might have felt Finley's loss more keenly, as he kept room out here with you."

"It's a sore loss, for true." The groom looked honestly touched.

"It's a kind thing, to have thought of us." He hurried over to clear a game of checkers from a barrel top. "You can place it here, if you please."

Grooms, drivers, and tack men began drifting out from every corner of the yard and its buildings. "Please," Kara said. "Help yourselves."

They converged upon the treats, tugging forelocks and offering thanks, but Kara's attention was drawn to a short stack of boxes standing outside a door. Balanced on top were two long poles with thick ends. "Oh," she exclaimed sorrowfully. "Are those Mr. Finley's golf poles?"

"Golf clubs, miss," someone corrected her respectfully.

"Clubs," she repeated. Walking over, she picked one up. "Mr. Finley had offered to teach me the game," she said sadly.

"He must have liked you, indeed," the first groom said, swallowing a pastry nearly whole. "He didn't make such offers to everyone."

"He was fond of Niall as well," Kara said with a smile at him. "He got the first offer to learn to play." She sobered. "In the kitchens they said Finley had no family. Is it true? Is there no one to take charge of his belongings?"

"No family," the groom said, determinedly *not* looking at the other lads.

"Closest thing he had was young Tom," someone else said. "That pair fair doted on each other. Thick as thieves."

"It's hit the lad hard," the groom said sadly.

"Is the boy here?" asked Kara.

"No, miss. He's out in the paddock with the mules. He's scarce left the spot since the news come."

"Oh, the poor dear. Well, he must have his share of the treats, surely?"

"He won't come. I'm not even sure he's eating at all."

"Well, then. Something must be done." Reaching into her reticule, she pulled out a handkerchief. "Would you mind if I give a try at getting him here?"

"We'd be grateful if ye could give the lad a bit of comfort, miss."

"Very well." Wrapping up two pastries in the linen, she assured Niall she would return soon and started out in the direction they pointed out.

"Wait!" The first groom came running behind her, bringing a couple of carrots with feathery tops. "You'll need something for the mules, as well, or they will never leave you be."

She offered her thanks and followed the curve of a riding ring, passed the largest barn, and came to a green field beyond. A boy lay prone on the ground, his face turned away and his hand idly picking blades of grass. Two mules grazing nearby looked up as she approached. "Good morning," she called.

The boy scrambled to his feet, but his head hung low.

"Are you Tom?"

"Aye, miss." He did not raise his eyes.

"I'm pleased to meet you, Tom. I am Miss Levett. I've just moved to Tallenford Priory with my fiancé, so that makes us neighbors."

"Aye, miss."

"I've brought carrots for the mules. Will you show me the right way to offer them?"

He looked at her at last, and she could see the ache behind his eyes. Taking a carrot, he called the mules with a click of his tongue. "Just hold your hand flat and out." He demonstrated. "Let Victoria take it from you, but be careful if she bares her teeth. She does bite, sometimes."

"Victoria?" she asked.

"Aye. And this here is Albert."

Kara bit back a laugh. She had met the queen, and she doubted Her Majesty would appreciate the honor. "I've brought you a treat, as well."

"I thank ye, miss, but I'm not hungry."

"Very well, then." Kara sat down in the sun-warmed grass. Throwing her head back, she gave the lad a nod of approval. "No wonder you like this spot. It's quite pleasant, isn't it?" Opening the linen, she took a small pinch of pastry, eating it with a sigh of pleasure.

Tom watched her, staring. He opened his mouth, then shut it again before plopping down beside her.

They sat in companionable silence for a time.

"Life is hard sometimes," she said eventually.

He let out a long sigh. "Aye, miss."

"It's difficult to lose someone you love," she said after another moment. "My mother died when I was not much older than you. My father passed several years later."

"Did he?" Tom frowned. "Did someone kill him?"

"No. His heart gave out." Silently, she offered him a piece of the pastry.

He took it and tasted it carefully, and his eyes widened.

"I know. They are good." She offered him the rest, and he took it. "I'm so sorry you lost Mr. Finley." She said nothing more while he ate, but when he'd finished, she sighed. "I had only just met him, you know. Mr. Finley. We were not close like the pair of you, but I liked him. He was going to teach me to play golf."

He blinked up at her. "He must have liked you, too, if he offered to teach you."

"That's just what the other lads said," she told him with a smile as she passed him the other pastry.

"He was going to teach me, too," he said around a mouthful. "Now I'll never learn."

"It's a terrible thought, isn't it?" Kara asked sadly.

"Terrible."

"Did you ever help him create his special clubs?"

"He let me sand the club heads sometimes." He straightened.

"Did he work on them in his room here?" she asked. "It doesn't seem as if there would be space enough."

"No. He had another place. Somewhere with room enough for his equipment. He would go there on his free days. Sometimes of an evening, if he wasn't too tired."

"Did he ever take you with him?"

"No, miss."

"So you don't know where his spot was?"

"No. 'Twere secret." He finished the last bite and looked away.

"I suppose he couldn't be too careful," Kara said. "Sometimes when you have a new idea, you have to protect it."

"Aye." Tom nodded sagely. "Finley had to be careful. He had a vival."

"A vival?"

"Aye, miss."

"What is a vival?"

"He were someone who watched Finley close. He followed him betimes. Spied on him. Stole his ideas."

"A *rival*," she said thoughtfully.

"Rival," he repeated dutifully.

"It does make sense," she mused. "A fine idea like Mr. Finley's for a special place dedicated to golf holidays? His passion for the game and for the idea could have infected anyone who heard him speak of it."

"He spoke of it to ye?" the boy asked, incredulous.

Kara glanced down at him. "He did. The night of the unveiling of the new statues. He told both me and the duke about it. He seemed quite excited."

"Was there anyone nearby?" the boy demanded. "Listening? Watching?"

"No. In fact, I noticed Finley was careful to lower his tone when he told us, but we were quite alone."

Tom sighed in frustration. "I don't even know who he is, but I hate that rival! He stole Finley's dream. That's what he told me. It made him so sad and angry. I wish I knew who he was." He glowered a moment, then spoke in a whisper. "I think he's the one what killed Finley."

Kara considered. "You might be right, but you must trust Mr. Darrow to find the culprit."

"Is he the gent who come 'round, asking questions?"

"He is. He was appointed by the lord advocate himself, so I know he is very capable. He will undoubtedly find the person who harmed Mr. Finley. Our job is to help him, however we can."

"But how do we do that?"

"Well, we tell Mr. Darrow anything we know about Finley's habits, where he spent his time, whom he spoke to … That sort of thing."

"Finley used to spend time with a girl, but she hurt his feelings."

"How did she hurt his feelings?" This was the first hint they'd had of a woman.

"She dropped him like a hot rock. That's what Finley said. Weeks ago, it happened."

"Oh dear."

"He was sulky about it for a while, but he got over it. Finley said a friend who betrays you hurts the very worst, but there was nothing like hard work to heal a broken heart."

"He was likely right. Good for him." She thought a moment. "You know, I might have another idea that might help."

"Help what?"

"Help ease our hearts, our sorrows, perhaps. It might even become a sort of tribute we make to Finley's memory."

"What is it?"

"We can learn to play golf."

The lad looked much struck. "How?"

"Surely we can find someone who can give us lessons. Finley said it was a popular sport in this area." She gave him a measuring look.

"You know, I have a ward who is near your age. His name is Harold. I'll wager he would like to learn as well." She tilted her head back to look up at the sky. "I could find a teacher and we could learn, the three of us. We could schedule lessons on your free days."

"Miss?" He stared at her in disbelief. "Do ye mean that?"

"Of course. If you are interested, that is." She canted her head to look at him.

"Are ye daft?" He made a face. "Sorry, miss. I don't mean to be insolent. Yes, please. I would like that. More than I can say."

"Good. We'll do it, then."

Silence stretched out again.

"Miss?" he asked after a few quiet minutes.

"Yes?"

"Maybe there's something I can tell the man looking for Finley's killer. 'Twere a secret, but there's no use keeping it now, is there?"

"Perhaps not. Would Finley be hurt if he knew you were sharing it?"

"No. Not if it caught the one who cut him down, I don't think. And if it were his rival who killed him, I don't want him getting Finley's dream, ye see?"

"I do see."

"Finley's girl, he visited her in the city, but his workshop had to be closer. He could make it there and back of an evening." Tom sighed. "He said he would take me there, once it truly belonged to him. But the old baxes ruined all of his plans."

"Old baxes?"

"Battaxes? Lattaxes?"

Kara searched her mind. "Old back taxes? Or perhaps owed land taxes?"

Tom frowned. "That sounds sommat right. Whatever they are, they stole his land away. Where he meant to set up his golf course. He couldn't get it back without a lot of money. And he was afraid his vival—*rival*—was getting the money quicker." He frowned over at her. "Is that something I should tell?"

She nodded, keeping her expression serious. "I think it is, Tom. It's very brave of you to offer to tell Mr. Darrow something so important. Finley would be proud."

"Do you think so?"

"I do. Mr. Darrow is staying with us at the priory, in fact. When you have your next day off, you could come and see us there. I'll introduce you to Harold. He will be delighted to meet you, I know. And I'll stay with you, if you like, while you talk to Mr. Darrow."

He stared at her, frowning. "May I touch your hand, miss?"

"Oh? Yes, of course."

Very tentatively, he reached out and let his fingers rest on the back of her hand. "Ye're real, miss?"

"Ah, yes?"

"Not one of the fair folk? Not seelie?"

"Oh. No. Just normal, regular human."

He drew his hand away, satisfied. "Aye, ye're warm. Not cold at all." He shrugged. "I just didn't know real ladies could be so carin' and nice."

The statement, so matter of fact, struck her hard. Blinking back tears, she gave him a nod. "Well, I did know that boys could be so brave and loyal to their friends. I'm glad to know you are one of them."

He thought a moment. "So am I."

"Now." She stood and held out her hand again. "Why don't we go and get you some more of those pastries before they are all gone?"

NIALL AND KARA had much to discuss on the way home. He told her of the confrontation in Mrs. Grier's office. "Honestly, the excuse I gave her is the truth. It makes no financial sense, on my side, to sell that land. Is that what I wish to be reported as one of my first transactions as owner of the priory?"

"Well, there is a certain social value to the idea," she mused. "A chance to help a neighbor, build connections in the community. Especially if the land has no special use or sentimental value to you."

"It all has sentimental value to me," he grumped. "Every one of those fourteen hundred acres."

"Then don't sell," she said.

"I'm certainly not going to make the decision until I know if the woman was involved in Finley's death," he added.

"Speaking of which," Kara said eagerly, "let me tell you what young Tom had to say."

He listened with rising respect. "Very well done, indeed. Another lead. Darrow will be impressed with our morning's work." He took the reins in one hand and reached over to cover her hand with his. "I'm even more impressed with how you drew out young Tom. That was the perfect notion, learning golf. Harold will love the idea. And it will be good for him to have a friend his own age up here."

"I thought the same thing. Harold was arranging one of his experiments in the schoolroom this morning, but he seemed listless. Surely a friend will help." Her nose wrinkled. "Though there will be remarks," she said on a sigh. "Someone will comment on the ward of a duke being encouraged to befriend a stable lad."

"You are likely right, but people here don't know or understand Harold's background."

"Nor do they need to."

"Correct." He squeezed her hand. "Nor do they understand your generous heart. But you struck exactly the right note, calling it a tribute to Finley. I would like to join you, if you don't mind."

"Of course! I'd hoped you would, but I didn't like to speak for you."

He took up the ribbons with both hands, then, turning his mind back to the information Tom had revealed. "It is fascinating that both of our leads in this case seem to be pointing us to the same place—to Finley's hideaway. Surely it is the same as the land he mentioned to us. I wish I could recall anything identifying he might have said about it."

"He probably did not mention anything specific on purpose."

"Yes. But we can hope to find his mysterious documents there."

"If they are documents."

"Whatever it was that Mrs. Grier seemed to pay significant money to hide."

"That same land seems also to be the reason he needed the money. But how will we find it, short of riding up and down the coast?" She frowned. "It cannot be far, but we are uniquely unqualified to discover it. Even Darrow is unfamiliar with the region. We must think of whom he would ask, were he able to move about the area. Then we can summon them to the priory."

"No need. I know who to ask."

"Who?"

"Cannot you guess?" He grinned. "It was the *baxes* that gave me the notion."

She gave a laugh. "It was a Herculean effort to keep a straight face, I tell you. Josie Lowe could not have done so well."

He laughed. "I applaud you now and will reward you later."

She eyed him cheekily. "Is that a promise?"

"A solemn vow."

"Good." She grew serious. "Surely the lad meant old unpaid taxes, didn't he?"

"He must have. And that is exactly how we will find the place."

"How?"

"We ask someone who is a high-standing member of the burgh and also a councilman. If there is a local property that has been confiscated for past due taxes, then he would know it, would he not?"

"But who is he?"

"Dalwiddie," Niall told her with satisfaction as they turned onto the lane that would take them to the priory. "And that means, when we get back, we will check on Harold, tell Darrow the latest news, and inform Mrs. Pollock of the triumphant reception of her confections, and then you must change into your riding habit so that we can set out for a visit."

"Goodness, you've thought of everything."

He laughed. "I try, my sweet, I try."

She was still worrying, though. He could tell as she frowned up at him. "Won't it seem a bit … forward? Turning up in a riding habit? As if I'm expecting an invitation to ride?"

"She will be delighted. You must trust me. Kate Dalwiddie will be disappointed if you *don't* come prepared to ride out with her."

"Very well. I will trust your judgment."

She harbored doubts, he could tell, but he knew he was right. Kara had gained a bit of support this morning in Balburn House, with the cook and the staff. He thought Mr. Norris at the Sheep's Head would also champion her against any gossip. But Kate Dalwiddie already seemed inclined to like Kara, and having her influence on Kara's side could be a boon.

He loved so many things about this woman. Her confidence and strength. Her determination to learn, to develop new skills and explore new horizons. She never hesitated to step outside the small circle that Society wanted to confine her within, but he knew that all of these things that he so admired had also won her detractors and critics. She'd learned to ignore them, but the lessons had come hard won. Now she worried he would face the same censure.

All he could do was reassure her. How could he not adore every inch and facet of her? How could he not place the unique wonder of her above small-minded considerations from anyone or anywhere else? But reinforcements would not come amiss, and he hoped Kate

Dalwiddie's friendship would ease her worries.

"Look at that," he said quietly. They'd come to the spot where they emerged from the wood and could look down on the priory.

Her expression softened. Harold rolled a hoop in the walled garden. One of the maids swept the front steps. The windows stood open and, from what must be the dining room, a rug unrolled.

"It will be grand when we are through, won't it?" she whispered.

He let his gaze roam over her. Her ebony hair had come a little loose and moved softly in the breeze. Her dark eyes shone warm and full of hope. "It will be grand, as long as you are there," he said softly, and then he urged the horse on so that they could arrive home.

Chapter Ten

"KARA! KARA, COME and see!"

Harold came running from the walled garden as the cart swept down the drive. Niall pulled it to a halt. "Go on," he urged. "I'll take the cart back to the stables and let Jamie pamper the mare a bit before we set out again."

"We'll meet you inside," she agreed as she climbed down. Harold swept up in a hurry, and she reached out to embrace him. "You look like you are feeling better. You looked a little peaked this morning."

"I'm fine. I ate too many of Mrs. Pollock's cakes," he said sheepishly. "But come and see what I found." He tugged her along. "I'm not sure if it is a good thing or bad." He sounded a little anxious.

Curious, she followed him to the back corner of the garden, eyeing the place as they went, thinking it needed soft borders of bright, blooming plants and perhaps a piece of Niall's art. Harold led her to a spot at the corner of the house where a curtain of ivy covered a section of the back wall.

"I was chasing a little lizard. He had a pretty pink throat. I lost him when he ducked into the ivy. But just look!"

He moved a section of the vines away to reveal a carved face peering from a stone circle covered in lines and symbols. It was a stern visage with knowing eyes and a great, proud nose. From his brow, cheeks, and beard grew swirls of vines and leaves.

"Is it a demon?" Harold asked nervously. "Old Mean Moll, who sold cabbages in Covent Garden, always told us she would send demons to eat us if we riled her nerves."

"No, no. No worries," Kara told him. "It's a Green Knight. Or sometimes called a Jack in the Green. These sorts of faces are very popular with the men who design places like the priory. You can find them in churches and old buildings all across the land."

"It doesn't mean sickness and doom?" Harold asked in relief.

"No. Not at all."

"Where does he come from, then?"

Kara grinned. She loved his curiosity, loved that he was comfortable enough to ask all the questions that sprang to his mind. She was happy to indulge him. "Well, I once had a teacher who knew about such carvings and architectural embellishments." She didn't tell him that the man was a failed scholar who had turned thief by trade, known for his ability to scale nearly anything. Her father had hired him to teach her the fastest, safest way of climbing buildings in London. It was just part of the most unusual curriculum of her childhood—how to evade and escape capture. "He told me all about gargoyles and about these green men. It is an old symbol."

"As old as the Picts?" Harold asked, excited to relate his newly acquired knowledge.

"Older still. Some believe he originates in these isles, but others think the idea of him came from faraway places, brought back by merchants and crusaders. But he's been a part of British lore for a long time. You'll likely have seen him in some of the street festivals or in the May Day processions in the city."

"Wait." The boy frowned. "The man in the great wicker cage, covered in leaves? That's him?"

"It's a version of him. He's part of the celebration of spring and rebirth. The man who taught me also said there used to be green men who came first in great parades or before a marching troupe of actors.

They would carry clubs that had fireworks embedded in them and use them to scatter the crowds and make way for the processions."

"But how is he a knight? You said Green Knight? Does he carry a sword?"

"He does, in the version that is part of the old tales of King Arthur. There is a very famous tale about Sir Gawain, the youngest of the Knights of the Round Table. He has an adventure in which the Green Knight teaches him the importance of honor and honesty."

"Niall has said that I may learn to make a sword, once I learn enough about forge work," Harold said, slashing away at the air with glee. "Then I shall be a knight!"

Kara looked the figure over again. "You know, the way his lips are pursed, it makes me wonder …" She began to pull at the ivy, separating the vines further down. "Look! It's a fountain," she said as she uncovered a stone basin. "There must be a spring here, but it's been clogged or dried up."

"My lizard!" Harold cried, scooping up the little creature, who appeared to be nesting in the bowl. "Look at his little pink throat. And his yellow stripe."

"I think he's called a newt, hereabouts," Kara told him.

"Can I keep him?"

"He certainly doesn't appear to be frightened of you, but I doubt he would be happy inside the house. You could visit him out here, though."

"Can I take him inside and show him to Mr. Darrow? Mrs. Pollock says he needs cheering."

Kara laughed, picturing the serious man's reaction. "Yes. I think it's a good idea. Mr. Darrow might be better for a little shaking up."

"Let's go!"

"Keep a good eye on him," Kara warned. "Turner won't be happy if he gets loose in the house, and I shudder to think of what Mrs. Pollock would do if she found him in the kitchens."

"The maids would shriek." Harold's eyes lit up.

"Yes, but Mrs. Pollock just might put him in a pot."

The boy protectively closed his hands around the little creature. "I'll bring him straight back out."

They met Niall on the way in, and he walked upstairs with them. They both laughed at Darrow's helpless reaction to Harold's enthusiasm. After a few moments, she sent Harold and his new friend back out. She hovered in the doorway with Turner while Niall caught the fiscal up on the morning's developments.

"He looks a great deal better," Kara said to the butler. "I can see you've been after him."

"He needed a wash, shave, and clean linens, which wore him out and convinced him to sleep. The surgeon came by and gave his approval, although he insists Mr. Darrow must stay in bed for several more days, at the least." Turner cleared his throat. "Since we are short of staff, I took the liberty to ask the surgeon for a recommendation for a caretaker to watch over our patient. She'll be arriving later tonight."

"Good thinking. Thank you."

"I've also written to an agency in Edinburgh, asking for them to send a few select gardeners for interviews, at His Grace's request." He gave her a direct look. "And the dining room is ready. Meals will be served there, moving forward."

Kara laughed. "We will behave appropriately."

Turner snorted.

"Is Gyda out readying the new forge?"

"Since you left this morning. I sent her out a basket for luncheon."

"Will you ready one for us? We are off to make a visit with the Dalwiddies, our nearest neighbors. We can eat on the way."

"For business?" Turner looked significantly at the procurator fiscal. "Or pleasure?"

"Both, hopefully. And will you send Brigitte to my room? I need to change into my riding habit, and I'll need help tying up the skirts."

"Of course."

She turned to go, but paused, searching her oldest friend's face. "What do you think, Turner?" She gestured, taking in the house, but meaning everything else as well.

He considered. "It's not Bluefield," he said carefully. "But I think we will be happy here." He raised a brow. "For *part* of the year."

She bit back a laugh. "I feel exactly the same."

>>><<<

THE DALWIDDIES' HOME was obviously old, but also clearly well cared for. Tall evergreens stood close to the house, like soldiers at attention. Bright flowers in pots stood between them, and ivy grew in spots up the three stories of local tan stone. A rounded tower stood at the far end of the house, and it boasted a multitude of windows that must surely denote a bright interior. At the edge of the drive, a discreet sign pointed the way to the stables.

"There's no use stopping at the house," Niall said, driving on. "Kate is always in the stables."

"But what of Mr. Dalwiddie? We need to speak to him, do we not?" Kara asked.

"He once told me he set up an office out in the stables, just so he could be sure to catch a glimpse of his wife during the day," Niall said, chuckling. "We'll check there first and leave the horse and cart."

The lane, lined with finely crushed shells, led around an ornamental garden, lush with blooms, and past a couple of outbuildings. As they came around a copse of trees, they caught their first sight of the stable block.

"Good heavens." Niall eased the horse to a stop, the better to take it in.

"It is magnificent," Kara breathed. "Like it was built for a king."

The building was set up in the shape of a quadrangle, constructed of rendered brick with a slate roof. They sat now before a central two-story entrance pavilion with a tall, arched passage. It was flanked on both sides and around the square with one-story wings. Passing through, they found the great square was formed by sides containing twelve bays each. The shelled drive continued around, lining the edges, but there was a large square of lush grass in the middle, holding a tiled pump and basin. Curious equine heads poked from stall doors, and grooms moved efficiently about. One came running to take the hired horse in hand as they drew to a halt.

"Mrs. Dalwiddie?" Niall asked him.

The groom gestured, and Niall looked down the left-hand side of the square. Near the end, a stall door opened and Kate emerged.

"We'll change the bandage daily for several days," he heard her say. Turning, she gestured, and another groom led a mare out from the stall and walked her in a small circle. "Very good. She's steadier on it now. We'll leave it for a day or two, but it must be kept covered. The laceration is closer to a tendon than I am entirely comfortable with, so we'll want to watch it closely."

A figure stepped out behind her, his focus entirely on the injured animal standing quietly, her head drooping a little. "Thank you, Mrs. Dalwiddie. I beg of you, do your best for her. That mare may just be the only true companion I have on this earth."

"With care and good fortune, she'll be fine in a fortnight," Kate replied gently.

The groom holding the horse bent to examine the bandage. As he knelt there, his gaze drifted over. Niall saw the moment he recognized them. A scowl bloomed on his face, and he caught the other man's attention and nodded in their direction.

The young man turned, and Niall stilled as he recognized the wide face of Will Grier. The young man's heavy brows lowered as he spotted them. The gratitude on his face quickly shifted to surprise, then unease.

Kate turned to follow where Will and his groom were looking. Her reaction was quite different as she broke into a broad smile and strode toward them, the heavy green skirts of her habit swinging. "Niall!" She strode forward to take Kara's hands. "It seems utterly ridiculous to call you Miss Levett when I call the duke by his given name, so let me bid you welcome, Kara. And you must call me Kate." She looked her over. "And you've come appropriately garbed! How clever of you."

Greetings were exchanged all around, and Kara looked to the young man and gave him a nod. "Good afternoon, Mr. Grier. Has your mount suffered an injury? I'm sorry to hear it."

Grier gave a negligent wave of his hand that belied his earlier emotion. "My fault, I'm afraid. I rode in an unfamiliar part of the wood and my mare got a tear from some rock or protruding stick. But if anyone can set her to rights, it's Mrs. Dalwiddie."

"And I am happy to do so." Kate smiled around at all of them. "Just as I am happy to recruit you all to come out for a ride with me. I've several of my budding hunters that need the exercise."

"As you noted, we came prepared to help," Niall answered with a grin. "But first, if we may, we have a small matter to discuss with Jacob."

"My husband is out in the fields, but he should not be far. We can ride out and collect him and tear him away to accompany us."

"Then we are at your service."

"Excellent. Niall, you have already made friends with my beautiful sable Seamus. Kara, I shall introduce you to Morag, who is very mannerly and gentle." She turned to the young man. "Come along, Mr. Grier, and make yourself useful. I shall find just the right mount for you, as well."

"I fear I must offer up my excuses," the young man returned. Shaking his head, he adopted the cheeky tone he'd used when they first met him. "I fear I am far too dissipated to be comfortable making myself useful. I'm far more skilled at making myself scarce."

"Very well, then, but do come back to visit your mare," Kate ordered him. "Your presence will reassure her and may well speed her healing."

"I shall try to find the time."

Kara, who had been watching the young man with a curious expression, suddenly spoke up. "Mr. Grier, as a boy, did you ever read the tale of Sir Gawain and the Green Knight?"

He looked puzzled. "I believe I did." Suddenly he quirked a smile at her. "Do you count it as a favorite, Miss Levett?"

"It's been many years since I read it, but I have just recently resolved to reacquaint myself with the story. Perhaps you might, as well."

He gave a rakish laugh. "Do you wish to remind me of my honor, as the Green Knight did for Sir Gawain?" His laughter turned dark. "I'm afraid it's gone too late for that." He swept a bow before them all. "Good day to you."

Kate watched him go. "It cannot have been easy for him, with his father gone, left with an uninterested uncle and such a mother. And yet I think he's not quite the roque he pretends to be."

"I hope you are right," Kara said softly.

Niall snorted. "You just like him, Kate, because he carries a soft spot for his horse."

"You cannot deny that it is an admirable trait," their hostess replied. "Now, let's get mounted so we may free Jacob and enjoy a good, long ride."

Chapter Eleven

THEY FOUND JACOB Dalwiddie standing mid-field with a group of his tenant farmers, examining the progress of a half-grown crop of oats. Spotting them, he spoke a little longer to the men, then lifted a hand and came over to the edge to greet them.

"Well met, my darling," he called. "This was our last field of the day." He came to stand by his wife's splendidly muscled hunter. "And I see you've found some recruits. Good day to you, Sedwick. And welcome to our home, Miss Levett."

"It's no use, dear," his wife told him. "Your manners are lovely, but I have already resolved that we are to be Kate and Jacob and Kara and Niall. Now, come. You must ride out with us."

Obediently, he was up and ready in moments. "Where shall we ride today, my dear?"

"Actually, I meant to ask you something before we set out." Kara watched as Niall expertly moved in closer to speak to his friend—and wished she'd spent a tad less time in the laboratory over these last months, and more in the saddle.

"I wanted to ask, Jacob, if you knew of any local properties that might have been seized due to unpaid taxes?"

Dalwiddie looked surprised at the question. "As a matter of fact, yes. Old Blister MacCallum's place. It's a small farm holding further out along the road toward the city. Why? Were you thinking to add to your holdings?"

"No, but I do have a reason to look it over."

"It's just as well. George Gibbons is the local tax commissioner. Honestly, I wonder if he didn't pay old Blister's taxes himself a time or two. But he will have to charge the new buyer the unpaid balance. I understand he has a buyer lined up already." He looked over to his wife. "More fresh blood in the area, my dear."

"The buyer is not a local?" Kara asked.

"No. A man from the city, I believe."

The rival, perhaps? Kara raised a questioning brow at Niall, but he was watching Jacob. "Is it close enough for us to ride out to inspect the place?"

"Of course. You know the farmstead I mean, don't you, Kate?"

"I do." His wife looked somber. "I often met Mr. MacCallum when I was out with one horse or another. I ride all over the area, and old Blister wandered as well, especially since he grew too old to keep the farm going."

"Riding out to meet strange men, my dear?" Jacob asked with a laugh.

His wife tossed her head. "I nearly always have a groom with me. You know all the horses need constant exercising. But I quite enjoyed old Blister's company. He knew an astonishing amount about these lands. I swear, he could whistle the birds out of the sky or tickle a trout from a stream with just his fingers. He loved to stroll out along the cliffs over the sea. We would sit there, sometimes, while he told me tales of the old ways." She gave Kara a sad smile. "This way, then. It's a good choice for today, for the way is easy."

"Is my inexperience so obvious?" Kara asked ruefully as they set out. "I rode more often in my youth."

"It is only because I have a trained eye," Kate answered. "And actually, your inexperience is useful. My hunters need to be able to adjust to different riders and their various skill levels. Some of my trained beauties will be kept by huntsmen as their treasured mounts, but others might be loaned out to guests of the hunt."

"I'm happy to oblige with my rusty seat," Kara said with a laugh.

Kate continued to discuss her burgeoning enterprise as they made their way along the coastal road. "This is a uniquely ideal area to raise hunters. There is such a natural variety of conditions to explore. I can teach my horses to handle the sand beaches and forested trails, the climbs over the cliffs, and the rocky riverbanks. They learn to adjust to different terrains with equanimity."

"That makes sense, but I can only assume your rapport with them is a large part of your success." Kara reached out to pat her mare's neck. "Morag is very polite and extremely responsive."

"She is a sweet, sweet girl. I will be sad to see her go, but Mrs. Clarke, who rides with the Duke of Buccleuch's hunt, is interested in her."

"It must be difficult to part with them."

"I make it easier, I admit, because I am very particular in who may have one of my darlings. I daresay it is bad business, but there you have it." She shook her head. "Enough about me. Tell me how things are going at the priory."

"They are progressing far more quickly now that the ever-efficient Turner is here. He is my assistant, butler, and friend," she explained.

"How unusual," Kate said. "But how lovely it sounds."

"He is a treasure, without a doubt. And with him in charge, I am sure we will soon be ready to receive guests—and you will be the first, of course."

"I cannot wait. But did you find the place in terrible shape?"

"Not at all, which was a relief. It just needs a thorough cleaning and an overhaul. A bit of organizing and an update. I'm quite looking forward to getting back to it—" She stopped, but Kate had caught her slip.

"Back to it?"

Kara glanced back to where Niall and Jacob rode behind them. They had been carrying on their own conversation, but clearly Niall had heard her exchange. She sent him a questioning look, and he gave a shrug.

"Well," she said slowly. "We do have an unexpected guest." She spoke of Mr. Darrow's accident, leaving out the bit about it possibly being meant for Niall.

"The fiscal? Hurt here, and so soon after Finley's death?" Jacob asked soberly. "That will cause talk."

"Mr. Norris said the same thing."

"Is the fiscal seriously hurt?" Kate asked.

"He is," answered Niall. "He will be some weeks recovering."

"It won't look good, the delay in investigating Finley's death." Jacob sounded concerned. "Another procurator fiscal could surely be brought in—"

"Darrow does not wish it."

Jacob's eyes widened. "Is that why we are going to look at old Blister's farm? For Darrow?"

"The fiscal does not wish it to be known that we are assisting him," Niall warned. "But I know we can trust the two of you to keep it quiet."

"Of course," Jacob said.

"Yes, yes," Kate said with a squeal. "But it is so exciting!"

"Well, then. Let us get on with it." Jacob indicated a branch that left the main road and climbed upward and inland. "This way."

They urged their mounts up the steep trail.

"The edge of the plateau marks the boundary of Blister's land," Jacob said as they made it to the top.

"What a view," Kara said, gazing out at the sea. "No wonder he liked to walk here."

"His home is this way." Kate turned her mare onto another track leading inland. "He was a curmudgeon, but I miss him."

The grassy plateau gave way to overgrown fields gone wild again, and then to a dense wood. Kara worried that the dim quiet might bother her mount, but Morag had clearly been this way before. "Mr. MacCallum had no family?" she asked.

"Oh, he was a distant relation to the Balstones, but the connection is tenuous, and there was some bad blood generations ago that continues to be carried by the different branches today. They mostly ignored each other, although Blister did like to mock Balstone's obsession. *Digging for shells and bone,* he used to call it. Like a boy making mud pies."

"When Blister lay dying, a rumor circulated that he meant to leave the farm to someone in his will, but the tax collector stepped in as soon as he passed." Jacob gazed around. "It's a pretty little piece of property, but whoever wants it will likely have to pay the owed taxes on top of the price of the land."

Kara's thoughts took up that thread. Could it have been Finley the old man meant to will the farm to? Two spurned relatives of the Balstones—they could have bonded over their dislike of the family.

"There it is," Jacob said, and she looked ahead to catch her first glimpse of the place.

The house sat low to the ground and spread out. Made of stone, it had lead-paned windows that had once been painted white. The roof needed looking after. The whole place looked ... lonely.

Niall glanced around at her, then swung down to try the door. "Locked."

"Are there outbuildings?" asked Kara.

At the same time, Kate said, "There's a barn around back." She grinned at Kara. "And a shed just through there." She pointed toward the side of the house, overhung with hawthorns, sycamores, and mountain ash. "I think it was meant for tools."

"Tools?"

"I'll take a look," Niall said. "The rest of you should stay here."

Kara swung down just as Kate laughed and followed suit. Jacob took up their reins and went to tie them to a post. "Sorry, Your Grace," he said, his eyes twinkling. "This is a joint endeavor now."

With a roll of his eyes, Niall turned to lead the way. He pushed through the overgrown thicket of trees. Branches entangled, as if purposely blocking the way. Jacob followed him, holding the worst of it aside as the ladies moved through. Kara brought up the rear. She had just stepped into the tiny clearing when she saw Niall try the door of the little shed.

"Not locked," he said over his shoulder. "Warped." He gave it a good shove, and the door gave way. Turning, he held up a finger, warning them to wait, then he slowly stepped over the threshold and into the dark.

Built of the same stone as the farmhouse, the shed had no windows. It would take several moments for Niall's eyes to adjust. Kara held her breath until she heard his call.

"It's fine. You can come in."

She was first at the door and entered just as Niall, rummaging in a corner, managed to light a lamp. The place smelled like sawdust and varnish. Looking about in the dim light, she felt triumph and relief building in her chest.

"Finley," she whispered.

Reverently, she reached out to touch the lathe that took up much of the right side of the wall. It was old and made of wood, but it had a foot pedal that would allow one man to run it. A stack of long, straight branches sat at one side, and a row of several finished shafts lined the other. "Did you know that the first metal lathe was developed by a man who also made automatons?" she asked low.

"No." Niall was busy rooting over a workbench at the back.

"The Digesting Duck was accounted to be his most famous work in that field."

Niall moved the lamp over a collection of chisels, planes, and other shaping and measuring tools, as well as several of the club heads in various states of production.

Jacob and Kate stood in the doorway still, but Jacob made a sound of pleasure and Kara turned to see him approach a line of finished clubs along the other wall. He hefted one and gave it a swing. Suddenly, he looked up. "Finley?" he asked. "I have a pair of his customized clubs. This was his workspace?"

"It appears so, but the fact must not travel beyond the four of us," Niall warned.

"You can trust us," Kate assured him. "But was it Finley that Blister meant to leave the farm to?"

"It's possible." Niall lit another lamp. "Now, we must look through every nook and cranny of this place. We are looking for documents. Letters. Papers. Anything personal." He paused. "And a leather wallet full of … something. We are not sure what, just that there was a lot of it."

"How exciting," Kate said. She moved over to the pile of branches and began to sift through them. Jacob began testing the floor, as if looking for loose boards.

Kate stood for a moment, looking around. Then she looked up. The wooden rafters were braced on the ends and in the middle with thick trusses made from crossed beams. Three triangle shapes resulted with each truss, two on either side of the cross point and one above. The shadows lay so deep in here, they were almost hard to notice. She studied them. The one in the middle would be the most difficult to reach. She was heading for the chair placed at the workbench when Kate spoke up.

"I'm sorry. I know it is frivolous and has nothing to do with the work we are doing here, but I must know." She was lifting branches aside and peering under the lathe. "*What* is a Digesting Duck?"

Kara laughed as she dragged the stool into the middle of the room. "Jacques de Vaucanson was a well-known creator of automatons. The

Digesting Duck was a marvel, seeming to drink water and eat grains. Afterward, it would produce green droppings, just like a real duck."

Niall looked up from beneath the workbench he was exploring and made a noise of exasperation. Rising, he rushed over to steady the stool as she climbed up. "Warn me, please, before you mean to do something that might break your leg. One patient at the priory is enough."

Kara merely reached her hand along the beam. With a sigh of disappointment, she wiped her hands on her skirts. "Nothing but dust, but I cannot reach along the whole of it." She reached out to Niall, who helped her down. "I need to move the stool over."

"But the duck didn't really digest the grain, did it?" Jacob asked. He'd found a small cabinet and was looking through it. "It couldn't."

"No. Vaucanson had created a secret compartment where he'd stashed a mixture of breadcrumbs and green dye. It was an illusion, but it was amusing to the French court, and that's what he needed to attract a patron."

Kara climbed again and explored the rest of the lower beam, then moved to the other side and did the same. "Nothing," she sighed. "But I cannot reach the highest spot. Do you want to try?" she asked Niall.

"Hop down," he said obligingly. She held the stool while he climbed up. He reached up to explore the space—and she saw his eyes widen.

"What is it?" she demanded.

He pulled something down from the shadowed spot. A closed folder, tied tight with string. Without a word, he jumped down and began to unwrap it.

"Oh!" Jacob exclaimed from the floor. He'd opened a sack of nails. "This is what you meant, I think." He pulled out a leather wallet. Opening the flap, he let out a long, low whistle. He reached in and pulled out a handful of banknotes.

Beside her, Niall made a strangled sound. Kara turned to see what he'd found.

"Marriage lines," he said. "Old Lord Balstone wed Finley's mother in 1834. In Canongate Kirk."

Kara stared up at him. "We have to get back."

"We have to talk to Darrow," Niall said grimly.

Chapter Twelve

"I WILL MEET her downstairs, damn it," Darrow growled. The fiscal was beyond furious. "By God, she *will* respect my position. And I will meet her downstairs and fully dressed."

Darrow had been convinced by the marriage lines, torn out of the church register, and the banknotes, issued by the Royal Bank of Scotland. "There's a witness who can place her with the victim and the wallet. The maid will have to be recalled," he'd added. "I will need to take her precognition myself. The recording of the marriage provides unassailable motive for murder. It had to have been her—or the son. I will flush out the truth, damn it all." He'd clasped Niall's hand and shot Kara a look of approval. "Damned fine work, both of you."

The fiscal had sent out a summons for Mrs. Grier to appear before him at once, though it had been late afternoon before Kara and Niall had got back to the priory and told their tale. The earl's sister, however, had returned his messenger with a curt refusal. *I do not leave home so late in the day* was all it had said.

Darrow had exploded into a temper, railing against both the recalcitrant woman and his injury. He'd earlier sent the constable, Mr. Creel, out to the cliff tops above the Viewing House, where footprints had been discovered, as well as signs that the boulder had been pried loose by something long and thin. The constable had made a credible job of creating plaster casts of the evidence.

"Who knew Cabbage Creel had it in him?" Mrs. Pollock had marveled.

"I'll get them for that rock fall, too," Darrow had raged. "Even if I have to wring the truth out of them."

The fiscal had then sent Hamish to Prestonpans to summon a pair of policemen. They had arrived this morning, and he'd briefed them and sent them straight over to Balburn House. "I don't care if you must haul her out of bed in her night rail and hair rags. I want her here *this morning!*"

Now Darrow was refusing to have Mrs. Grier brought to him in the bedroom. "Put me on the damn door again and carry me down," he insisted. "And I don't care how much it hurts to put on my damned pants."

"I'll remove the leg of a pair of your trousers," Turner offered. The butler had been solidly in agreement with Darrow over presenting a dignified front. "We'll cover your legs with a blanket. No one will know."

"They are right," Gyda said from the back of the room. "That Grier woman is a snob and a bully. He needs to present an intimidating front."

"But there are no receiving rooms ready," Kara protested. "There's only the dining room."

"Then I will meet her in the dining room," Darrow vowed.

He got his way in the end, and Kara had to admit that the fiscal did look imposing, despite being stretched out on a chaise placed at the end of the table.

She gazed about with pleasure. This room would need no further refurbishing. The walls were painted a rich blue below, and a gorgeous blue green—just the color of foaming waves pounding ashore—above. The great squares that had been covered with sheets were revealed to be filled with delicate filagree designs of plaster. The furniture was of fruit wood and polished to a sheen. The room managed to look both rich and welcoming—except for the scowling figure on the chaise, dressed in a navy coat and white linen and looking as if he'd been born to dispense justice from this exact spot.

"Turner, you are a marvel," she murmured as the butler straightened a deep blue blanket over Darrow's legs.

"So you keep telling me," he said with a hint of a smile. Straightening, he cocked his head, listening. "They are coming down the drive."

"I'll be lurking in the entry hall," Gyda announced. "I want to hear it all." She gave Darrow an encouraging grin. "Wring her dry, man. It's about time someone did."

Mrs. Grier entered minutes later, clearly in a temper. "I want to know the meaning of this," she demanded, yanking off her gloves and glaring at Darrow. "If you wish to speak with me, then you come—" She stopped when she'd got halfway down the table and realized his situation. She turned a scowl upon Kara standing next to him at the head of the chaise. "What have you done, girl?"

Kara gaped, but Niall spoke up instantly in response. "You will use your manners when you address Miss Levett," he ordered her from his spot at Darrow's feet.

"I believe the relevant question is 'What have *you* done, Mrs. Grier?'" Darrow said coldly.

"I? I have done nothing. Certainly nothing to warrant being dragged over here." She arched a brow at Niall. "Unless you have reconsidered selling that bit of land?"

"You are here to discuss other matters, ma'am." Darrow reached under the table to the seat of the nearest chair, where Kara had placed the evidence they had discovered. "You are here to discuss this." He placed the marriage lines onto the table before him.

She stepped closer, peering to see. Kara saw her pale when she realized just what Darrow had.

"You recognize it, then?" the fiscal asked.

The woman shook her head.

"Still, you know what it is."

"I have no idea what you mean. Or what you want from me."

"There is no use lying. We know you paid Finley a great deal of money to keep him from publicly exposing these marriage lines."

She shook her head again.

"A *great* deal of money," Darrow repeated. He reached again and placed the wallet on the table. "You were seen handing this over to Finley at a secret meeting, in the dead of night."

Her eyes closed. She gripped the back of the closest chair.

"You paid Finley to keep quiet the fact that he was your true brother. But he didn't turn over the proof he had. He kept it and hid it away. You couldn't have that, could you? He could displace your son as the heir to the title. Finley would be the next Earl of Balstone. Your brother would inherit, not your son. You killed him to prevent it."

The woman slid into the seat. For a moment, she allowed her head to fall into her hands. "Half-brother," she said fiercely. "And I did not kill him."

"Come now, Mrs. Grier," Darrow chided. "We both know better. And so will a judge and jury."

"Marriage lines can be faked," she clipped out.

"But these will match the torn edges of the register at Canongate Kirk, will they not?"

She sighed. "I had no reason to kill him. Finley wasn't even interested in the title. Why do you think he didn't come forward years ago? He arrived here under false pretenses to discover what he could—and he found the truth. The earldom comes with no power, not since the Scottish Parliament was dissolved. Balburn loses more money than it brings in. My brother has drained the coffers in pursuit of shell necklaces and bronze plates—trinkets that he cannot even sell. Finley was no fool. He wasn't willing to take on the responsibility if there was to be no reward."

"Then why did he stay on?" Darrow asked.

Mrs. Grier shot him a look of dislike. "For the steady pay. So he could play his wretched golf in the area. To be a thorn in my side, I suspect. And to keep his eye on the main chance. If the tides were to turn at Balburn, or if my brother were to discover something valuable, he would want to know."

"I don't understand why your father didn't acknowledge him, and the marriage, earlier," Kara said.

The other woman snorted. "That is because you did not know my father. All he dreamed of was being the same sort of great leader he imagined our ancestors were. He wanted to be a lord of old, holding court over a large family, a throng of obedient subjects, dispensing orders and justice, directing a large brood of sons into marrying well, growing the family, working to increase our standing and wealth."

"Except his wives kept dying," Niall said.

"Yes. He never intended on marrying Finley's mother until after she gave birth and proved she could bear him sons. But it was the girl's sister who thwarted him. She forced him to marry the girl before the babe came. The sister threatened to kill the girl and babe both if he did not wed her, and right away. She would blame the curse that was whispered to be laid upon him and cry up and down the countryside that my father had collected yet another dead woman."

"He capitulated," said Niall.

"Yes. And then he rejoiced when the child was born. Since she had given him another son, he planned to bring her to Balburn, to make her his true countess. But the girl died soon after the birth."

"And your father didn't want to claim the boy because he came with another dead wife," Niall finished. "He didn't want future potential brides to be frightened by the idea of the continued strength of the curse."

"The aunt agreed to take the boy for a princely sum, but she wasn't stupid," Mrs. Grier said bitterly. "She stole away the proof of the marriage."

"Your father gave away a living, breathing son, for the hope of enticing another woman into marriage, so that he could have more sons?" Kara said, incredulous.

"So that he could have a raft of sons," Mrs. Grier corrected her. "Dunstan was small and bookish. I was a girl. My father could not give up on his dream of a houseful of strapping warrior boys who would broaden his influence and wealth." She sneered. "The irony of it is, Dunstan is just like him. He cannot give up on the idea of digging something spectacular out of the dirt, to broaden his influence in the archeological community."

"And his wealth," Niall said.

Mrs. Grier lifted her chin. "Finley was not raised to hold a title, nor even to be a part of our family. He grew up grubbing around the docks. He was not fit to become Dunstan's heir, nor to take over Balburn. And he agreed! Don't you understand? He didn't truly want any of it. He just wanted money to pursue his own ridiculous dreams."

"It sounds like he fit in your family rather more than you'd care to admit," Kara said.

The woman glared at her. "Finley wanted to move on, and I wanted that, too. He knew that Dunstan and I could have fought his claim in the courts. Such papers can be falsified, as I said."

Darrow slapped another paper onto the table. "But Finley didn't fake the letter written by the clergy who married your father and his mother and confirmed his claim. It's signed and witnessed by a banker and a bishop."

Her shoulders slumped.

"You were hoping Finley had lied about that, weren't you?"

"I wanted no such gossip or drama overshadowing my son's inheritance. I found the money he wanted. Finley and I had an agreement," she said plaintively. "I paid him what he needed, and he vowed to keep quiet. Our bargain was struck and we both followed through. He was leaving to pursue his own interests."

"Except he came back wanting more, didn't he?" Darrow said. "You were seen and heard arguing about it on the night of the unveiling."

"That was your fault," she spat at Niall. "Finley knew you were being paid for that ridiculous statue. He knew the party would incur extra expenses. He thought I was lying about the state of Balburn's finances, that I was holding back money somehow. I told him that I had practically bankrupted us to pay for it all—and for his silence. I finally convinced him. He believed me. I had no need to kill him, as I keep telling you."

"Except that he still held tight to the proof of his birth—and you could not find it, could you?" Darrow asked. "And your son's inheritance was still in danger." He sat back. "If you didn't kill Finley, then your son did."

"Nonsense. My son went to Edinburgh the night of the party. He is still there."

"Are you sure he hasn't returned?" asked Darrow, watching her closely.

"Of course I am sure."

"We saw him yesterday at the Dalwiddies'," Kara told her.

Mrs. Grier paled again.

"Whichever of you did it, I will find out," Darrow stated. "I will question your son. I will discover the truth. And until then, you will be confined to your rooms at Balburn. I will send over officers to be sure you stay put."

"Absurd." Fury coursed through the woman. She stood, her face gone red. "You know nothing, you fools."

Darrow gestured at the two constables still standing just outside. They came in to flank Mrs. Grier. One of them tried to take her arm, but she pulled away.

"If you want to know who killed Finley, look to the man who cheated him in business," she cried. "Look to Riley Wolford."

She continued to struggle, but the constables escorted her out, one at each arm.

"Have a lovely day, Mrs. Grier," they heard Gyda say merrily.

When her cries of protest had finally died away, Darrow turned to look at Kara, then at Niall. "Who the hell is Riley Wolford?"

Kara raised a brow. "I would say that Mrs. Grier has given us the name of Finley's rival."

※※※※※

"We'll have to look into him, this Riley Wolford," Darrow said morosely, after they had got him settled upstairs again. "Although I hope that woman turns out to be the culprit." He looked to Niall. "You'll have to go to Edinburgh, right away."

"No. *We* will not," Kara interjected.

Darrow began to protest.

"She's right," Niall said. "What would you have us do? Wander the streets calling his name?" He shook his head. "I am going to go to the Dalwiddies' again and ask Jacob to introduce me to George Gibbons."

"Oh, yes. The tax commissioner," Kara recalled. "Brilliant, Niall. If Riley Wolford is Finley's rival, he might be the one pursuing the purchase of Blister MacCallum's farm."

"And if he is, George Gibbons would have his address, at the least," Niall finished. He cocked his head in her direction. "Would you care to accompany me?"

"No, I don't believe so," Kara said. "I think I need to spend some time with Harold. It's not like him, not being in the middle of a commotion like we had here this morning."

"That is true." Niall looked concerned. "Shall I go and look in on him with you?"

Darrow looked ready to explode.

Kara bit back a smile and darted a glance in the fiscal's direction.

"No. You go and find out what you can. I'll check on Harold. But perhaps later you can take him out to where the new forge will be? I know he'd love to be included on the planning."

"You are right. Tell him I'll come to find him when I return."

Kara walked Niall downstairs, then went in search of her ward. She looked through the house, and was both charmed and concerned when she found him curled up in a window seat in the schoolroom, fast asleep. He started awake when she ran a hand over his hair. Kara was alarmed to see the shadows lurking beneath the boy's eyes. He'd changed so much from the thin, dirty, brave boy who had lived on London's streets. She never wanted to see a sign of ill health or neglect in him again. "Are you quite well, dear?" she asked gently, suppressing a surge of worry. "I cannot ever recall you napping during the day."

"I was still so tired when I woke up this morning," he said, sitting up with a yawn. "I was going to look in my books to see what sort of swords the Picts used, but I couldn't keep my eyes open."

"I've been thinking about your Green Knight out in the gardens," she said, settling down next to him. "Niall and I might have to go into Edinburgh for a day or two. I thought I would find a copy of the story about Sir Gawain and the Green Knight. We could read it together, if you like."

"Oh, yes. I've been thinking of him too. I heard Ailsa tell Catriona that the rocks and trees here have spirits. I thought our Green Knight might be their protector."

"That's a lovely thought. I was wondering if we shouldn't make him the subject of our next project?"

"An automaton?"

"If you like the idea, we could start designing him today."

"I have drawing paper!"

He hopped off the seat with his usual energy, and some of her worry eased. They spent a long while discussing what their Green Knight would look like and what his qualities would be.

"He should have a sword, of course," Harold declared.

"What would his sword look like, do you think?"

"It should have vines and leaves on it. Perhaps we can carve them into the metal, the way that Gyda carves runes on her axe heads." He looked into her face. "I could make the sword in the forge. I know I could do it, if Niall helped me."

"Oh, yes. I forgot. When he returns, he wishes you to go out to the site of the new forge, to help with the planning of it."

Harold was delighted with the notion, and she took the opportunity to ask him what he thought of the priory.

"I like it," he said thoughtfully. "It's fun to run down the colonnade and in the walled garden. I'd like to go back to the Viewing House sometime. But I miss the laboratory, and it will be better here when we get it all cleaned up and have more people living here."

"Speaking of new people, I met a boy over at Balburn House the other day. His name is Tom. He's recently lost someone he loved and is very sad about it."

"We should do something to cheer him up," Harold said immediately.

"That is just what I thought, and I had an idea about it. There is a game they play about here, a game with long clubs and small balls."

"Golf! Mrs. Pollock said she played it when she was young."

"Did she?" Kara was momentarily diverted, trying to visualize such a thing. "Well, that is the very game that young Tom's friend was going to teach him. He's lost that chance, but I thought we might engage an instructor to teach us, and invite Tom over to attend the lessons as well."

"Anyone would like that," Harold said with a nod.

"Tom is employed as a stable lad, so we might have to wait until his days off," she warned.

"Oh? Maybe he'll tell me about his job. I asked Jamie, and tried to tell him about the stables in Bluefield, but he wasn't interested."

Kara nodded. "Jamie is a bit older than you. I suspect he's more interested in talking to the young maids."

"Is Tom the same age as me?"

"Close to it, I would guess."

"Good. I'll tell him all about how I sell pies for Maisie."

"I'm sure he'll be fascinated."

Harold shot her a shy glance. "Will you like the golf lessons, do you think?"

"I hope so."

"Will they remind you of the lessons you took when you were young?"

Kara stilled. "Who told you about that, Harold?"

"Oh, Maisie did. And Elsie, back at home. Different people." He looked at her avidly. "Is it true? Your father hired people to teach you to fight? And climb? And escape? All sorts of different things?"

"It's true. Do you know why he did that?"

"Because bad men wanted to kidnap you, to get money."

She nodded. "They succeeded once."

"But Turner saved you." Harold hesitated. "Kara?"

"Yes?"

"Do you think I would like lessons like those?"

She pursed her lips. "You might. Would you like to try some lessons of that sort?"

"I think so."

"Do you mind telling me why?"

"Because Turner is growing older. And Niall can't be around all the time. If someone comes to try to take you, I want to help."

Kara's heart wrenched. She pulled the boy in to hold him tightly. "You can have any sort of lessons you'd like."

"Miss Levett? Master Harold?" Brigitte stood in the schoolroom doorway. "Mrs. Pollock sent for the lad and says his luncheon is ready in the kitchen."

"I'm not all that hungry," the boy said. "But I'll go."

"I'll go with you," Kara announced. She moved down the stairs with them while they chattered.

<hr />

"Don't tell Turner I'm eating in here with you," Kara said, buttering a piece of fresh bread while Harold played with a bowl of soup.

"His appetite has dropped off," Mrs. Pollock said to her, while Harold told Ailsa about the Green Knight.

"He doesn't seem his usual energetic self," Kara whispered back. "I'm starting to worry."

"He's complained about a gripe in his belly," the cook said. "I swear, it cannot be anything I've fed him."

"I would never think so," Kara reassured her. "We've all eaten the same dishes." She shook her head. "I wonder if he's homesick for London?"

"We'll keep an eye on him," Mrs. Pollock vowed.

"Yes. Let's all do so. If he gives you or the maids a hint at anything that might be bothering him, please let me know right away."

The cook moved away, nodding, as Niall came pounding down the stairs and into the kitchen.

Kara glanced up at him expectantly.

"It's him," he said. "Riley Wolford. I ran into Jacob on the coast road, and he took me right into the village to meet Gibbons. He's the one who made the offer to buy Blister MacCallum's land. We have an address for Wolford, in Edinburgh." His eyes twinkled. "But don't tell Darrow I'm back. Not yet." He gestured to the lad. "Come, Harold. We have some planning to do if we are to fit out our new forge."

Chapter Thirteen

NIALL AND KARA left for Edinburgh the next morning. The drive along the coast was chilly but gorgeous. Niall had had the foresight to hire a coach and pair, so they rode in comfort, watching the sun rise. Turner had provided warm bricks, and Mrs. Pollock a basket of still-warm rolls and boiled eggs.

"If these are the perks of being a duke, then I am happy to count them," Niall said, letting loose a long sigh.

"I would feel spectacularly spoiled, if only we were heading into town of our accord," Kara said. "I hope Ailsa is not cold up there."

They had brought the maid along as a nod to propriety, but she had preferred to ride up on the box with the hired driver, who had turned out to be somehow, somewhat confusingly, related to her.

"Ah, well. I do have a list of supplies to order for the forge." He patted his coat pocket.

"And I've got a grocer's list and an order to look at paint colors. And I cannot forget to stop in a bookshop."

"Ah, but we also have a bit of privacy for once." Niall moved over to her bench and kissed her softly for several enjoyable moments, before tucking her into the corner of his arm. She sighed and rested her head on his shoulder.

"Gyda and I both received letters from Beth," Kara told him after a few quiet moments.

"How is she?" Niall asked. The young girl was a good friend to them all. A quiet and nervous young woman, she was learning to be more confident. She'd come a long way from the shy, skittish waif who jumped at shadows and noises. He grinned. How could she not grow bold, with Kara and Gyda as examples?

"She is faring well. She asked if we had seen Rob and asked us to pass on her good wishes." Kara twisted to look up at him. "I don't think her feelings for him have faded."

"I'm not sure how he feels about her. He did show a certain reluctance to go back home."

"And he did treat her so gently and kindly."

"He did."

She hesitated a moment. "I was thinking of inviting Beth to come to the priory for a visit."

Niall shifted. "I'd hoped to take you to my home, to show you where I grew up. Show you my first forge. Visit with Rob and his family."

"They will be amazed to welcome you home as a duke," Kara said.

He laughed. "It won't matter a stick to them. Rob's brothers will still try to dunk me in the mill pond, and his mother will stuff me with her game pie. They will love to know you. They will delight in spoiling Harold. We could talk with Rob, get an inkling on how he feels about Beth." He sighed in frustration. "But it will have to wait until we resolve Finley's murder. Why does it always seem as if we are postponing our lives until an investigation is solved?"

"Because we are," she said. "But it cannot go on forever. Eventually we will settle down into a simpler life."

He stared down at her in amazement. "I cannot believe you just said that. Can you truly imagine our lives ever being simple?"

She made a face. "I suppose not."

He moved so that he could cup her face in his hands. "It does not matter if our lives are complicated, or even if we continue to get wrapped up in these entanglements. It only matters that we are together. Scientist, artist, creator of automatons, duchess, detective, friend, lover. Any of them and all of them. All the facets of you, by my side. That is all I will ever need to be happy."

Tears sprang to her eyes, and he kissed them away. With soft murmurings and lingering touches and long kisses, he strived to tell her what she meant to him. And she said as much to him, using the same language. And so they traveled on, the coach barreling along the coast road, as they stole moments of comfort and contentment while they could.

Their pace slowed when they reached the city. Niall gazed out at the familiar mix of stone buildings, winding cobbled streets, busy crowds, and green spaces, lost in memories.

"You spent time here before we met," Kara said. It wasn't truly a question, and yet he could sense the query behind the words.

"Yes. After Malina. And in between my other travels, I would sometimes stay here."

"You haven't spoken of it. Not even when we were here for the parliamentary elections."

He lifted a shoulder.

"You must have friends. Acquaintances."

"A few." He exhaled, letting go of old burdens. "I was different then. I was numb for a time. I was busy making art and building walls. Gyda was my only true friend." He smiled. "Until you came along and started chipping away at those walls."

"Smashed at them, I think you mean," she said. She laughed a little, but she ducked her head, too.

"And I thank the heavens every day that you did," he said softly. "No one else has ever believed in me, fought for me—even against my own fears and protestations—the way you did. You saved me, Kara. From lonely, misunderstood duty, from detachment and seclusion. You've given me friendship and love and laughter and tears—a full life.

You saved me."

"You saved me right back."

He gripped her hands. "Darrow gave me a name. David Taggart. He's the one who was to talk to the banker, Mr. Dunn. We are to go to him if we need help in our enquiries." Leaning down, he pressed his forehead to hers. "I don't want to need his help. I want to find Wolford, listen to his story, and get back to the priory. I want to build your laboratory and workshop, and my forge. I want to come back here sometime, when we wish to, to visit with you and make real memories. I want to plan our wedding and build our lives."

"I want that, too," she whispered.

Niall could hear the apprehension in her voice, though. And he knew it came both from the fear that Darrow had instilled, that someone wished to harm him, and from her worries of somehow harming his reputation or acceptance with her own differences.

He clenched his jaw. He would finish this enquiry. He would untangle himself from the mess of it all. And he would sweep the way clear for her to drop such burdens, for he knew how insidious such fears could be. He'd worried about her in a similar fashion, when they had been waiting to see what consequences would come from his exposed secrets. She'd been patient with him, and he could do no less for her. All he could do was reassure her, in the end, for she was grappling with ghosts and insecurities from her past as much as worries for his future.

It was frustrating as hell, when all he wanted was to brush her path free of anything dark and worrisome. She deserved all the light and love and laughter that she brought to so many others.

The coach slogged through the traffic, heading north for Leith and the docks. The driver had to ask directions a couple of times as they wound their way through the streets, but Ailsa was a help. Men were happy to answer the pretty girl's questions. Finally, they reached Mill Lane, near the Water of Leith.

It was a relief to climb out of the coach. The driver waited while Niall left Kara and Ailsa on the pavement outside the shabby, narrow house while he went to pound upon the door. His knock went unanswered. Glancing back, he repeated it, but to no avail.

Kara was staring across the lane when he came back to them. He looked over at the inn that had caught her attention. The Siren's Blade. Its colorful, swinging sign featured a mermaid holding a gleaming sword.

"Didn't Finley mention that he had experience running an inn?" she asked. "What are the odds?"

"Damn low, I'd say, but it's worth looking at. You said Tom Harden hinted it was a friend who betrayed Finley. Perhaps they knew each other from this neighborhood?"

The three of them crossed over, trooped inside and headed for the dining room. It featured a crackling fire, a shining bar and the smell of bacon in the air. This early, the customers were sparse, but the place was not empty.

The man behind the bar was older, but still solidly built. He had lost a good bit of his hair, but not his brawn. He eyed Ailsa with appreciation as they entered.

Kara pulled the girl close. "We'll take a table. You go and order an ale for the duke and a couple of lemonades for the two of us. He looks like he might flirt with you a bit."

"Am I to flirt back, miss?" Ailsa asked, her eyes wide.

Kara laughed. "I leave that entirely to your own discretion, but do ask him if he knows Edmund Finley. You can tell him the duke is looking for someone who knows the man."

"Aye, miss." She paused and looked between them. "Am I investigating? As you and His Grace are wont to do?"

Niall wondered what the girl had heard. "Yes. I believe you are."

"I never would ha' thought it!" Ailsa shook her head. "I am that glad to be working for you and the duke, miss."

Kara pressed her hand. "We are glad, too, Ailsa."

The girl went to the bar. Niall held out a seat for Kara. He watched surreptitiously as the girl gave their order. The man appeared jovial as they spoke, but Niall saw when he stilled and looked over her shoulder at them.

Ailsa came back, nodding as she took her seat. "He knows him."

The barkeep took his time about pouring their drinks, and stepped to the back to call for someone to watch the bar before he carried a tray over to them. Passing the drinks out, he looked to Niall. "The girl says ye be a duke. I thought Edmund was working for an earl."

"He did, in fact," Niall answered quietly.

"Did? What's the boy done now? Got hisself fired? Run off? Leave a good position to chase a dream of gettin' rich?"

"I'm afraid Edmund Finley is dead." Niall said it gently.

The man took a step back, shock on his face. "Dead?" he repeated.

"Under questionable circumstances, I'm afraid."

The barkeep looked stunned.

"Please, have a seat." Niall moved to pull another chair close. "Mr....?"

"Spanner," the man said flatly. "Name's Spanner. Edmund is truly dead?"

"I'm afraid so."

Spanner shook his head. "The boy and I had more than our fair share of disagreements, but I never wished him dead."

"You knew Finley well?"

"I should say so. I near raised him, didn't I? After I married his aunt, who had the keeping of this inn. He were just a lad. We butted heads, but that was just the way of it, with a new man come into his life. I always tried to do right by him." He sighed. "We had a real tosser of a row after my Jean died, but I would not wish him ill."

"What did you fight about, if I may ask?" Niall looked around. The inn was not in the first stare of fashion, but it was clean and looked cared for. It likely did a steady business, this close to the docks. "This place?"

Spanner flushed. "The boy thought the inn should come to him." He shook his head. "But I married Jean and what's hers became mine. Edmund thought he could fight against the natural order of things, but when it came clear he wouldn't wrest this place from me, he left. Didn't see him for a while, but in the last years, we made peace. He would stop in when he came to town."

"Was he coming to Edinburgh to see Riley Wolford, by any chance?"

Spanner sat back, frowning. "Riley? That wee scoundrel? Edmund was not mixed up with him again, was he?"

"The procurator fiscal has heard Finley's name linked with Wolford's in a possible business deal."

"Surely Edmund would have known better by now."

"They had a history?"

"Aye, they ran together as bairns. Nothing but trouble, that Riley. He was always hanging out here, every chance he got. The pair of them were always sneaking ale, snitching something from the kitchens. I caught that little rat, Riley, stealing from my cellars more than once." His head swung in amazed remembrance. "The little blighter got right through my locks. I changed them, but that didn't slow him down a bit."

Niall glanced at Kara, who had more than a bit of skill at lock picking, herself, but she only gave him a slight smirk.

Spanner sighed. "I beat Edmund good and told him to keep that boy out of here. Riley's got a crooked streak a mile long. Edmund should have known that." His expression darkened. "If the fiscal thinks he had a hand in harming Edmund… by God, I'll have his guts for garters, myself."

"The fiscal just wants to understand their business dealings, for now," Niall soothed. "I gather Riley lives across the lane?"

"Riley? No. His father's still there, nigh on to crippled, now, after years of working the docks. His sister moved in to care for him."

"I knocked over there, but no one answered."

Spanner shrugged. "If the sister is out at the market or something like, then Paul would not be able to get to the door."

"Is Riley still in Edinburgh?"

"Aye. Him and his own sister keep a place closer to his work at the warehouse. Down by the new Victoria Dock, I think it is."

Kara spoke up. "Do you know Riley's sister, Mr. Spanner?"

"Aye. Lily. She's a pretty thing. Edmund always had a soft spot for her."

"Would you know which warehouse Riley works in?" asked Niall.

Spanner made a face. "It's one of those down near the Vaults on Henderson. Stores wine, mostly. I don't know which one, must be a hundred of them. But if ye want to know aught of him, ask at the Blue Dog. That's where I heard he takes his pints."

"Thank you, Mr. Spanner. You've been very helpful."

The man nodded and stood. "Ye be careful, asking after him. Rats get mean when they are cornered."

"We will go carefully. Thank you."

The barkeeper wrung his apron in his hands. "Do you think the fiscal would let me know what he finds, in the end? I'd like to know what happened to Edmund. I hate to think of him gone, so young."

"We'll make sure you are informed, sir," Niall promised.

"I thank ye." The man returned to the bar, deflated. Niall looked back once, and gave him a nod, before they left.

⋙⋘

THE CLOSER THEY got to the docks, the more crowded the streets grew. Their driver stopped at a livery to get directions to the Blue Dog and they made their way through a maze of warehouses and past crowds of sailors, stevedores, clerks, businessmen, and every sort of costermonger. Ailsa rode inside with them now and she pressed herself close to the window, agog at the busy scenes outside. She looked back suddenly. "Miss? Why did His Grace give you such a look, when Mr. Spanner spoke of his locks?"

Kara grinned. "I'm sure I don't know. I haven't picked a lock since well before we left London for Scotland."

Ailsa looked shocked.

Niall shot her an amused look and spoke to reassure the maid. "Don't worry, Ailsa. Miss Levett's father arranged for her to learn to pick locks, but only so that she might protect herself. I've seen her get herself out of serious trouble with those skills—and she's rescued me from danger more than once."

"Aye, then. Well, that's different, isn't it?" The maid regarded Kara with approval. "I always feared a life in service would be dull as ditchwater."

Kara colored a bit, but Niall only laughed. "Miss Levett is a woman with many sterling qualities, Ailsa, but dullness is not one of them."

The carriage pulled to a stop and the coachman climbed down to tell them that the pub sat down a narrow lane where the coach could not go. They left him waiting on the main thoroughfare and set off.

Kara crinkled her nose. The cobblestones were uneven and the lane was smelly and dirty. Several times she was forced to pull her skirts aside as they passed noxious puddles or piles of garbage. She was very glad she'd donned one of her altered outfits, with special changes that allowed her to carry, hidden, several useful implements.

No one else traveled the lane, although there were several worn shops along it. They passed a tobacconist and a general store, but saw no customers inside either of them. Her heart dropped as they reached the decrepit door on which hung a tattered sign proclaiming it as the Blue Dog. The door was shut tight. The shutters over the one window were closed.

"It's not open," she said with dismay.

"The Blue Dog is not the sort of place to open before the sun is going down."

They all turned to see a woman standing in an open doorway across the lane. She watched them with amusement. "It's not the sort to take ladies into, neither."

Kara gave her a nod. "Thank you for the warning."

The woman was dressed in blue skirts with a patterned bodice covered in unlikely blue roses. Her hair was teased high in the front and hung in long, sausage curls over her shoulder, almost like the hairstyle of a court lady of old. A girl in a scruffy, worn gown stood behind her, in the shadows.

"We are truly only searching for a man who is a frequent patron of the pub."

"Which one?" the woman asked. "There's a fair number to choose from." She gave a laugh. "And none of them likely worth yer time." She gave Niall a careful scan, from head to toe.

"We are looking for Mr. Riley Wolford," Niall said.

The woman straightened, interest blazing in her eyes. "Have ye got news of his sister, then?"

"Lily Wolford?" Kara asked. "No. Why? Has something happened to her?"

The woman slumped against the doorframe again. "Gone missing, ain't she?"

"For how long?" Niall asked sharply.

"Several days?" The woman shrugged. "How should I know?"

"Do you happen to know which warehouse Mr. Wolford works in?" Kara asked her.

"Aye. It's a big one, down near the Shore. He's a manager for Lander's Imports." She turned her attention to Niall again. "Are ye an importer, too? I hear they got some interestin' things making their way through Lander's."

"I'd thought it was mostly wines," Niall said, as if he knew more than the single note that Spanner had given them. Kara bit back a laugh.

"There's wine there, among other things. Exotic things, I heard." The woman made it clear she found Niall to be exotic.

"Thank you," Niall said abruptly. "We'll be off to find Wolford at his work, then." He held out an arm to Kara.

"That warehouse ain't the place to be taking ladies to, neither. But you could leave them at the Fishwife's Parlor, down at the Shore. It is a place designed for ladies. They may even dine in there. Quite fancy, as the queen herself complimented them when she was here, years back."

The girl moved forward out of the shadows. "Riley's not likely to be at the warehouse," she said in a low voice. "He's been leavin' work to look for signs of his sister."

"Do you think she's in trouble, then?" Kara asked, keeping her tone gentle.

The girl nodded, but the woman looked displeased. "Go back inside, Mary."

The girl quickly ducked back behind the older woman.

"I'm very sorry to hear it," Kara told them both. "If you see Mr. Riley Wolford, please tell him we'd like to help him find Lily, if we can."

"So we will. So we will," the woman said in a way that conveyed that she absolutely would not.

Niall tugged at Kara's arm, and she sent Mary a last smile before letting him lead her back toward the coach, with Ailsa stepping right in behind them.

"I didn't like her eyes," the maid whispered, once they'd gone far enough away. "Not a bit."

They had nearly reached the main road when footsteps sounded behind them, coming fast. The girl, Mary, breathed heavily when she caught them up. "Lily *is* in trouble," she gasped. "If ye truly mean your offer to help, I can have her meet ye at the Fishwife."

Kara glanced at Niall. "Yes, of course. We will do what we can."

"Thank ye." Mary looked truly grateful. "Lily is my friend. I thank ye fer helping her. I'll get word to her, and she should meet ye within the hour."

The girl turned to run back, and Niall sighed. "This is starting to become complicated."

Kara shrugged. "We need to take what leads we can get. And could we say anything different, in any case?"

"No, you are right."

She started toward the carriage. "Let's go, then. We don't want to miss her."

Chapter Fourteen

KARA WAS CHARMED by the Shore. Grand stone buildings, with the water before and the hills over Edinburgh towering behind, the great sweep of the old harbor and pier, the tall masts of the ships, the bustle of commerce, and even a few ladies and gentlemen strolling the pier for pleasure—it all made for a busy, inviting scene.

The Fishwife's Parlor was just as charming. At the bottom of a stone building on a street corner, with a rounded edge and large-paned, curved-top windows, it welcomed one inside with lovely smells and a bright interior.

"I understand you have a dining parlor for ladies," Niall said to the hostess who greeted them.

Kara eyed her white, winged hat and colorful petticoats with interest.

"Aye, sir, and so we do." She gestured to the grand portrait of the queen that dominated one wall. "Our establishment sent dishes to be served to the queen when her ship docked in Leith in 1842. She complimented them nicely and later remarked on the prettiness of our local fishwives. We created the dining parlor for ladies in her honor." She beckoned them to follow her. "Please, allow me to show you."

She led them to a lovely room, lined with those large windows, filled with plants and delicate chairs and tables covered in fine linen and china.

"It's like a garden," Ailsa said, gasping.

"Fit for a queen," the hostess agreed. "We hope one day the queen will return and we will have the honor of serving her ourselves."

Groups of ladies sat at several tables. One group also contained a pair of gentlemen. Another man sat in a corner, his newspaper raised like a barrier to the others in the room.

"As you can see, it's perfectly respectable for ladies and gentlemen to dine here, either alone or separate," the hostess assured them. "Our parlor is proper, estimable, and well regarded."

"It's lovely," Kara told her.

"Do you think you will be safe if I leave you two here to meet Lily while I check the warehouse for her brother?" Niall asked. "Wolford is our main objective here, and if we split up, we'll get more accomplished."

"Of course," Kara told him. "Ailsa and I will have tea and see what we can do for the girl."

"Be careful," he whispered, with a secret squeeze of her arm.

Then he was gone, and their colorfully garbed hostess was leading her and Ailsa to a table next to a white stone fountain. The falling of the water played a soft background to the clink of china.

"Oh, miss!" Ailsa's eyes had gone wide. "I've never been anywhere so grand!"

"It is lovely," Kara agreed. "But it is welcoming and friendly, too, and I think that is so much more important, don't you?"

Ailsa looked doubtful, but a serving girl approached and Kara ordered a pot of tea.

"We've a lovely plate of Parlies to go with it," the girl offered.

"Parlies?" Kara looked to Ailsa, but the maid shrugged.

"They are tasty shortbreads, flavored with ginger and black treacle. They used to be a favorite of the men of the Scottish Parliament of old. Perfect with tea."

"They sound wonderful," Kara said with a nod. "Thank you."

They sipped their tea while Ailsa let her gaze wander over the others in the room. "I think that bloke is waiting for someone, like we are," she said in a whisper. "He hasn't turned a page of that newspaper, and he keeps watching the door."

"Well spotted," Kara said. "Don't let him see you watching him."

The Parlies were devoured before Kara found her attention caught. A young woman entered, pausing in the doorway to glance around. She had honey-colored hair and darker brows. A sharply pointed nose dominated a face that wore a certain hard expression, as if the girl had dealt with a number of life's harsh truths, and she knew more were coming.

"Do you think that's the sister?" Ailsa asked.

The newcomer's gaze had settled on them. She hesitated, then moved toward them.

"I believe so," Kara answered.

At the same time, Ailsa sighed in disappointment. "No. She must be here for the gentleman. He recognizes her."

Kara glanced over at the man with the newspaper. He had abandoned it and got to his feet, all of his focus on the new arrival.

The girl followed Kara's gaze. She stopped in her tracks. Kara's fingers were working on the concealed pocket in her skirt even as the fear bloomed on the girl's face.

The man left his table and started toward the girl. With a last, despairing glance at Kara, she turned and fled.

The man rushed after her.

"Stay here," Kara ordered Ailsa. "Do *not* leave. I will come back for you, or Niall will. Stay until then." She set off in pursuit of the pair, the hidden pocket in her skirt only half unfastened.

When she reached the pavement outside, Kara's gaze caught the end of Lily Wolford's skirt flitting around the far end of the building. The newspaper man was still several lengths behind her. Kara ran, pushing as fast as her skirts would allow.

She turned the corner and saw that the girl had crossed the street. She was aiming for an alley that was blocked by a wagon carrying a full load of hay. Ducking and sliding, she went under the wagon and into the alley. The man chasing her cursed as he dodged traffic, but he made it across, then followed suit. By the time Kara got there, the wagon had moved, allowing her to gain a precious few moments in her pursuit.

She caught her breath as she plunged into the alley. The man had caught Lily and had her pushed up against a wall, down at the end, close to an intersection with another street. Kara freed the last fastener on the hidden flap of her skirt and reached inside, moving carefully toward them.

"Let me go!" Lily was panting and fighting to get away. The man had pinned both of her shoulders, but she'd got a hand under his chin and had his head pushed back.

"Stop fighting," the man ordered her. He jerked his head, but she held fast, keeping his face pointed high. "I'm to take you to Grier," he bit out. "He doesn't want to hurt you!"

Kara froze, her hand still buried in her pocket. *Grier?*

"Like hell," Lily said. She wiggled frantically, trying to break free, but couldn't get loose. The pair of them were in a stalemate.

Kara pulled her hand free—and her pistol with it. She held it steady as she approached, aimed at the man.

Lily quit struggling, but she kept her captor's chin pushed as high as she could make it.

Kara placed the end of her pistol right behind the pursuer's ear. "Let her go."

The man only snarled and held on, straining to see her from the corner of his eye, caught in his awkward position.

"Let me tell you about my pistol," Kara said conversationally. "It's quite small, as it was made for me specially by Mr. Samuel Colt, the American gun manufacturer. I saved him a vast amount of money, you see, when I exposed a scheme to steal the designs for his six-shooter. He created this pocket pistol just for me, in gratitude. The gentleman is astonishingly skilled. It's quite compact, but dead accurate. Not that it needs to be at the moment, though, does it? Now, why don't you do as you're told? Let. Her. Go."

The man growled.

Kara cocked the pistol.

With a vicious curse, he let go of Lily, spreading his hands wide and holding his head still.

The girl shot Kara a grateful glance and slipped away.

"Wait!" Kara called. But the girl stepped around the corner and was gone.

The man's feet shifted, almost imperceptibly. He was going to grab for her pistol.

Kara stepped back and fired, just past his ear. He yelped and ducked, coming up from his crouch and reaching for her.

But she held the pistol steady. "If you move again, I'll be obliged to put the next bullet in your brain."

He straightened slowly, his gaze murderous.

She felt a jolt in her gut. The man looked familiar. But where had she seen him? "Stay just there," she ordered him. "Give the girl a chance to get away."

"Bitch," he snarled.

She laughed. But her brain was whirling. "What does Will Grier want with that girl?"

"Ask him your damned self," he said, lifting his lip in derision.

She sighed, staring and trying to recall where she'd encountered him, but after a few moments, she judged Lily had had enough time to disappear into the streets again. She motioned for him to leave.

His gaze narrowed.

She shrugged and lowered her aim. "I don't have to kill you," she said. "A bullet in your knee would keep you from chasing either of us."

Cursing again, he whirled and took off at a run.

Kara sighed. She waited until he was well gone before she turned to head back and fetch Ailsa—but she kept her gaze sharply focused and her pistol in hand and buried in the folds of her skirt as she went.

※

NIALL FOUND THE correct warehouse without too much difficulty, now that he had a name to work with. He had to work a little harder to be admitted, but he managed to convince a guard that he was a businessman seeking a contract for rented space and wished to view the place. "I have an appointment with Mr. Wolford," he told the wary man, at last.

The name cleared the man's expression. "Ah, that makes sense, then, but Wolford's not here. Should be, and normally he's right on top of things, but he's got a bit of a jumble in his personal life. Ye'll have to deal with Mr. Irving, then." He made a face. "Though, if I was ye, I'd wait for Wolford. He's the one who really runs things here."

"I appreciate the advice." Niall raised a brow. "But I'm here now. I might as well have a look about, even if I must come back later to finalize matters."

"Suit yourself." The guard led Niall through hundreds of wooden wine barrels, all waiting their turn to be clarified and bottled. The huge space smelled of old wine, the air filled with the heady aroma of dried fruit, spice, smoke, and leather. Niall kept his gaze moving as they walked, looking for any sign of "exotic" goods, but spotted nothing. He climbed a narrow set of stairs behind the guard, crossed through an office occupied by several clerks, and stepped forward toward the open door the guard indicated. The man gave a shrug. "Good luck with that one," he whispered.

Niall paused in the doorway. The man inside sat at a wide desk. He was shifting the objects on the surface, rearranging a stack of files, an inkwell, a wax jack, and a blotter, then moving them all back again. As Niall watched, he reached inside a drawer and drew out a decanter and a glass. With shaking hands, he poured himself a tall drink, downed it quickly, then shoved away all the evidence.

Niall cleared his throat.

The man nearly lunged out of his chair. When he spotted Niall, he collapsed back again, his hand on his chest, his expression radiating relief and reprieve. "Saints! Ye gave me a fright. I thought they'd come early."

"I have an appointment with Mr. Wolford." The lie had worked so well the first time, Niall trotted it out again.

"Ah. Wolford. Well. He's not here, I'm afraid. Should be, of course. But he's not. There's just me."

"Mr. Irving?"

"Yes. That's me. I'm the night manager. Shouldn't be here during the day at all, should I? But here I am, left holding the bag. Waiting to be squashed."

Clearly that had not been the man's first drink this morning.

"Do you perhaps know when Wolford will return?"

Frowning, Irving appeared to consider the question. "When his sister is found?" He grimaced. "No, no. I am doing the man a disservice. He must search for her, must he not? He's spending his days searching for a sign of what's become of her, but Wolford does come in early for a few minutes, and stops in at odd times, to be sure all is well and nothing else has gone missing."

"Nothing besides his sister?" asked Niall.

"No! I mean, yes. I mean … I'm garbling this all up, aren't I? Of course, you cannot blame the sister. Pretty girl. She would smile at me, betimes, when she stopped in to bring her brother a bit of dinner, should he work late. Hope nothing serious has befallen her, of course. But honestly, she could have timed it better, if you think on it."

"Timed her disappearance?" Niall asked. "Do you think it's possible something serious has befallen her, then?"

"Well, who knows? Pretty thing like that, left alone a good deal of the time, wasn't she? With her brother working all hours? A hard worker, that Wolford." The man's head listed to one side as he gazed up at Niall. "He was the one that brought Lander's in, did ye know?"

"Lander's Import Company."

"Aye." Irving shook his head. It kept shaking for a long moment. "I told him not to take that account, but he met those gents in a tavern somewhere and got all worked up over it." He heaved a sigh. "I told him. Wine is easy. Wine is steady work. No messes. Oh, you might lose a cask or two to leaking or a moldy cork, but there's wine all through these docks. Don't have to worry over someone breaking in and stealing it, do you? Not like gold. And now look. I was right, wasn't I? More trouble than it was worth." He dropped his head into his hands.

"Lander's Imports is storing gold in your warehouse?"

"African gold. Shh ... It's secret." Irving looked up suddenly. "Who are you, again?"

"I'm looking for Wolford," Niall reminded him.

"Renting space, I hope," the man said mournfully. "We'll need ye, should Lander's pull out. Ohh," he moaned. "Wolford will be so angry. He worked so hard. Hired extra guards to keep those Lander's trunks safe. Came up with a variable patrol system through the warehouse, so that those trunks were never unchecked for more than a quarter of an hour. And at different times, every day. Genius!" He slumped again. "Didn't matter in the end, though, did it? Gold's gone, isn't it?" Irving slammed a hand flat on the desk. "Irony of it is, that gold could have been stolen at any time since it was put here. Though how they got such great, bloody pieces out without getting seen—I cannot fathom it!"

"Gold was stolen from the warehouse," Niall repeated slowly.

"Not just any gold. A great, bloody pipe, nearly three feet long—

solid gold! And a breastplate. Huge. Heavy. Just decorative, of course. Not for real warfare. But gone. And all discovered on my watch. Wolford's out looking for his sister, so I get the blame. He didn't heed me, so here we are. I'll have to tell the men from Lander's. I'm left to pay the piper. I'll be sacked. Ruined."

"You will, if you don't sober up before they get here," Niall told him. He stuck his head back out into the larger office. "Bring this man some coffee. Strong black coffee. And a lot of it."

The nearest clerk scrambled up and out. Niall turned back to Irving, who had put his head down on the desk and commenced moaning again. Niall's mind was whirling, putting pieces together.

This morning they'd heard Riley Wolford described as slippery and known to take what didn't belong to him—even at peril to a friend. As warehouse manager, he'd taken on an unusual account to store gold. He'd arranged a complicated security strategy—so intricate that only he might know the short intervals when it would be left unattended? He was known, or at least suspected, of having lock-picking skills.

"Irving," Niall said. "Irving!"

The moaning stopped.

"How was the theft discovered?"

Irving stared.

"The gold. Who discovered the theft? How?"

"Oh. Yes. The lock had been opened. Scratches showed it had been worked at. But the trunk was spun around to face the wall, and who knows how long it took for one of the guards to notice that?" He groaned again. "I'll have to tell them—these men from the Lander's group. And they are hard men. You can see it. They've seen things, Done things. In Africa. Who knows what they will do to me?" His head went down again.

Perhaps Irving was right, then. The theft could have occurred at any time. Had Wolford stolen the gold in order to buy the land in Highfield? How else would he have been able to make the offer himself and cut Finley out of the deal? Becoming a man of property with an inn and a golf course was a far cry from making a living as a warehouse manager in Leith. Worth stealing for? Perhaps. And what of the sister? Was her disappearance only a cover? A way to get Wolford out of the way while the land taxes were paid and the sale went through? A way for someone else to take the blame when the theft was discovered?

The clerk came back with the coffee, and Niall gestured for him to administer it to the morose manager. "Irving, have you done anything to try to trace the gold?"

"Trace it?" The man looked bewildered.

"Have you contacted the police?"

"The insurers had them in."

"And?"

"And?" Irving echoed.

"What have they found?"

"I'm the *night manager*." Irving sounded aggrieved. "They are not going to tell me."

"You are the one who is going to have to report the theft to the owners. Don't you need information to report? A plan? Have the police looked into pawn shops and local fences? Collectors?"

Irving continued to look blank.

Niall sighed. Surely this was the sort of thing that Darrow's contact could help with. But was it necessary? Did it matter to the investigation into Finley's death, where Wolford got the money to cut him out of their deal?

Likely not. But he did need to talk to Wolford. Discuss the status of his relationship with Finley and find out where the man had been the night Finley died.

"When do you expect to see Wolford again?"

Irving snorted. "I wish I knew. He should be the one in this meeting. But he does usually stop in sometimes, later in the day."

"Fine. I will be back then." Niall sighed. "In the meantime, sober up. Talk to the police. Prepare yourself for your meeting."

"They'll only sack me."

"Then meet your fate with dignity, man. If I discover something useful, I'll send word. If you see Wolford, tell him I need a word with him." Turning on his heel, he marched out. "More coffee for him," he told the clerk.

Niall was making plans before he reached the stairs. He would leave word with Darrow's contact. And it looked like they were going to need rooms for the night. This wasn't going to be over quickly, damn it. He needed to fetch Kara and Ailsa. Perhaps they had learned something useful from the sister.

From behind him he heard a muffled exclamation. "But I don't even know your name!"

He kept walking.

Chapter Fifteen

WHEN KARA EMERGED from the narrow alley, traffic had grown thicker on the ground, both in the street and on the pavement. She kept her gaze moving, watching for signs of either Lily or her pursuer, but both seemed to have melted away into the city and its crowds.

Carefully, she crossed the street. She was drawing near the waterfront Shore when she spotted a familiar figure approaching the intersection from the opposite side of the street.

Niall. Relief rushed through her. He wore a frown and a distant look, as if his thoughts were far away, even as his long stride carried him closer. She watched him when she could, her view of him briefly blocked now and again by the people on the pavement ahead of her. But she caught sight of him again as she approached the intersection. She'd reached her side well before he reached his, but he must have felt her regard, for he looked up and met her gaze.

He grinned, and she automatically returned his smile. His chin rose, he increased his pace—and at that moment, someone walking away from her and toward him reached out a long arm and shoved him hard, sending him stumbling to his left, tripping over the curb and sprawling into the street.

"Niall," she gasped. "Niall!"

She scanned for the villain from the corner of her eye, but all she caught was the tall form of a man quickly losing himself in the confused, milling crowd. Her main focus was on Niall as he lifted his head and slowly attempted to push himself to his hands and knees.

"Niall! Get up! Quickly!" she shouted over the noise of the traffic and the crowd. Bursting out into the street, she darted in front of a cooper's wagon, ignoring his derisive calls as he pulled his horse to a stop. She kept running. "Niall! Watch out!"

Even from here, she could smell it—a great tar wagon, pulled by a mismatched team, stained with black and carrying a dozen barrels of the stuff. It was moving faster than it ought to in this traffic. And it was heading straight for Niall.

She reached the other side of the intersection, but he was still a dozen feet away. "Niall!" She wasn't going to reach him in time. He was shaking his head and trying to get to his feet. "Niall!"

Suddenly there were young men in the street, inserting themselves between Niall and the wagon. They shouted and jumped, waving their hands and their hats. The wagon's team shied and faltered, slowing to a stop and milling in their traces. Another young man helped Niall to his feet and pulled him out of the street. They all ignored the shouts of the wagon driver as he swerved his horses out of the way and moved on.

"All right there, sir?"

"He's coshed his noggin."

"Sir? Can you stand on your own?"

Kara pushed her way toward them.

"Yes, yes." Niall was standing upright, if a bit unsteadily. "Thank you. I'm fine."

"Niall!" Kara reached him at last and clutched his coat. "Are you all right? Saints alive, you nearly died!"

"Some damn fool pushed me." He sounded aggrieved. Reaching for her, he missed, clutching at the air beside her. "I'm fine, but there seem to be two of you."

"Come. Sit down a moment." With the young men helping, she guided him over to a step in front of a tea merchant's shop. "Thank you all, so very much. You saved his life."

"He was going to be flattened by that wagon," one of them said, indignant. "Couldn't let it happen."

"Thank you, gentlemen." Niall spoke formally to the air on one side of the furthest lad. "Students, are you?"

"Not today, sir," one of them answered cheekily.

Niall laughed, then clutched his head. "I cracked my skull on a cobblestone, I think."

"Here, sir. Take this." The third young man pulled out a flask. "It's the good stuff. Just take a long pull and let it settle while you close your eyes for a bit. It'll put you to rights."

With a grateful murmur, Niall did just that. Kara hovered while he leaned his head back, and when he opened his eyes again, he gave a grunt of approval. "Just one of you now. That did the trick, lad. Thank you." Climbing to his feet, he reached in a pocket and pulled out several coins. "You lads have a round or two, with my thanks."

With a chorus of appreciation and sincere wishes for a quick recovery, the three young men moved on, slapping each other on the back and hooting in delight.

Heedless of the crowd moving past, Kara leaned into Niall. "This is getting out of hand."

He snorted and grimaced at his dirty hands, coat, and knees. "You are right about that. Odin's arse, but my head is pounding."

"Let's get back to Ailsa, and we'll get you some tea and clean you up."

Moving slowly, they made their way back to the Fishwife's Parlor. The hostess was at first relieved to see them, then dismayed at Niall's appearance. "Your young friend has been worried. But sir! I did tell you earlier—we are a respectable establishment!"

"The duke has had an accident," Kara told her. "Perhaps you have a private parlor where we can set him to rights?"

"Duke?" The woman gaped.

"Sedwick, at your service." Niall gave a short bow, then grimaced.

"Oh! Your Grace! I'm sorry. I had no idea. Of course, come with me, if you will." The woman quickly saw them settled in a small, pretty room. She sent in hot water, clean cloths, a comb, a maid to take Niall's coat for brushing, and a spread of luncheon.

"I was frightened to death, all by myself," Ailsa confessed when she was led in. "But I took up that bloke's newspaper and acted as if I dine alone every day."

"Very well done, Ailsa," Kara told her. She got Niall's scrapes and bruises clean and cleaned the grit and blood from his hair. While he ate, they exchanged stories of their findings, then sat grimly regarding each other.

"So the girl is indeed in danger," Niall said quietly. "I thought the story might be a ruse. Something her brother cooked up to cover his tracks."

"No. The threat was real. I saw her expression. Lily Wolford truly is afraid—and of someone named Grier," she said darkly. "I assumed it was Will Grier, and her assailant did appear to confirm it." She stood and began to pace. Angry fire crawled in her veins. "Everywhere we turn in this enquiry, there is a *Grier*. One or the other of them. And I'm not sure which one is worse." She turned to face Niall directly. "And do not tell me they weren't behind that attempt on your life just now. For that is what it was. Don't even try to explain it away." She raised a sardonic brow. "Who else could it have been? Unless you have a mortal enemy tucked away in Edinburgh that I am unaware of?"

He shook his head.

"I will *not* have it." Every time she pictured him stumbling into the street, her fury rose higher. "Surely this means we are getting closer to the truth? But close is not enough. They go too far, again and again. I want this solved. I want these nonsensical attacks on you to end. And I want them *punished*."

Ailsa's eyes had gone wide.

A knock on the door sounded, and the maid returned with Niall's brushed coat. Kara thanked the girl and helped him into it.

"You are right," he said. "About all of it. It's time to settle this. But clearly, we will have to go carefully."

"You will not go anywhere alone," she said fiercely.

He didn't argue. Not at this moment. But she could sense it coming.

"First thing," he said patiently. "We need to get rooms for the night. I know a place. I left word for Darrow's man that he could reach us there."

He meant to leave her there, leave her behind. She knew it. But before she could object, he forestalled her. "It's the best thing, too, if you want to help Lily Wolford. We can get word to her, get her in. A safe place for her to retreat to."

She pressed her lips together. "We need to speak to one or the other of them. Lily or Riley."

"We need to know where they were when Finley was killed," he said with a nod.

"We need to know how they are mixed up with the Griers and what they know of them." Kara gestured for Ailsa to take up her wrap. "Let's go, then."

She set her anger aside for a moment as Niall settled the bill and saw about sending word for the coach and driver to come for them. Kara pulled the hostess away. "I wanted to thank you for your help today and for making sure our Ailsa was safe and comfortable." She glanced over at Niall. "The duke will doubtless be called to the queen's court before long. I will do my best to pass on word of how you have honored the memory of Her Majesty's visit and your hope to welcome her here one day. I will speak of it to her ladies, if I can. The word may just reach her." She shrugged. "There's no way to know if anything will come of it—"

The woman stopped her with a hand on her arm. Her face shone with delight and excitement. "Thank you. It's enough to know that the queen might hear of our devotion. I'm very grateful."

Kara smiled at her. "As am I. Thank you for all of the help you have given us."

"I hope you will stop in again."

"Of a certainty, we will."

They stepped outside then, and Kara donned her indignation and determination again, imagining it wrapped around her like a cloak. As they set out, she fervently wished Mrs. Grier and her blasted son could feel her wrath coming closer.

"THE WITCH'S PRICE?" Kara asked.

Niall nodded carefully, trying not to set off his already aching head.

"That's the name of the inn?" Ailsa whispered. She stood at the top of the stairs on one street, looking down into the dark, winding length of another below. She looked terrified.

"It is." He beckoned them on, taking the stairs slowly. "It looks ... questionable, I know. But it is safe. Everyone in Edinburgh knows, if you are accepted as a guest at the Witch's Price, you are safe as houses."

"A witch's protection?" Ailsa sounded curious, but still frightened.

"Something like that," Niall agreed. "Superstition is a powerful tool."

He led them down the narrow street to a tall building of stone sitting on a curved corner of the road. Every other building on the street featured a pointed gable topped with a cross. This one featured three gables. None held a cross, but the middle one sported a tall weather vane with an elaborately crafted man in the moon. Below it flew a shooting star with a spreading tail, and each directional letter carried a different phase of the moon above it.

Kara stopped and stared up at it before turning to him with raised brows. "You made that," she declared.

Surprised, he nodded. "I did. Come along. I'll introduce you."

He led them up the stairs and into the reception hall. The place had not changed in all the time since he'd been here last—all shadows and dark, carved paneling, the only light shining from a small lamp on the high desk at the back. Sitting there, as ever, was the woman he'd been expecting. "Good afternoon, Beryl."

She looked up, utterly unsurprised. "There you are, boy."

"A new hat?" It was the only thing that differed about her. Tiny and black, it sported raven's wings and smushed down a section of her wild and wiry nimbus of gray hair. Her dress was black, her collar blinding white, as always. Perhaps the paint was applied a little thicker. Her cheeks were ruddier with rouge than he recalled, though her brilliant blue eyes still stared out from the heavy kohl with the same clear, knowing look that made him feel like she saw through his soul and out the back of him.

"Aye. I wore it for you, though I was expecting you earlier."

Ailsa had edged closer. "You knew he was coming?" she whispered. "Do you have powers of divination?"

Beryl looked through her, too. "No, dear. A man came looking for Niall earlier today, saying he'd had word he was staying here."

"Apologies, Beryl. We were delayed. If you will allow me, I will make the introductions?" He pulled Kara forward. "This is my fiancée, Miss Kara Levett," he said with pride.

"So it's true, then?" Beryl put down her huge, old-fashioned quill and, with a grunt, slid down from her seat and came around the desk. "Well, then. Let me have a look at you. 'Tis glad I am to meet the woman who could crack this one's shell."

"I'm very happy to meet you, as well."

Beryl looked pleased. Reaching out a hand, she paused and gave Kara a questioning look.

Casting a glance over at him, Kara gave the older woman her hand.

Beryl held it between her own for a moment, her eyes closed. Then she turned Kara's hand so that she could examine her palm. She let out a snort of laughter. "Oh, ho, boy. You'd best keep on your toes with this one."

Niall only rolled his eyes and gestured toward Ailsa. "And this is Ailsa, our sometime maid and current colleague."

Ailsa looked gratified at the description and bobbed a curtsy. "I've always wanted to meet a real witch," she murmured.

"So have I," Beryl said. Shuffling back behind the desk, she took a couple of keys from a drawer. "I gave ye yer auld room. The one across is empty. The ladies can stay there. Water's fresh. Fires will be lit at sundown."

"That sounds perfect," Niall said. "Our coach and driver will arrive shortly. He'll have our portmanteaus, and he'll need a place for the night."

"Already have the room in the stables made up." Beryl shook her head as if he might have known she would be utterly prepared.

Kara stepped forward. "If I may ask, might your hospitalities extend to a pot of willow-bark tea? Niall has suffered a blow and his head is aching."

"Aye, I'll bring it on up. Quickly, as yer friend will be back soon."

"Thank you."

Climbing back onto her high seat with effort, Beryl shot Niall a sharp look. "Rate's gone up since last ye were here."

"Your friendship and hospitality is worth a price above rubies, my dear," he answered.

"Go on with ye," she said, but she gave a hint of a smile.

Niall led the others down a dark passage and up a rickety set of stairs. Each step had its own special creak or groan.

"I begin to understand the place's reputation for safety," Kara said low.

"It is extremely difficult to skulk in here," Niall said with a laugh. "And that is only one of the place's endearing qualities." He led them to the third floor and opened the door to the room across from his usual haunt.

"I'm glad to see the lighting is better up here," Kara said, crossing to a large window.

"I quite like it," Ailsa said, gazing around at the heavy furniture and the ancient tapestries on the wall.

"My room is across the hall," Niall said. "It has a little sitting room. We might as well wait there, and we'll see who arrives sooner, Ailsa's cousin or Darrow's man."

He opened the door and heard Ailsa gasp as they all spotted Beryl waiting in the passage with a tray bearing two steaming pots.

"Get the door for me, boy, and I'll set it up. I brought tea for the ladies, too, but you need a good tisane to set you right."

Niall knew from experience how well the woman's remedies worked and that they tasted nearly as good. He opened the door to let all the women through, then sank down on a seat and took a cup from Beryl with a sigh.

"You'll be all right, then," she said, tilting her head and watching him critically. "Drink it down. Your man is here."

Without another word, she left, pulling the door closed behind her. A mere moment passed before they heard the squeak and creak of a heavy tread coming quickly up the stairs.

"Wait!" Ailsa exclaimed. "I didn't hear *her* come up!"

Kara went to open the door. There was no sign of Beryl, as Niall had suspected there would not be.

Ailsa gasped.

"Secret passage?" Kara asked over her shoulder.

Niall grinned and shrugged. Kara, of all people, would catch on to that particular trick, as her own Bluefield Park was riddled with secret passageways—and Niall was one of only a handful of people who knew it.

Ailsa sighed in relief.

Niall downed the last of his tisane and climbed to his feet as the heavy footsteps left the stairwell and advanced toward them, down the passage.

"Mr. Taggart, I presume?" Kara said as the man moved closer.

"Aye, and so I am." The man stared appreciatively. "Miss Kara Levett, you would be, then? Darrow has spoken highly of you." He caught sight of Niall over her shoulder. "Your Grace." He advanced and gave a short bow. "I admit, I'm looking forward to working with the pair of you. Darrow is a hard man to impress, but you've managed it."

"Please, come in." Niall gestured.

"Tea?" Kara took the seat Niall held for her and lifted the pot.

Niall glanced over and raised a brow at Ailsa, who had crept into a corner. Shaking her head, she took a seat and folded her hands.

"Thank you." Taggart sat and sighed as he took the cup she passed. "This is a far cry from how I usually offer up my reports."

"You have something to report?" Kara sounded surprised.

"Several somethings," Taggart answered. "But let me start with the first task Darrow set me to."

"Mr. Dunn, of the Royal Bank of Scotland," Niall reminded her.

"Oh, yes." She looked to their guest. "You have spoken with the gentleman?"

"I have not," Taggart declared. "Dunn has disappeared."

"Disappeared?" Niall repeated. "On purpose? Or as a victim of foul play?"

"He's on the run, or at least, that is my opinion," Taggart stated. "I could use your help in confirming that, as a matter of fact."

Niall waited.

"There are signs that the man is in trouble. I spoke to members of his household. Servants, to clarify, as Mr. Dunn never married and appears to be without family. They reported that the gentleman has been acting nervous of late. Giving orders to refuse any visitors, watching out of windows, jumping at small noises. His valet told me that he was ordered to pack a valise with clothing and sundries for several days. When he asked where Dunn meant to travel, he was told just to leave it in the wardrobe, at the ready."

Niall leaned forward. "And is it still in the wardrobe?"

"It is. It appears that the last time anyone saw Mr. Dunn was several days ago, at the bank. I've spoken to a number of clerks and various underlings there and heard similar reports of Dunn receiving a disturbing visitor in his office."

"Disturbing?" asked Kara.

"There was shouting," Taggart explained. "From both sides. Threats. One of the clerks reports hearing the words *opium* and *whores* repeatedly."

"Blackmail," Kara breathed.

"Dunn was said to have been talking loudly of mortgages."

"Is there a description of the visitor?" asked Niall.

Taggart pulled a notebook from his pocket and flipped through several pages. "Tall. Thin. Angry."

"It was a tall, thin man who shoved you earlier," Kara said. "I shiver every time I think of that long arm reaching out of the crowd for you."

Taggart shot him a questioning look.

"A minor incident," Niall demurred.

"A minor incident that might have killed him," Kara objected. "And likely the second attempt. Third, if you count that note that was delivered the night of Finley's murder."

"That does put an interesting spin on things," Taggart said. "Any notion on why they are targeting you, too?"

Niall shook his head.

"Which means we must be vigilant and careful," Kara said with a significant look at the other man.

"Message received," Taggart acknowledged her.

"Can we get back to Dunn?" Niall suggested.

Taggart nodded agreeably. "He appeared to be greatly agitated after his visitor departed. He paced. He issued curt orders. He ordered coffee and dosed it with alcohol hidden in his desk. He went through a storm of paperwork, then he disappeared into the bank vaults for an unusual length of time. Long enough for it to be remarked on. Most damning—when he left work that afternoon, it was noticed that he carried a case that no one recalled seeing him enter with."

Niall grunted. "But he did not go home."

"He did not. He has not been seen since. Not that I can uncover."

"A storm of paperwork," Kara said suddenly. "Mortgages. Miss Simmons mentioned that the servants were all convinced that Mrs. Grier had mortgaged the estate at Balburn." She looked to Taggart. "Would it be possible to find out if any of that paperwork related to Balburn?"

"That's where I hoped the duke would help," Taggart said, glancing at Niall. "In my opinion, Dunn was frightened. I believe he took either money or valuables from the vaults and went on the run. But though I've spoken to the lower levels at the bank, none of the more prominent men, those who actually know anything, are eager to speak to me, a mere constable, for a case not even centered in the city. But a duke? Doing a favor for an investigating procurator fiscal? They will talk to you. Hell, they will roll out a royal welcome. You could discover if anything went missing, or if any of the accounts of your suspects were tampered with."

"They might agree to speak with me," Niall said slowly. "But is it necessary? Dunn was likely either threatened or blackmailed. He was frightened. He ran. Do we need to know what he did before he left?"

"We do, if he didn't run," Kara countered. "What if he was taken before he could run? Or worse? After all, he never made it home to fetch his ready-to-go bag."

"The question is, why?" Niall said. "Why would they bother with him?"

"He did something, or he knew something," Taggart suggested.

"He knew Finley had a legitimate claim to the earldom," Kara said suddenly. "Judging by Miss Simmons's story, he was the one who broke the news to the family."

"That is true." Niall sat back. "I hadn't considered that aspect of it before. Finley didn't break the news to his siblings himself. Why not? Because it was smarter to have someone else know the truth?"

"Safer," Kara corrected him.

"Not safer for Dunn, if you are right," Taggart said.

"What you are postulating is too simple," Niall mused. "Elfred Grier murdered Finley to protect her son's claim to the title, then scared off Dunn—or worse—because he knew the truth?"

"Did anyone else know?" Taggart asked. He raised a brow at Niall. "Did you? Is that why someone has been after you?"

"No. I wouldn't know any of it at all, had Darrow not been injured."

"But does anyone else know?" Kara insisted. "Mrs. Grier didn't expect us to find those papers proving Finley's claim. That much was clear."

"That's one problem with your theory. Her brother knows," Niall reminded her. "And I cannot see Balstone going along with murder or any of the rest of it. As far as I can tell, he bears no great love for Will Grier. He spoke almost scornfully of him. Honestly, I don't think he gives a damn who gets the title once he's gone, he's so intensely focused on archeology and his place in it. In fact, I would imagine he would have favored Finley over his nephew. Finley at least understood the workings and scope of the dig site, even if he didn't share Balstone's passion for it."

"You are right," Kara mused. "It must not be that simple. For it doesn't explain why someone is after you. And it would mean that Riley Wolford was meant merely to be a distraction, when now we know that somehow he is mixed up with the Griers—or at least, his sister is."

"We are missing some piece of the puzzle."

"Several pieces, more like," Kara said glumly. "Which is exactly why we should perhaps be exploring more into the various threads that are poking out at us. Dunn's fate. Riley's motives. And why Lily Wolford is hiding from Will Grier."

"Wolford, oh yes," Taggart said, as if she had reminded him. "I did get your note asking about men who might be able to move stolen gold, and brokers who might cater to men who collect antiquities or artifacts."

"Were you able to find anything?"

"Well, there are several in the city. And that's the beauty of a man like Darrow. Foresight, that's what that man has. He keeps contacts and informants in many useful places. And that includes inside one of the most prominent shops that clandestinely deals in exactly that sort of thing. I sent out a feeler, and his contact can meet us tonight."

"Fine, then." Niall was happy to realize that his headache had left him. "We've got quite a list, then. Talk to the bankers. Investigate Riley Wolford's stolen gold." He could see that Kara was about to protest. He held up a hand. "One, I won't be alone."

"I'll keep him safe for ye, miss," Taggart said with a grin.

"And two," Niall continued, "that means I'll need you to get another start on finding Lily. If you will write a note to that young girl, Mary, inviting her to bring Lily here, you can both get her story and keep her safe. I'll leave it for the girl, first thing, before we move on to the rest of it."

Kara wanted to object. He could see it. But he was right and she knew it. She agreed, though she didn't look happy about it. After writing the note, she pressed close and whispered in his ear, threatening bodily harm if he wasn't careful.

Niall laughed and kissed her. "I love you, too," he said low. "You be careful as well."

Chapter Sixteen

KARA WATCHED OUT the window as Niall and Taggart set off. Her mind was busy sorting the people and connections and possibilities of Finley's murder even after the two men disappeared down the curving street. Finally, she heaved a sigh and turned around. "Come out from the corner, Ailsa." She beckoned the girl. "There was no need for you to hide away there."

"You and the duke had business, miss. And I don't want to seem too forward, poking my nose where you don't want it."

"Your nose has been in exactly the right place all this long day. You've done well. Now, if you can prove yourself discreet once we are back at the priory, then I will be entirely happy with you."

"I'm sure I will, miss, if only you will tell me what it is."

"Discreet?"

"Aye, miss."

"It means not revealing all the details of our adventures. To anyone, not even our friends at home. It's a matter of knowing what is right to share and what should be kept between ourselves."

The girl considered. "You mean something such as—I can tell that I dined at a fine spot like the Fishwife's Parlor, but not that I flirted with Mr. Spanner, even if it was just a little?"

Kara grinned. "Yes. That's what I mean."

"And I can say the duke is friends with a witch, but not that he presses a kiss behind your ear when he thinks no one is looking?"

"Just so." Kara reached for the hidden slit in her skirt, where her pocket pistol was concealed. "Might you have a needle and thread in your reticule, Ailsa? I'm afraid I loosened this button earlier."

"Oh, aye, miss. Mrs. Pollock told me to bring along a few trinkets that might come in handy." Ailsa brought out the implements and waved Kara away when she would have taken them. "Please, allow me, miss. You'll be all twisted about at an odd angle unless ye take off yer skirts. I can get it done quick as a whistle if ye sit still, like."

"Thank you."

They sat quietly for a moment while Ailsa sewed. "If ye don't mind my asking, miss, why dinna ye have a regular lady's maid? Ye'll be a duchess soon enough. Surely ye'll need help managing ... everything."

Kara sighed. "Elsie is the maid I have at Bluefield Park. She's been with me since I put away my pinafores, but she said she was too old to go gallivanting to Scotland. I almost convinced her when I told her how much the queen and Prince Albert enjoy it here." She shot a grin at the girl. "But at the risk of being indiscreet, I will tell you that I suspect Elsie has a bit of a *tendre* for Mr. Bell, the widowed head gardener. I don't believe she wished to leave him for so long."

Grinning, Ailsa finished the button and bent down to bite off the thread. "There ye are, good as new." She glanced toward the door. "Are we truly just going to wait again for that poor girl to find us?"

"Yes. For a while, at least. But if neither Mary nor Miss Wolford turn up, then I may have to go out looking. Then it will be your job to wait here, in case I missed them." Kara watched the maid carefully. "Will you be too frightened to be left here alone?"

"Och, no, miss! Not with that Beryl on the watch. Ye heard what His Grace said. Here, we are as safe as houses."

A sudden knock sounded on the door, and Ailsa jumped, belying her words.

"Miss Levett, ye'd best come," Beryl called. "There's sommat outside, and I think it's meant for ye."

"Stay here," Kara said to Ailsa in a whisper. "Lock the door." Rising, she went out. Beryl gave her an enigmatic look and jerked her head. Kara followed the older woman downstairs and out onto the front step.

Beryl gestured. "She's here for ye, aye?"

The sun still hovered on the horizon, judging by the colors in the sky, but the shadows lay deep in this lower street level. Kara could just make out the form of the young girl, Mary, holding on to the curved iron bars of the gate. Tears coursed down her cheeks. When she looked up and spotted Kara, she let out a hoarse sob.

"Mary, what's wrong?"

"It's Lily," she croaked.

Kara started forward, but Beryl reached out to grip her arm and stop her. The old woman held her head cocked, as if she listened to something Kara could not hear. "There's more afoot here," she said ominously. "Get back inside. You need to get behind your door and bolt it."

"Come, Mary," Kara called. "Come inside and tell me what's happened."

"I daren't!" Mary said, gazing up at the place with fear in her wide gaze. "It's known! Ye don't go in there unbidden, lest ye pay the witch's price!"

Beryl stepped forward. "I bid ye to come, then!" she said in a harsh whisper. "And hurry, girl, afore it's too late. Whatever it is followin' ye, I've no wish to let it in."

Mary's eyes grew wider. She glanced behind her. Kara beckoned her again, and she slipped through the gate, coming closer with halting steps.

Beryl ushered them both inside and locked the door behind them. "Up the stairs," she ordered them. "Quick, now."

She followed them up but stopped as they drew near the top floor. "Blasted bone and marrow," she cursed darkly. "Too late."

Behind them came the loud creaks and groans announcing others on the stairs. Looking down, Kara saw two figures step onto the first landing.

"Mary! Stop there!" The woman they'd first met with Mary, outside the Blue Dog, glared up at them, a man moving close behind her.

"Oh, no," Mary groaned.

"Go on." Beryl hustled them up to the top of the stairs and down the passage.

"Is this where you've stashed that wretched Lily?" the woman behind them called as she came up after them. "Damn ye, girl, fer holding out on me!"

Kara grabbed the girl's arm and headed for Niall's room, but Beryl stopped her. "It's too late. She's spotted ye. She won't get in the room, but she'll never stop hounding ye." She glanced closely at Mary. "And ye've work to do, aye? The pair of ye?"

Mary stared at her wildly.

"Do we? Can we?" Kara asked. "Can we do something to help Lily?"

Mary nodded frantically. "I hope so, miss!"

"Ye can, if ye are not trapped here, playing cat and mouse hole with that one." Beryl sighed. "Fine, then. A bit of trumpery is called for." She pulled them both to a stop partway down the passage, between rooms, and turned to face the pair that emerged at the top of the stairs. "Ye're not welcome here," she said, her tone low and menacing. "Leave now or pay the price."

The woman laughed, but she paused. "I'm not afraid of ye, old witch. I've come fer the Wolford girl. She's got a pretty price on her head, and I aim to collect it. Give her over and we'll go."

Mary groaned.

Beryl looked bored. "What ye seek is not here. Begone."

The woman's eyes narrowed with menace as she began to stalk toward them. Her companion stepped in close behind.

"I warned ye." Bracing her feet apart, Beryl gave a sudden shout and made a throwing motion with one hand.

A loud bang sounded behind the advancing pair. Smoke billowed up in great clouds, obscuring the two of them completely.

They cursed and coughed behind the smoke, but Beryl quickly stepped to the wall, where she pressed a bit of molding. A narrow panel slid open. She pushed Kara and Mary onto a tiny landing. "Go all the way down," she whispered. "I'll meet you there."

The door closed. Kara and Mary were left in darkness. Kara gripped the girl's hand. "Wait a moment for our eyes to adjust," she whispered.

"Damn you, you witch, and your flummery, too!" The woman sounded furious—and perhaps a bit closer than she had been.

"They are gone!" The man sounded spooked.

"They've ducked inside one of these rooms, you idiot." The sound of a door rattling on its hinges echoed in the passage outside.

Mary pressed against Kara's side. Kara gripped her tight. Her eyes were growing accustomed to the dark, enough to see a narrow set of stairs behind them and a faint glow reaching up from below.

"Ow!" The man's voice sounded close outside their hiding spot. "Something touched me!" He sounded panicked. "What? What is it? There's nothing there!"

Creaking footsteps, moving fast, sounded on the main stairs.

"They slipped past us, you fool! After them!"

"Let's go," Kara whispered to Mary. She held on to the walls as she started down the narrow, spiraling stairs.

Behind them came a great thud, as if something heavy hit the floor. "It's pricked me!" the man shouted. "What is it? Get it off me!"

Kara moved faster. Mary kept up. They were both careful to set their feet gingerly and make no sound. They passed another landing and a narrow walkway stretching from it, but they kept going, heading down as the light grew brighter.

The stairway spilled them out into an unexpected room, extraordinarily long but merely ten feet or so across. Close to the stairs it resembled a snug sitting area, with a stuffed chair and ottoman, a lit brazier, and a lamp on a shelf of books. A basket of yarn sat next to the chair, and on the ottoman sat a brindled cat blinking yellow eyes up at them.

A panel slid open across from the chair, and Beryl stepped through. Behind her, Kara glimpsed the high chair and reception desk. The old woman closed the door behind her. "Come," she ordered them.

Kara took Mary's hand, and they followed as Beryl moved through the long room. They passed a cluttered desk, then a worktable covered with pestles, pots, and powders and over which hung various dried plants and herbs. A cot made up with plump pillows and woolen blankets came next. At the end of the room was a narrow wall with a shuttered window.

Beryl threw up the sash and opened the shutters. "You cannot go out the front. She'll likely have a watcher out there. Probably out back too, if she's smart. And that one seems just intelligent enough to be dangerous. You'll have to go out here."

Kara looked out into a narrow alley between the Witch's Price and the building next door. Below, a thick shrub grew, stretching across the entire, slender space.

"Look closely," Beryl said. She pointed down, and Kara realized there was a barrel standing in the midst of the bush, with the greenery growing all around it. "It's just the right height for you to climb down. Head toward the back, but stop before you reach the kitchen garden back there. There's a gate into the neighbor's garden. Go through there and around their house. You'll come onto the street around the curve and won't be seen."

Kara nodded, absorbing the directions. "What of Ailsa?" she whispered.

"That girl has a head on her shoulders. She stayed behind her stout door during all of that ruckus. She'll be fine in there until one or the other of you gets back."

"And you?" asked Kara.

Beryl chuckled. "Don't worry your pretty head over me, girl. I'm going to go and exact the price from that wicked pair."

"You won't harm them, truly, will you?" Mary asked.

"Not me, girl."

"But we heard him fall ..." Mary sounded worried.

Beryl shook her head. "There's nothing pricking him except a bit of itching powder mixed with the smoke and his own guilty conscience. But there are ways and ways to pay, and the price must be met. They will settle their balance for the wrongs done here." The old woman eyed them critically. 'Now, go. Find the girl they seek. She has need of ye."

"Let's go, Mary." Kara turned, hitched up her skirts, and threw a leg over the windowsill. She fixed a stern look on the girl. "We'll get you safely away from here, and then you will tell me exactly what is going on with Lily Wolford, do you hear?"

With a swallow, Mary nodded. Kara lowered herself down until her foot touched the barrel, and then she let go.

<hr />

"Good afternoon, Your Grace." Mr. Marsden, of the Royal Bank of Scotland, gave a shallow bow and gestured for Niall and Taggart to enter his office. He offered Niall a seat, but pointedly did not extend the same courtesy to Taggart, who took up a position behind Niall, near the door.

"Now, then." Marsden settled into the grand leather seat behind his mountain of a desk and looked Niall over with bland regard. "I assume I must congratulate you on your recent ascension to the title, Duke."

"You've heard the story of it, then," Niall said mildly.

"There was a great deal of talk in the city when you were summoned to the parliamentary election." The banker paused. "We are, of course, happy to welcome you to Scotland and pleased to extend you an invitation to bank with us."

"Thank you. I look forward to working with such a fine institution."

"What sort of account can we interest you in? We do make loans at very competitive rates." Marsden's polite tone held an edge.

Niall steepled his fingers. "Thank you. A loan will not be necessary. As a matter of fact, today I am not here in pursuit of my own business, but that of Mr. Darrow, the procurator fiscal."

Marsden shot Taggart a dark look. "As I explained to the constable, that is not possible." His tone made the word *constable* sound as if it left a foul taste in his mouth. "We would be happy to speak with the fiscal directly. Barring that, I'm afraid we must decline to discuss the matter he is investigating."

"There are some unusual circumstances at play—"

Marsden interrupted smoothly. "The Royal Bank of Scotland does not deal in unusual circumstances, sir."

"The Royal Bank of Scotland is neck deep in this particular pit of unusual circumstances," Taggart snapped.

"I'm afraid Mr. Taggart is correct," Niall said dryly. "The fiscal is unable to come to you, as he is currently lying injured at my home. He was hurt, I might add, in pursuit of a murder investigation that involves not only one of your clients, but one of your employees."

Marsden's expression tightened. "We wouldn't know anything about that."

"That is odd, as many of the underlings in your bank do, in fact, know about it."

The banker sat back, his face a mask of indifference. "The situation involves clients of long standing and ancient bloodlines. Perhaps you would understand, had you not been so recently elevated yourself."

Niall raised a brow. Anger rose, as hot and heavy as lava pooling in his gut. "Very well. You have made your position clear, sir. Allow me to do the same. I am here today acting with the authority of Mr. Darrow, on his behalf." He leaned back. "And as you claim to know my story, then you may well understand the avenues and depth of authority that I may call upon, should I so choose."

He had never regarded his bloodline as more than a complication in his life and would never have imagined himself throwing the weight of it or of his new title about, but Niall had to admit, watching the color drain from Marsden's face felt immensely satisfying. He stood. "You will tell me what I need to know *now*, sir. Or you will tell me tomorrow morning, when I return with the lord advocate at my side."

The banker shifted in his chair.

"You may explain to him, then, why you feel entitled, in your unmitigated gall and snide self-importance, to impede the Crown's pursuit of a killer."

Marsden's jaw dropped. "I ... I ... No, of course I did not mean ..."

"Then speak, sir," Niall commanded. He was enjoying being a duke more by the minute.

Still, the banker hesitated.

"Very well." Niall turned to go. "Until tomorrow morning."

He was halfway to the door before the man gave in.

"No. Wait, then."

Niall turned halfway back, his gaze expectant.

"You must promise that word of this does not get out," Marsden said anxiously.

"I will repeat everything relevant to Mr. Darrow. He will decide what is to be used in his reports and presentations to the courts, as well as how he portrays the Royal Bank of Scotland's handling of this volatile situation."

"I don't mean to obstruct the Crown in any way, of course. It's just …"

"The Earl of Balstone is a client."

"Yes. The family has been with us for many years."

"Which is why you agreed to extend them a mortgage on their failing estate, I assume."

"I … Yes."

"Mr. Dunn had charge of the account. I presume he has recently recorded some … changes to it?"

Marsden swallowed. "Mr. Dunn recently recorded the mortgage as paid in full."

"And is there a proper record of such a substantial payment?"

"No. Dunn appears to have emptied his own accounts to transfer toward the debt."

"I would be very much surprised to imagine he could cover the entire amount."

"He could not, of course. The rest of the balance appears to be … fabricated."

"And Dunn's other customer accounts? There have been irregularities noticed?"

The banker shot an ugly look at Taggart, as if he blamed the constable for Niall knowing so much. Which, of course, was entirely correct. "A large sum of money and valuables has disappeared, taken from several accounts that Mr. Dunn had charge of."

"You've had no word from him? Of him? Since he disappeared with his stolen largesse?"

"None. And we have looked."

Niall paused, thinking. "The missing valuables. Might they be of gold?"

Marsden blinked. "Yes. Most of them."

"And were they pieces with historical significance or value?"

"You could say that, I suppose. They were all of French origin, I believe. Very old. Treasures snuck out by families during the bloody revolution. Several elaborate frames, a religious icon, and a set of tall, heavy candlesticks from a family chapel." He frowned. "How did you know?"

Niall settled his hat on his head. "Thank you, Mr. Marsden. I'll be sure to tell Mr. Darrow everything."

The banker had the grace to appear worried. "I hope he will appreciate and record our cooperation."

"I hope so as well. But as I said, that will be at the fiscal's discretion. My own involvement will end with the unmasking of the murderer, as I'm sure we will solve that before Mr. Darrow is on his feet again. After that, the fiscal will take over the prosecution and court matters. And I will be returning to my own business."

"Yes, of course." Marsden waved a hand. "I know that your estate has long been untended and may take time to become profitable again. If we can help in some small way, do be sure to appeal to us. We will regard your application with all fairness."

Niall stared at the man for a drawn-out moment. The banker had been disdainful from the first moment, and grown increasingly more so. He suffered a brief moment of sympathy for Kara, who often had faced members of Society who found her wanting. Ridiculous notion. They knew only the surface, not the rich depths of her. Just as this man thought he knew something of Niall, but clearly did not comprehend the whole story. He considered giving the man the edge of his tongue, but decided to laugh instead. "Your offer is as unnecessary as it is condescending, sir. For a man dedicated to money matters, you appear remarkably uninformed."

"I know that the family that once held Tallenford Priory had no ready money to go along with it."

Niall raised his chin. "Perhaps you just do not understand, then, that the Crown generally does not grant a title and estate to a man who cannot afford the running of it."

"Perhaps Mr. Marsden doesn't understand your career as an artist, or the extent of the long line of clients clamoring for a piece from you, Your Grace," Taggart suggested.

Niall shrugged. "Or perhaps the gossip he indulged in did not extend to the gratifying annuity that I was granted from the Civil List, for services to the Crown."

The banker's eyes widened.

Taggart gave the man a pitying look. "For a certainty, he must not be aware that your betrothed is in possession of one of the largest fortunes in England."

Marsden slumped in his chair.

At Niall's pointed glance, Taggart lifted a shoulder. "I do my research, sir, even if the Royal Bank of Scotland is remiss."

"I must assume that there are other institutions in the city who keep more up to date on these matters."

Taggart looked thoughtful. "I do have a mate who works in the Bank of Scotland, and that one is hundreds of years older than this paltry place."

"Excellent, Taggart. Good day to you, Mr. Marsden," Niall said over his shoulder as he turned to go.

"Oh, yes. Good day!" Taggart sang out as he closed the door behind him. He grinned as he moved after Niall.

"Gold," Niall said to him as they strode away. "The missing piece in all of this—it must have something to do with gold and antiquities. Let's get to that meeting with Darrow's fence connection."

Chapter Seventeen

Kara hurried Mary up the stairs at the end of the street and along the road above. "Are there no cabs to be had in Edinburgh?" she muttered.

"We're a walking city, miss. Although we'd likely have more luck on the next street over."

"Earlier, we walked a good distance here from the docks. I assume we are heading back in that direction?"

"Aye, miss. I hopped on the back of a fish wagon to get here, but we won't find one heading back, and I doubt we'd both get away with it anyways."

"Come along. We'll find a proper cab so we can be rested when we get there, and along the way you can tell me everything."

It took two streets and several minutes, but Kara heaved a sigh of relief as they finally settled back in a hansom. "Now, Mary," she said firmly. "Tell me all you know about Lily Wolford, Edmund Finley, and Will Grier."

Mary looked like she wanted to answer. Her mouth worked a moment, but clearly she didn't know where to begin.

Kara closed her eyes. "How did Lily know the two young men?"

Mary's expression cleared. "They were her beaus."

"What? Both of them?"

"You mustn't think badly of Lily. She didn't allow them to court her at the same time. Well, not exactly. Not for any length of time."

Kara reached for patience. "Hold just a moment. Let us start at the beginning. How do you and Lily know each other?"

"Oh, that's an easy one. We practically sprouted together. There's not so many small lassies running about in Leith. We knocked about together since we could toddle." Mary drew a shuddering breath. "People say things about Lily. They call her a sharp one. Or they say she's always lookin' out for herself."

Kara snorted. "I've heard the same myself. As if it is a bad quality in a woman. As if all the world wasn't built and arranged for men, and we are not left to carve out a spot in it as we can."

"Aye, miss! Just so. And it weren't true, in any case. Lily always looked after me. And I tried to do right by her, too. But I owe her a greater debt, for she put herself between me and Glade, and that is no small thing."

"Glade?" Kara eyed the girl. "Is that the woman who followed you to the Witch's Price?"

"Aye." Mary sighed. "She's my auntie. My da's sister. He's a sailor, ye see."

"Gone for long stretches, then?"

"Aye. He pays Glade for my keep when he's gone to sea. He bids me to stay with her, but I swear, it's scarcely safer than bein' on my own." Her color rose and she ducked her head. "It grew worse when I first became a woman." She raised her gaze to see if Kara understood. "See?"

Kara nodded sadly.

"Lily stopped her from hiring me out. She said she'd turn Glade in fer runnin' a bawdy house. And Lily, she knows her letters." Mary said it almost as proudly, as if it were her own skill. "She can read and write, both. She told Glade she'd write to my da and tell him what she was up to. Glade didn't want that regular money to stop comin' in, I'll tell ye. She let me be after that."

Kara gripped her hand. "It is completely understandable that you would want to help Lily, then. But I'm afraid I don't know just what sort of trouble she's in. Can you tell me about Lily and Edmund Finley?"

Mary nodded. "Oh, Edmund grew up running with us as well. He lived right across from Riley and Lily. He and Riley were close, in the same way as Lily and me. But Edmund always had an eye fer Lily. He'd watch her with such a look on his face ... Like she was the sun and he wanted to soak in her light."

"You said Edmund courted her."

"Not at first. Lily didn't want a boy from Leith. She wanted a gent, a toff, someone who could take her somewhere away. Somewhere finer. And she's that pretty. It could happen. She just had to find the right man. So she pushed Edmund away, though he was tall and good lookin'. After his aunt died, he moved on. He hinted to Lily that he had prospects, but he wouldn't explain right out, and she couldn't risk it."

"So what changed?"

"Edmund came back after a few years. He looked more handsome than ever. Sun-brown and well fed, with fine clothes and saying he had steady work and his own prospects on the side. He told us that he was going to come into some land and that he meant to run his own inn and host city toffs that liked to play at outside sports."

"Golf," Kara murmured.

"Aye. That were it. I saw a man once, on the deck of a ship at dock. He were swinging a stick and knocking balls out toward the sea. Lily said he was playing at golf." Mary's gaze drifted to the street beyond the cab. "Edmund was that excited about his plans, and Riley was on fire to be a part of it. He nagged and teased at Edmund and promised to put up part of the money. You could tell that Edmund wasn't keen on the idea. He'd always wanted to take over his aunt's inn. He'd talked about it enough when we were tykes and dreamin' about what our lives would be. It were plain he wanted his own chance at a similar sort of dream, now. And he knew what Riley is. Edmund kept turning him away. So Riley asked Lily to convince him."

"Convince him?" repeated Kara. "How, exactly?" She was afraid she knew the answer before she asked it.

"Lily agreed to step out with Edmund. Oh, he was over the moon, to be courtin' her at last. And I think Lily quite liked having such a handsome man on her arm. She was coming around to the prospect of being married to a man running his own business, like Edmund planned."

"And she did change Edmund's mind about including Riley," Kara mused.

"So she did. Edmund agreed at last, because Lily wanted him to. And because Riley's promised money meant he could get it all up and running that much faster."

"Where did Riley get that amount of money?"

"Stole it, I'd wager," Mary said bluntly. "Riley never made that much working at the warehouse, not even as manager."

"Edmund didn't suspect Riley was using ill-gotten gains?"

"Dirty money, do ye mean?"

Kara nodded.

"Oh, aye. Edmund suspected it. He told Riley and Lily both that he had no wish to be starting out on a bad foot, using bad money. Riley told him he'd won it gambling on the cockfights out behind the Blue Dog."

"And Edmund believed him?"

"Lily backed her brother up, like she always does. There was another reason she kept quiet, too. It was because whatever scheme Riley was into, he brought Will Grier into it, too."

Kara leaned forward. "So, how does Will fit into the picture?"

"Well, Edmund was coming into the city right often, to see Lily and to make plans with Riley. He loved to step out with Lily, take her to the parks, or to stroll the Mile, or just on the strut through Leith. But he began to notice he was being shadowed."

"Followed?"

"Aye. Lily saw it, too. Someone was watching Edmund. Following in their footsteps. Edmund couldn't explain it."

"Or wouldn't?"

"I don't know which of those is the right answer," Mary admitted. "He chased the follower off a time or two, but they always would show up again. He said even at his job in the country, he could feel eyes on him."

"So what happened?"

"Lily," Mary said with a sigh. "It nigh drove her mad, not knowin' what it was all about. Wonderin'. One night, after Edmund set out again fer the country, she noticed the shadow stayed with her. He hung about her home, standin' outside and starin' up at the rooms she kept with Riley. It put her back up, so she threw up the sash and stared right back down at him."

"What did he do?"

"He grinned up at her. And Lily noticed his fine coat and expensive hat."

"And that intrigued her, I'm sure," Kara said.

"Enough so that she marched herself right down there and asked the bloke what he was about."

"Oh dear."

"Aye. She told me what his answer was. I remember it clear."

Kara waited, expectant.

"He told her he'd been admirin' her beauty from afar, but he was glad fer the chance to experience her spirit up close."

"It was Will Grier? It sounds like something that young buck would say."

"It was. Lily demanded to know what he was doin', stalking her beau like a hound to a deer."

"And what was his answer to that?"

"He said he come from the village where Finley meant to set up his business and he was checking into him, looking for bad habits or tidings, making sure Edmund was above board and harbored no bad connections or hidden purposes."

"What was he really after?" Kara said cynically.

"I don't know, but I know what he ended up with."

"Lily?"

"Aye. Oh, how he sweet-talked her. He told her he'd never met a girl so straight and forthright and full of fire. Lily liked that, I tell you. And he was rich. A real gentleman with manners and all. Money. Just like she'd always dreamed of. She flipped for him, arse over teakettle, as Glade put it."

"Lily threw over Edmund?"

"Quick as a wink, once she met Will."

"But Grier could not have been serious about her. Finley meant to marry her. Grier could not have promised so much." Kara thought Lily sounded smart enough to take the practical into consideration.

"Lily said he did. He told her he'd make her a real lady."

Kara shook her head. "His family would never countenance such a match." They'd already escaped one such pairing, with Edmund's mother.

"Lily refused to hear anything against Grier. She broke off her courtship with Finley without telling him who she'd thrown him over for."

"It must have been a blow to him," Kara said sadly.

"Worse was to come. Edmund threw himself into the plans for the business, but something happened. Some sort of setback."

The past due taxes, Kara thought. That must have been when Finley found he couldn't inherit the land without paying what was owed on it.

"Whatever it was, Riley took it as his chance," Mary continued.

"He'd cooked up some scheme with Grier. The two of them definitely had something going on. Their heads were always together. They crowed about it when they'd had too much to drink. They were making plans fer being rich and idle. And Riley decided he would go ahead with the business without Finley. He said he didn't need a partner."

"But the whole thing had been Finley's idea," Kara protested.

"Aye, but *fair* and *right* ain't never been two words that held any kind of acquaintance with Riley Wolford. He made a move to get the land without Edmund's involvement. Grier helped him do it, somehow. Talked to someone in the local council or somethin'."

"What happened?"

"Finley found out about it. He come roaring into town to shout it out with Riley, but he found only Lily at home. They had a ragin' fight. I don't know what was said, but something bad happened. I think Edmund must have found out it was Will who stole Lily away, and who was workin' against him with Riley."

"He didn't hurt Lily, surely," Kara said. "I wouldn't believe it of him."

"Oh, no. But they fought hard enough to shake the rafters. He left, but something he said rattled Lily. Shook her hard. Real hard. She was just ... not herself. White as a sheet. Starin' at the wall. *It was all ruined.* That was all she would say. She didn't cry, didn't rage. She scarcely moved. Until a couple of days later, when we heard the news that Finley was dead. Killed, they said. Lily dropped right into a faint." Mary pressed a hand to her chest. "Scared me bad, she did. I never seen her in such a state. But when she woke up, she stared at me, then she got up and started packing her things. She said she had to hide, to disappear. I had to help her."

"And you did."

"Of course. I had to." Tears sprang again into the girl's eyes. "She was so scared, she scared me, too. She said she'd be as good as dead, too, if Will found her. So I hid her. I tucked her in with the old woman who sells oranges down the docks. She mostly keeps to herself. She's one of those that people look at every day, but never really see, aye?"

"Aye," Kara said softly. She leaned forward abruptly, realizing where they were. "That lane we just passed? Isn't that the one that leads to the Blue Dog and the rooms you share with Glade?" At Mary's nod, Kara gripped the girl's hand. "Where are we going, then? What's happened to Lily?"

"Gone, I think," Mary whispered. "I was heading for the old woman's rooms this afternoon, bringing food, when I saw him."

"Who? Grier?" Kara asked sharply.

"Not him. But he's not likely to do his own dirty work, is he? No, it was the fellow who has been all through Leith, offering bribes, beatin' the bushes, lookin' fer her, tryin' to flush her out. He had a couple of men with him, and they were headin' into the boardin' house where Lily was hiding." The girl's head dropped. "I knew there was nothin' I could do. I couldn't bear it." Tears dropped onto her hands. "I should ha' stayed, but I couldn't. I ran home—and that's where the girl found me, the scullery from the Blue Dog. Yer man paid her to deliver his message to me. But I couldn't bring Lily to ye, could I? So I thought I'd bring ye along here. There might be somethin' to be found out. If they spared the old woman, or she hid away, she might be able to tell ye somethin'."

Kara sat back, her thoughts grim. She felt close to tears herself. Too late. They were too late to save Lily Wolford. The image of the girl's face flashed in her mind. She'd only had a fleeting glimpse of her, but she'd seen both fear and hope in her pretty face—and Kara knew how it felt to live with both of those emotions struggling for dominance.

The cab stopped. Kara paid the driver and stared at the rickety boarding house before them. Beside her, Mary still fought back tears.

There was no telling what they would find in there. A body. Bodies. Likely nothing at all. "Which room?"

"Straight to the left from the door, middle room."

Throwing her shoulders back and unbuttoning her pocket pistol once more, Kara marched inside.

Silence lay over the place—a heavy quiet, weighted with aftermath. The middle door sat cracked open. Stepping carefully, Kara approached. Standing to one side, she pushed the door slowly open.

It was only one room inside, mostly bare and grimy. A cot and a pallet on the floor took up one side, and a small table and chair were overturned on the other. The old woman lay stretched out on the floor beside the fallen chair. Beside her knelt a man.

Kara raised her pistol, but the man was helping the woman to sit up, murmuring quietly. He looked up and she was caught, frozen. The man from the alley. The one she'd prevented from taking Lily.

He glanced at her from his crouching position, the candlelight caught in his chestnut hair. And abruptly, memory returned.

"You are him. The groom at Katherine Dalwiddie's stables." She was surprised into speaking out loud. That was why he'd looked familiar. She'd seen him tending to Will Grier's injured mare. She steadied her pistol, holding it pointed directly at him. "You are Will Grier's groom."

"Ye shouldna' ha' interfered with me," he growled. He gestured at the empty room and the bruise darkening the old woman's eye. "This is all your fault."

"What have you done with Lily Wolford?"

He gaped at her, still angry. "I don't have her, do ye hear? I was her best chance at getting out o' this alive, and ye ruined it."

"Grier wants the girl dead." Kara tossed her head. "Because she knew, didn't she? Edmund told her the truth. She knew who he was. The irony of it must have struck him a harsh blow. Lily chose the money and the title, but it was Edmund's all along. The truth of it must have knocked her adrift. She chose the wrong man, in every way. And since she knew his secret, Grier sent you to silence her. Forever."

"He sent me to *save* her," the groom spat. "To get her safely away." He stiffened as Mary peered around the doorway.

"Stay back, Mary," Kara ordered the girl, still covering the groom with her pistol. "Stand clear. We have to make him tell us where Lily is."

"I dinna have her! Do ye never listen?"

At the same time, Mary asked a quiet question. "But who is he?"

Kara glanced over at her. "This is the man who has been chasing after Lily."

"Another one?" Mary said, shocked. "Who is this one, then?"

Dark foreboding flooded Kara. "Mary," she said quietly. "Is this not one of the men you saw coming for Lily earlier today? Is he not the one who has been trying to find her?"

"No. I've not seen this one before."

Fear and chagrin chased each other up and down Kara's spine. "Who is he? The man you said has been trying to flush Lily out. Who is he, if not this man?"

"I don't know him, do I?"

"Can you tell me anything about him? What does he look like?"

"He's tall, that one. Thin." It was the old woman who spoke in a gravelly voice. "I've been watching him for days, searching through the docks. He's the one that took her. He wears a fine coat. He's got a long face. Dark shadows under his eyes. And jowls that look like they would flap in a good breeze."

"Aye, and long ears on the sides of his head, too," Mary agreed. "He's like one of those dogs in a painting, running alongside the horses, chasing the fox in a hunt."

Kara's arm fell. She stared at the groom. He nodded grimly.

"Largray?" she whispered. "It's Largray, the butler from Balburn House?"

"Aye," the groom said with a nod. "He's Mrs. Grier's creature. Will is trying to save the girl from his own mother. But now she's got her."

Chapter Eighteen

TAGGART TOOK THEM to the outer edges of Leith, far enough from the docks that the street of houses they walked along looked entirely respectable and relatively prosperous. Niall wondered at finding a pawn shop assistant in such a location, but held his tongue as he followed the constable, who strode straight up the walkway to one of the residences and walked in without knocking.

He couldn't hold silent as they entered, however. The marbled entry hall was graced with busts and statuary of obvious antiquity. Taggart moved directly into a parlor to the right that held even more surprises. A Turner on one wall and a Titian on the other. Chinese porcelain on display. A glass case full of ancient Egyptian ushabtis. Niall actually gasped out loud when he turned to find a cabinet full of golden treasures—a model of a chariot with horses and a diminutive driver, drinking vessels, torques, rings, and a golden scabbard decorated with a scene of a lion hunt. "Are those Persian?" he asked in quiet awe.

Taggart laughed. "Are you asking me?"

"Someone has a good eye," an amused voice said from behind him.

Niall turned to find a young man entering through a door he hadn't noticed, as it was painted and paneled to match the walls. The newcomer wore a decent suit and a pair of spectacles. Only his long hair, curling at his shoulders, kept him from looking like any other clerk in the city. "Someone has exquisite taste," Niall returned. "All of these pieces look like they might be in a museum."

"They could be," the young man agreed. "However, they are all bound for collectors, instead. My master is very skilled at finding the right pieces for the right client. He always delivers, without fail. After collecting his commission, of course."

"Your master?" Niall raised a brow.

The young man shrugged. "I am his apprentice. He is my master. It is an old arrangement, one that has worked in many crafts and trades for many years."

"You are training under a master thief?" Niall allowed his amazement to show.

"No, no," the young apprentice said smoothly. "My master is not a thief. He does not steal. Ever."

"But he buys stolen goods?" Niall asked.

The young man shrugged.

"And by your own words, he sells them on."

"After taking his commission," the apprentice reminded him.

"It's much the same," Niall said with a lift of his shoulder. "Still unlawful. And amoral."

"Which is why his work is so profitable. He takes the risks."

"You are the one taking risks," Taggart interrupted. "Playing both sides is dangerous."

"Yet profitable," Niall said. "And perhaps it has led you to some knowledge that can help us unravel some tangles surrounding a murder enquiry."

"Murder? My master certainly does not condone any killing in pursuit of his goods."

"Tomb robbing, yes? A little light larceny is fine? But no murder?"

"I would say that is an accurate representation of the boundaries of his work."

"Good, then you won't mind telling us what you know of Riley Wolford," Taggart said. "As usual, Darrow will compensate you for the risk. He'll likely double the price if your information leads to the capture of a killer."

The clerk frowned. "I am always happy to help Darrow, as you know. Especially as he has agreed to keep quiet about my assistance. He has never betrayed me, nor broken his word, and I value that. But I am afraid I do not know this name. Wolford?"

"Weaselly fellow," Taggart said. "Short, cocky. Works as a warehouse manager at the docks."

The apprentice made a face. "This does not sound like the sort of person my master would do business with."

"Nonsense," Niall said sharply. "He's the sort of person who is in a position to take valuables that do not belong to him. The sort of person who helped himself to some very old, golden artifacts of African origin. Very unusual and hard to come by in the normal scheme of things, I should imagine." He eyed the young man with expectation. "Surely you and your employer would know of it if objects like these became available."

The clerk's brow smoothed. "Oh, yes."

"A long pipe? A chest piece? Other assorted golden badges? You know of them?"

"More than that. We have them." The young man indicated the hidden door. "In the workroom. I am cleaning them in anticipation of a sale. My master has a client who is quite excited about seeing them. But they were not brought to us by a warehouse weasel. A young gentleman brought them in. He said a family member of his had been involved in the Laird expeditions into the African interiors."

Niall exchanged glances with Taggart.

"A young gentleman? Dark hair? Wide face? Just barely more than a boy?" Niall asked.

"That sounds right."

"By the name of Will Grier?"

The apprentice hesitated only a second. "Well. Since you already know his name ... yes. That is him."

Niall paused. "And did he bring you anything else, after the African pieces?"

"He did, in fact. So recently that not even my master has seen them yet."

"French pieces, from before the revolutions? Frames? Candlesticks? Religious icons?"

The young man's interest was piqued. "No, actually. But we would be very interested in acquiring such a collection. Have you heard of such a group of objects coming to market? Do you have a lead on where to obtain them?"

Niall's mind was working. So it wasn't the goods Dunn stole from the bank that Grier had brought in after Riley's stolen African gold? "What else did the young gentleman bring you, then?"

"Pieces found at his family home, I believe. Ancient British origin. Bronze Age relics, if my judgment is correct. Gold rings and bracelets, hair decorations, and carved arm rings."

"But there have been no such treasures found at Balburn," Niall protested. "It's all been just tools and trinkets and everyday items."

"These are definitely not common items. It's my guess that they are grave goods. Likely they were interred with a wealthy figure. Or a leader, perhaps. Someone with power and wealth."

"Balstone hasn't found any gravesites. It's just common huts at his dig site."

"Surely it is a recent find, then? The young gentleman said there were more goods to be had. He mentioned coins, a belt plate, perhaps even a royal circlet."

Niall frowned, his mind working. And abruptly, all the pieces snapped into place.

"Keep those grave goods aside," he ordered the man. "Don't show them to anyone. I'll purchase them all."

"I'm not sure ..." the young man started.

"Don't," Niall snapped. "Darrow may have made an agreement to keep your activities secret, but I have made no such bargain. I want those goods. I'm willing to pay your cost, but Darrow might just take them as Crown evidence, and you'll be out your purchase price."

The apprentice sighed and gave him a slow nod. "Very well, then."

"Let's go," Niall said to Taggart. "There may be an entirely different reason for Finley to have been killed. One that none of us has remotely suspected."

ONCE AGAIN THEY were awake before the sun, preparing for another journey. This time they meant to get home as quickly as they could.

Kara had bidden Mary a tearful goodbye the previous evening, while Niall had been making arrangements to hire a change of horses halfway home—the better to speed their journey. Kara had promised the young girl she would do all she could to help Lily Wolford.

"Find her, please. Save her from these bad people. Send her all my best," Mary said with a sob. "And tell her how sorry I am, that I couldn't hide her better."

"None of this is your fault, Mary," Kara had said sternly. "Do not take on that burden. You did your best to help your friend, and I am sure Lily both knows and appreciates it."

"She's my dearest friend, miss." Mary couldn't speak above a whisper. "If something were to happen to her ..." The girl could not finish her thought.

"We will do our best," Kara had vowed.

Now, in the dark hours while the moon hung low in the sky, Kara hugged Beryl as they took their leave. "Thank you so much for finishing those orders for me," she told the older woman. "None are urgent, save for the order of books."

"It's no bother at all," Beryl insisted.

Kara paused. "I hope we can come back soon, when things are settled and at peace. I'd like to sit with you by your brazier and talk of how you met Niall and how you came to this place. Perhaps you could visit us at Tallenford Priory."

"Ah, it's hard for me to leave the Witch's Price, child, but you will come back for a visit."

"I would love to hear your stories," Kara confessed.

"As I would like to hear yours." The old woman took her hand and peered into it once again, although surely she could not see in the dim moonlight. "And if I'm not mistaken, we've stories yet to write together."

A sudden shiver slipped up Kara's spine, and she had the sense that this moment, standing in the dark with her hand in Beryl's, with the night breeze lifting her hair and the feel of the dark and the old stones of Edinburgh surrounding them, would come back to her in some future moment.

She whispered a goodbye, then hustled a sleepy Ailsa to the carriage.

Niall had opted to hire a mount for the journey, in case of trouble with the carriage. "It's happened once before, with you and Gyda," he'd reminded her last night. "And I've no wish to delay. This way, at least one of us will be back at the priory by midday."

"Niall Kier, don't you dare set foot in Balburn without me, no matter what happens," she whispered fiercely to him now, as she stood just outside the carriage.

He paused to press a kiss into her hair, and she relished, just for a moment, the warmth of his embrace and the strength of his large form. "I won't." He pulled away to meet her gaze with a serious one of his own. "Not unless it is absolutely necessary."

She had to accept that. She was just turning away to climb inside the carriage when a man rode up and stopped behind it. Kara stiffened. It was too dark to see clearly who it was.

"I'm going with you," he announced.

"Taggart," Niall murmured.

"I need to report to Darrow," the constable continued. "And you'll be a man down, with him still tied to his bed."

For a moment, Kara thought Niall might argue, but he only shrugged. "We'll be glad to have you," he replied.

With another glance at her betrothed, Kara climbed in and they set off.

The journey to the city had been a brief interlude of peace. Going back this morning, it felt interminable. Ailsa quickly slipped back to sleep, her head lolling back and forth across the back of the bench. Kara was envious, but she was too much a bundle of nerves to sleep herself. Her mind's eye filled with a jumble of images. It raced between Lily's frightened face, strange golden figures, Mary's sorrow, and the scowling visage of Elfred Grier. The one face that particularly haunted her was the accusatory glare of Will Grier's groom. *This is all your fault.* The words echoed in her head.

She tried to push it away, to take the advice that she'd given Mary, but the doubt and the guilt lingered. Had she made the situation worse? Was the Wolford girl in worse danger because of her? She fought against the anxiety and worry as the miles passed. It was a relief to stop at Port Seton to change horses. She took the opportunity to climb down and stretch her legs.

"I have made a vow to ride out more with Kate Dalwiddie," she told Niall. "I would feel so much better making this journey on horseback, as you are. And it would be faster."

"It also gives you a feeling that you are *doing something*, even if it's mostly illusory," Niall agreed.

Kara ordered a wrapped packet of bread and bacon from the innkeeper's wife. Ailsa had awakened both hungry and out of sorts. "You can eat in the carriage," she told the maid. "We'll be underway again soon, as soon as the team is changed out."

Taggart meant to keep his mount. "This old boy is a solid one," he said, patting the animal fondly. "We've been through enough together that I know he'll go steady all day."

Niall's new mount was a fiery specimen, prancing as he was brought out and saddled. They were admiring him when a clatter arose and a horse came into the courtyard at a fast pace. The beast blew heavily as the rider pulled him to a skidding halt. The lad jumped down, looped the reins over a post, and set out straight for the inn.

Kara saw Niall's eyes widen. He drew in a breath and took a step. "Jamie?" he called. "Jamie, lad? Is that you?"

The young man spun around on a heel. Shock lit his gaze. "Your Grace?" he said, his tone thick with relief. "Your Grace! I canna believe my luck!"

"What is it, lad?" Niall looked as serious as Kara had ever seen him. "What's brought you here?"

"I've come for ye!" Jamie said, striding toward them. "Turner and Mrs. Pollock sent me. Ye're to come home straight away. Thank all the little birds in heaven I didn't miss ye! I never expected ye to be on the road already."

"But why?" Kara asked. "What's wrong? Why were you sent?"

The young man's face took on a grim aspect. "It's the wee laddie. Young Harold."

"What?" Kara reached out to grasp his arm. "What of Harold?"

"He's sick, miss. Taken in a bad way, he is. Ye're both to come straight away."

Everything inside Kara crumpled. Tears welled. Instinctively, she reached for Niall. He pulled her close. Looking up, she saw his gaze go from his mount, saddled and ready, to the coach, still waiting for the fresh team to be put into the traces.

"Go," she said as the tears spilled over. "Go, now! You can get there far more quickly than we can."

Niall shot a look at Taggart, but the constable shook his head. "I'll only hold you up, with you on a fresh mount. Go on. Do as you need to. I'll see the ladies safely home."

"Thank you." Niall's face was a frozen mask as he vaulted onto his horse. Some of his anguish broke through as he glanced down at Kara, but she nodded and motioned him on. With a grunt and a kick, they were gone.

Chapter Nineteen

Kara's earlier anxiety was nothing compared to what she felt through the last half of that journey. As the carriage finally pulled down the drive and toward the front of the house, she already had the door open. As soon as they came to a halt, she vaulted down without waiting for the step or assistance.

She was through the door and racing up the stairs within moments. Somewhere she could hear Gyda's voice raised in anger, but she went straight to Harold's door, where she forced herself to stop and catch her breath, so that she might enter calmly and quietly.

Catriona sat at the boy's bedside, sewing. "Oh, miss!" she exclaimed in a whisper. "Ye came so quickly! He will be that glad to see ye, miss. He's been askin' after ye."

Kara knelt at Harold's other side, stroking his hair. She had to work not to recoil at the sight of the vibrant boy now so still and wan. "What is it?" she asked quietly. "Is it his stomach again?"

"So it started out, miss. He's had some pains in his guts, as ye know. But then he started with a bout of the flux, and vomiting, too. It were something fierce to see," Catriona said with a shake of her head. "We had the doctor in, but Turner wouldn't let him bleed the boy. He said he was weak enough. The doctor left in a snit, but then it got worse. The lad could barely walk a straight line. His hands started to shake. He couldn't sleep a wink, and he complained that his eyes were jumping about in his head."

"Good heavens. I had no idea it would grow so bad! Oh, I should never have left!"

"Oh, no, miss. Don't you go blamin' yerself. The most of it came on real sudden, and how could we ever be expecting such? They popped up, one odd thing right after the other. We sent fer ye straightaway, then, but we never thought to see ye so soon. He'll feel better just knowing ye're here."

Harold stirred then, and opened his eyes. He looked to Catriona, who gestured toward Kara. As he turned his head—so slowly!—his eyes lit up. "Kara! You are back," he said, barely above a whisper.

"So I am, and I'm so sorry to hear you've been so ill, my dear boy."

"Oh, I feel somewhat better today." Harold summoned a grin. "I made a sketch. It's how I think we can make the face of our Green Knight. I want to show you." His hand did indeed shake as he reached out to try to push himself toward her.

"I should love to see it, dear, but I think you should rest just now. We need to get you all back to rights. We've such plans and so much work to do. We'll need you up and about so that you may help and give your advice."

"Yes. I want to help," he said. "I think we should paint the forge blue, but Gyda says Niall will never allow it." He looked around. "Niall is here too? I thought he was in here earlier, but I was afraid I dreamed it."

"Niall is here too, dear one."

"Maybe I'll help tomorrow, then? I'm so sleepy."

"Sleep, then, dear. We'll be here."

Harold had drifted off even before she finished. She gave Catriona a questioning look. "I thought you said he couldn't sleep?"

"Mrs. Pollock dosed him with a bit of laudanum after a while. He was so wound up, it wasn't doing him any good."

Kara's heart twisted. What could this be? Something did not sit right about any of this. She'd never heard of such a collection of symptoms.

"Thank you, Catriona," she whispered. "You'll stay with him?"

"Aye, miss. We're takin' it in turns, never leavin' him alone."

"I'll be back as soon as I can." Kara had to see Turner. If she knew him, he would have already sent for her London physician. And he would know where Niall was now. She left and paused outside the door, listening, but the house lay silent now. She headed downstairs and found the butler standing in the open front doorway, directing the unloading of the carriage.

"Miss!" She saw the relief on his face when he spotted her, but also real trouble. "You've seen Harold?" he asked.

"I've just left him. He could scarcely stay awake."

"We had to dose him. His condition deteriorated so swiftly, and he'd grown so agitated. I've sent for Dr. Balgate, but who knows how long it will take for the message to reach London, let alone for him to travel here."

"I knew you would move quickly. And if I know Balgate, he'll be on the next train, as soon as he gets that message. Thank you, Turner." Kara could not count the number of times she'd had cause to feel so very grateful for Turner and his calm efficiency. Seeing the fear that still lingered in his expression set her on alert. "What is it?" she whispered. She listened again to the quiet house. "Where is Niall?"

Turner swallowed. "He was scarcely in the house a quarter of an hour before this came." He reached into his coat and pulled out a note. It looked like a piece of thick, roughened vellum, just like the note that had come the night of Finley's death. She snatched it away and opened it.

I know the boy is ill.
It is my doing.
I have the antidote.
Come at once. Alone.

You know where.

"Antidote?" She looked up at Turner. "Poison?"

Turner's face was set in a hard cast. "To do such a thing to a child ..." he said harshly.

"Get me a mount," she ordered him. "No. The carriage. Is it still at the ready?"

"Yes." He reached for her when she would have turned to walk out. "A moment. Mr. Darrow insists he must speak to you before you leave."

"I have to go after Niall, Turner," she said implacably.

"He insists. He was furious when Niall left without talking to him."

"Kara Levett!" The procurator fiscal's voice came booming from upstairs. "I can hear you down there! Don't you dare leave before I tell you what you need to know!" he roared. "Or so help me, I will drag myself down after you!"

"He's going to wake Harold," she snapped, her own anger rising higher and higher by the moment. She took the stairs at a run again, fury climbing inside her with every step she made. "What?" she demanded, throwing open the door. "I have to go, Darrow!"

Taggart stood inside, at Darrow's bedside. The fiscal's face was flushed. "I know, but you need to hear this! The boy! I only just heard of his illness. Gyda's just told me of it, before she stormed off after the duke. Listen to me, Kara! I think it's poison! They've poisoned the child!"

"I know!" She threw the note at him. "She's admitted as much."

He read the note and pounded his fist on the bed. "The bastards! Damn this leg to perdition! You think it's the Grier woman?"

"Who else?" She glared at Taggart. "Did you tell him?"

"Everything."

"I think they've put it in with the crown and the scepter," Darrow growled. "The boy has been sneaking in to the sitting room just there, where Sedwick stored them. He comes when he thinks I am asleep." He looked anguished. "I *pretended* to sleep, so that he would come in! He was just sporting about, wearing the crown and brandishing the staff. Just play-acting, whispering of knights and swords and entertaining himself. I didn't know! I saw the dust drifting off the objects, but I never suspected ... I should have stopped him." He'd gone red with anger and guilt. "But I swear, I didn't know!"

"You couldn't have known," Kara told him. "How could you?" But the image in her head, of Harold pretending alone, growing sicker every day ... All of the horror and fury she felt, her fear for Harold and for Niall and for Lily Wolford—it was all coalescing into a lump of righteous determination in her chest.

"Has Niall gone after the bitch?" Taggart asked.

"He has. And I am going after them both," she said coldly.

The constable strode to her side. "Count me in."

>>><<<

THE DOOR TO Balburn House sat partway open. Moving slowly, peering into the paneled entry hall, Kara opened it all the way. No one waited inside. No butler or footman moved to challenge her.

"Where is everyone?" Taggart asked in a whisper.

"I don't know." Silence lay heavy over the place. It didn't feel like the quiet peace of the priory. The atmosphere felt ... empty. Deserted. "Have they all gone? All the servants?" She took a breath. "Good afternoon!" she called. "Is anyone here?"

No answer came. "There are supposed to be constables here, watching over Mrs. Grier," she said. "Keeping her under supervision."

"I hope she didn't poison them as well," Taggart muttered.

"The dig site," she said. "They must be there."

"Or perhaps she's cut and run, like her banker," suggested Taggart.

"No," Kara said decisively. "Everything she's done, she's done it for this place, for her family name. She's here." She glanced to the left, at the parlor from which they had all departed for the unveiling. "Now, if I can only recall how to get out there."

The afternoon sun shone bright. The air was sweet and full of birdsong. It didn't match Kara's mood or circumstances. She spotted the well-worn path as soon as she left the terrace off the parlor. Taggart followed as she stalked along it. Something was shifting inside her. Fire was smoldering. She moved faster, fanning it with the flames of her passage.

The wooded path at last let out into the clearing. Niall's statues gleamed in the sun. Kara passed them, then came to an abrupt halt, so suddenly that Taggart nearly bumped into her from behind.

All of her focus lay ahead, to a spot at the opening in the sunken perimeter wall, where Elfred Grier sat on the ground. She looked disheveled. Bedraggled. Locks of her hair had fallen from her perfect coiffure, clinging to the sides of her neck. A smudge crossed one cheek. Her black gown bore streaks of grass and dust.

Largray, her butler, lay cradled in her lap. His head was pillowed on his mistress's thighs. He looked even worse than her. He'd passed out, his long face gone slack and covered in blood. Kara gasped when she spotted the unnatural angle at which his arm lay.

Mrs. Grier heard the sound. As she looked up, relief passed across her expression, but it was replaced almost instantly with impatience. "Come." She beckoned Kara and Taggart imperiously. "I'll need help getting him back to the house."

"What happened here?" asked Taggart.

"My son decided an insignificant tart matters more than his name, his title, or his chance at a decent life," she answered bitterly. "Now, get him off me."

Taggart started to move forward, but Kara blocked him. "No," she answered harshly. "You don't give orders." The fire in her chest burned bright. All the doubts that had plagued her since she'd learned of Niall's new title, all the insecurities that had come rushing back—fueled by the memories of slights, the harsh judgments of her varied and unusual pursuits, the pointed questions that were meant to highlight and disparage her differences—they were all incinerated by the indignation and furious determination rising in her.

Mrs. Grier, unwisely, did not notice the change in Kara's usual easy demeanor. "I think you forget where you are, girl, and that I do, indeed, give the orders here. Largray is hurt. Lift him away and get him back to the house."

Kara glared. "Largray is a bullying henchman with at least a handful of heinous crimes to his credit. You are the monster who gave the orders behind them. But the days of your haughty rule are over, Mrs. Grier."

The woman sat up straighter. "How dare you—"

"How dare *you*? Do you believe your evil deeds are still unknown?"

"I ..." The color drained from her face as realization dawned.

"Yes. We know," Kara told her. "We know you killed your own half-brother. We know you attempted to murder both the procurator fiscal and the Duke of Sedwick. We know you've taken part in a scheme to steal valuable antiquities and kidnapped an innocent girl."

The woman's shoulders dropped. "I ... Not all of that is true."

Kara was not going to debate with her. "Where is Niall?"

Mrs. Grier closed her eyes. "Gone looking for the girl."

"And the antidote?" Kara took a step closer, and the woman flinched at what she saw on her face.

"Antidote?" She sounded uncertain.

"I did not list the poisoning of my ward. An innocent child, suffering terribly right now, and at your hand. But I suppose the poison was meant for Niall, was it not?" Niall's description of Balstone's study came back to her. "Did you think he would leave the pieces out? Handle them with reverence as your brother does his finds?"

"Poison?"

"Do *not*! I have no patience for your lies! You knew what you were doing when you laced the Cursed Crown and the staff. You admitted as much in your note."

Now the woman began to look frightened. "Oh, no. He did not. Surely not?"

"Do not think to shift the blame," Kara thundered. "Give me the antidote." She stepped closer again, her worry for Harold fueling a loathing like she'd never felt. "I swear, by all that is holy, if that boy dies, I will personally watch you hang for it. The crowds will laugh and jeer. I will donate a fleet of ships to the queen, in return for the privilege of pulling the lever to stretch your neck myself. You said there was an antidote. I want it. *Now!*"

"I don't have it!" Mrs. Grier snapped back. Her face had gone white. "I have done wrong, I know it. It all went so far out of my control!"

"Mrs. Grier, we know what happened with your half-brother, and with all of the rest of it, too." Taggart tried to introduce a note of calm into the heightening tension. "You don't wish for the child to die as well. The papers will turn it into a circus. *Baby killer*. Your name will be reviled through all the kingdom and across the Continent."

"But I didn't know about the child, I promise you." She covered her face with her hands.

"Where are the constables that Darrow stationed in your home?" Taggart asked.

She blanched. "Dosed with laudanum." She flinched at his dark look. "You don't understand! It's all gone wrong! The servants have been sneaking out and taking valuables with them. Then Largray arrived, with a chit in tow. I had to get them out of the house! I don't understand all that's happened. I just wanted to pay Edmund off! I tried to work with him."

"You blackmailed Dunn, your banker, into granting you a second mortgage. Another crime to add to your list," Kara sneered. "Did you send your son to haunt Finley's footsteps in the same way? To find his weakness so that you could exploit it?"

"I had to force Dunn's hand! It was what Edmund wanted too, as I've already told you. He didn't want to be the Balstone heir. He wanted to build a golf course and charge sportsmen to stay in Blister MacCallum's dingy little farmhouse." She sounded both distraught and disgusted. "I already told you all of this. Even when he came back wanting more, I convinced him there *was* no more."

Kara recalled what Mary had said of the argument Finley had had with Lily, late the night of the unveiling. "But that was not the end of it, was it? You convinced him, but your son ruined it, didn't he? Not content with taking Finley's title, he stole the woman he cared for, too. And then he tried to cut him out of the MacCallum land altogether. What happened when Finley learned of it? But we know, don't we? He told Lily the truth. That he was the true Balstone heir. And then he came back and said the deal was off, didn't he? He decided to claim his birthright as your father's son."

"It wasn't right!" Mrs. Grier snarled. "He took the money. He made the agreement."

"But you didn't hold up your end, did you? You and your son made Finley's goals, his contentment and happiness, impossible. Unreachable. You stole everything that meant anything to him." Kara shook her head. "Do you know, I was so nervous, so anxious for your approval? I let myself slip back into the miserable morass of needing endorsement from someone. And from someone who turned out to be so ... unworthy." She felt incredulous at her own folly. "It's so easy to fall into that trap. It's so incredibly hard to break out, to know your own worth without looking for approbation from others. But that's what Edmund was trying to do. And even though it suited your own needs, you could just not allow him to be happy."

"You don't understand. He was going to take my son's inheritance!"

"No. You don't understand, and I suspect that you never will. Finley merely decided not to allow you to buy his birthright. It was a choice that he never would have made, had you just left him alone to follow his own path." Kara looked down at the woman with pity. "You crow about your family, your bloodline, your superiority. But you pick and choose, don't you? You don't embrace the concepts of true nobility. You don't serve or care for the people who look to you. You know nothing of honor. Of honesty or courage in the face of adversity."

The woman lifted her chin. Her haughty look returned.

Kara gave a surprised huff. "In a way, I should thank you. You've knocked me off the slide of doubting and insecurities I've been skidding along—just by your bad example. I remember who I am now. The woman I'm meant to be. And I do understand how a true lady acts."

She took the last step and leaned down to grip Mrs. Grier's wrist. "And I am willing to throw it all away right here and now, do you hear me? I know three separate ways to break these fragile bones right here. And that is just the start. I will move on up your arm and on to bigger bones. I will happily maim you, Elfred. I will rot in jail beside you *if you do not give me that antidote right this minute.*"

Largray stirred on her lap, but Mrs. Grier was too frightened to notice. "I've already said I don't know about any poison!"

With a sigh, Kara widened her stance, tightened her grip, and braced herself.

"Unfortunately, she's telling the truth."

Startled, Kara looked up. Will Grier was walking out from the dig site. As he passed the sunken perimeter, she saw Niall coming behind him.

"I heard that last part," Niall said, his eyes alight and his tone fervent. "And if we were not already betrothed, I would drop to one knee right here, Kara Levett. I would drag you to the village parson right this moment, in fact, if we did not have pressing business."

His words rushed in, filling the empty places her fears and doubts had left, but Kara had to brush away the warmth they brought. "Grab him up, Niall," she ordered him. "If his mother doesn't have the antidote, then he must. Snatch him up and make him turn it over."

"He doesn't have it, love," Niall said gently.

"Where is it, then?" Kara was feeling quite desperate now. "What is wrong with you?" she demanded of the young man. "Not content with ruining your uncle's life? You had to ruin Lily's too? And now you threaten an innocent child?" A sob very nearly escaped her. "Where is the antidote, then? And the girl?"

"I've made mistakes," Will told her. "But you made me think, ma'am. You reminded me of the Green Knight, and I began to remember who I am, too. Or, at the least, who I'd like to be." He shook his head. "I should not have pursued Lily, but I found her irresistible. I didn't cut my uncle out of the deal for the land, though. That was all Riley." He glared down at his mother and her butler. "But I made my biggest mistake when I told them that Lily knew the truth. That I meant to marry her, no matter what happened with the title. Now we must go after and rescue them both, I'm afraid. The antidote and Lily. We stand a better chance if we work together."

Kara let go of the woman's hand. Tears spilled over. "You were right, then?" she asked Niall, stricken to think that they still had another confrontation ahead of them before they could save Harold. "About the land?"

Niall nodded.

"Is that where they are, then?"

"Yes," Will answered, and he looked… concerned. "They are there with my uncle."

Chapter Twenty

"WHERE IS IT? Let's go," Kara said.

"Hold just a moment," Taggart interjected. Niall was glad to see that Kara had brought him along. "I have to secure these two." He gestured at Mrs. Grier and her butler. "I cannot just head off and leave them the chance to scarper away."

"Stay, then," Kara snapped. Her nerves were stretched thin, Niall could see. "You can catch up."

"We have to go after him," Will added. "He has Lily."

"Just wait a damned minute, will you?" Taggart asked. He was already clipping the two together with a set of wrist cuffs.

"It's my brother who is the real villain here," Mrs. Grier began. "As I tried to tell you—"

"You be quiet," Kara interrupted harshly. She moved away from the woman.

Niall followed. He had taken a firm hand of his emotions and pushed them down. He had to concentrate, to act. But beneath that shield of control, fear raged. He'd been struck with terror when he heard of Harold's symptoms, and worse when he'd realized the cause. He could not let the boy die. His own heart would break and crumble, but when he thought of what it would do to Kara …

He watched her closely, so glad to find that he still had room for pride above the pit of worry. He'd heard Kara berate Mrs. Grier, and he'd heard her find her own confidence again, even as she expressed her bewilderment and anger. Reaching out, he took her hand and pulled her aside. "I nearly burst when I heard you threaten her."

"With mortification?" She ducked her head.

"With pride," he said quietly. "You are a goddess. A lioness. As you said, a true lady is willing to do what it takes to protect those she loves, and those who love her." Hunger stirred in him as he held her. Not the sharp edge of want he'd felt often enough before, but a deep and abiding need. He would never be the same. She'd changed him in a hundred little ways, and he reveled in it. The realization came with the pleasant ache of knowing that she was his, as he was hers. "I don't deserve you," he whispered in her ear. "But I am grateful beyond words that you are mine. I never knew what a great and wondrous thing a true heart's mate could be, but every day you show me what a good woman is—and you make me wish to be a better man."

She leaned against him, and he welcomed her trust. "Thank you," she whispered. His hold tightened. He would do anything for her.

After a moment, she pulled back to look up at him. "I honestly didn't think you could be right," she said. "It's so hard to believe the earl could be behind so much of this evil. He seems so … scholarly. So kindly. So utterly focused on his work."

"That's what makes him so exasperating—and so utterly dangerous," Mrs. Grier called over. "He'll do anything, sacrifice anything or anyone, for the work, and most especially for his reputation. Dunstan didn't give two twigs when Edmund said he meant to claim the title. He doesn't care about who comes after him. He doesn't care for the family name or the estate. There is only one thing he thinks of—becoming famous, world renowned, for his contributions to archeology. He only took any real notice of our troubles when he realized he could use them to ease his. He told me he would eliminate the problem of Edmund, but only if I helped him get rid of the duke."

"All because he wants that parcel of your land?" Kara asked Niall.

He'd told her his suspicions, but she still sounded incredulous.

"He wants what is *on* the land," Niall clarified.

"It's your fault, too," Mrs. Grier said to him. "You made that pretty speech at the unveiling, talking about how Dunstan had inspired an interest in his work, in the field. In the *hunt*, is what he heard. It was the very worst thing you could have said. You already had something he would do anything to possess."

"But I didn't know it," Niall protested.

"It didn't matter." Mrs. Grier looked at him with pity. "You awakened all of his competitive instincts. It was the moment he decided he had to be rid of you."

"I was an ass who acted out of boredom, aimlessness, and selfishness," Will declared. "Who was I to be, if not the Earl of Balstone? My mother acted because she had been furious her entire life that she could not inherit. If *she* could not be the earl, then she *would* be the mother of him. But my uncle? He was mad with envy and thwarted ambition. He'd made the discovery of a lifetime—and then realized it was on *your* land. It was everything he'd always dreamed of. He could not bear the thought of your finding it, claiming it, and reaping all the glory he'd chased his whole life. The glory that should be his."

"Love, hate, envy, or glory. It's always one of those," Taggart said knowingly. He'd found a rope inside the dig site and was knotting it through the cuffs and around the wrists of Mrs. Grier and the butler, who, finally awake, seemed unable to do anything but press his broken arm to his side and whimper.

"He couldn't bear the thought of sharing the glory of the discovery, but he was fine with your selling off the goods from it?" Kara asked, disbelieving.

"He didn't know about that," Will confessed. "He's likely finding out right now. He didn't know I'd found his secret at all." He had the grace to look sheepish. "It's you I should apologize to," he said to Niall. "When Riley connected me with that antiquities dealer, he only wanted me to legitimize the African pieces so that he could get more money for them. But when it worked, I saw my chance. I meant only to sell some of those burial goods so that Lily and I could get away. Far enough away to start anew, make a life together."

His mother made a sound of protest.

"There is more to be had, though," Will told Niall. "More gold. More important pieces."

"We don't care about gold," Kara said. "It's the antidote we want. And Lily, if we are lucky enough to find her still alive. Let's *go*," she insisted.

"She's alive," Will said grimly. "I finally caught up to Largray when he brought Lily to my uncle and my mother out here. My own flesh and blood. They worked together to kill Edmund Finley, and they meant to take Sedwick out, too. Today, Largray dragged Lily before them, and they both looked right through that pretty, lively, funny girl. They didn't see her spirit, her spine, her heart. They saw only an impoverished girl from the docks. A girl without a pedigree, but with too much knowledge about their own misdeeds. And with cold-blooded detachment, they decided that she needed to die."

His mother looked away.

"Largray was going to do it, too, the evil worm." Will shot both his mother and the butler a look full of venom. "Lily has tried to tell me that I needn't follow in their wake. That I could choose my own fate. And she was right. I had to act, to put a stop to it. I'm glad I broke his arm. I hope I broke his nose. I hope they both fester in misery." He glared at his mother. "If you hadn't interfered, then Dunstan would not have been able to get away with Lily." He looked at Kara with anguish in his gaze. "He took her through to the huts. I thought he was going to push her into that sinkhole and kill her the same way they killed Finley. But there's a way out back there, a way to get to the gravesite on Sedwick's land. It must be where he's taken her."

"He knows his plan has backfired. That consequences are catching up to him," Niall said. "He'll be there gathering up any treasures left to take with him. He'll want to use Lily and the antidote to bargain for his escape."

"I don't care. Let him have them. Let him go," Kara said, fervent. "As long as we get Lily and what we need to help Harold."

"I'm not familiar with the route back there," Will said. "I only know the way I found the spot. I'll have to take you back along the path toward the house. There's a branch that leads to the orchard. Past there, we cross over into Sedwick's land and toward the gravesite."

"Let's go," Kara said.

"I'm ready," Taggart called. He'd tied the rope to a post at the perimeter wall on one side, and to the base of Niall's sculpture at the other, leaving the pair suspended between the two points and unable to move far from their current position. "Let's go get him."

They started back along the wooded path. "Listen," Niall said quietly, "Balstone projects a mild image, but he's intelligent. I spent enough time with him to know he's more than a bit wily. Now he's proved himself ruthless. He's had weeks to prepare for this, and he's cornered now. Likely desperate. We must go carefully."

"Tell us what we will find when we get there," Kara told Will.

"It's a ceremonial site, if I had to guess," the young man answered after a moment's thought. "A great mound with an old stone circle in the middle. It's a cist grave. Square, small, and shallow, and located on the west side of the circle. I believe it is a woman's grave. She would have been of very high rank."

Niall watched him in surprise. "You seem to know a good deal about it."

"I did learn what I could, when I was younger. I tried to enter into my uncle's interests. I'd hoped we could grow closer." He frowned. "My own father was … much like my mother. But Dunstan did not encourage my studies."

"It's a weak man who is fearful of competition," Kara said darkly.

"When I realized lately that he was sneaking off to another site, I couldn't follow him directly for fear of being caught. I circled around and came at the place from a different angle. By the time I found it, he'd already dug up one grave, but it appeared empty. Probably looted in the past. But this one, it's something he's been dreaming of. Completely intact. He already set up a pulley system to remove the capstone, but he left her mostly undisturbed. He's likely been making drawings and documentation. The woman was interred in a fetal position, wearing her finest jewels and surrounded by symbols of her status and wealth."

They had reached the orchard, and Will paused to scratch out a map in the dirt. "Here's what it's like. The mound, with tangled woods crowding around the base of it and climbing up at points." He glanced at Kara. "It's how I injured my mare, pushing through there. We'll have to move carefully and quietly, so we don't alert him. The circle in the midst, the empty grave to the south, the lady interred to the west."

"Let's just get close enough to see without being seen and we'll form a strategy," Niall said.

And so they did, moving slowly, taking step by quiet step as they drew near. They gathered in a tight group in a copse at the bottom of the south side of the mound, in an area covered by thickly grown trees and underbrush. The afternoon sun cast long shadows across the clearing. The wind blew in occasional gusts that pushed through from the sea.

"There he is," Niall said on a quiet breath.

Balstone lay stretched out perpendicular to the grave, draped over the stones lining it and reaching inside. Beside him lay a sack, half full of whatever he was pulling from inside. A wooden frame stood over it all, with chain and rope and pulleys hanging from it and a tarp covering it, to keep the site dry. Despite himself, Niall was impressed. It could not have been easy to remove that heavy capstone. It had been left at the bottom of the grave, set at an angle. In the middle of the stone sat a blue bottle.

"It must be the antidote," Kara whispered.

"Lily!" Will's cry was quiet but anguished. The girl had been secured to a column by a chain and her mouth was stuffed with a cloth.

Niall gripped the young man's shoulder. "Patience," he whispered. "Balstone is only expecting you and I to follow him. We have the advantage."

Will drew a breath and nodded. "The empty grave is right ahead where she is sitting. He's covered it with dirt and moss, but I'll wager there is only a tarp or cloth under it. He's set a trap, hoping I'll fall in if I move to free her. The hole is only a few feet deep, but it would alert him, and I could easily break an ankle or a shin."

"There may be other traps around, then. We must all be cautious." Niall considered. "Here's what we'll do. Taggart and Kara will move in behind Balstone to cut off his escape. I'll move over to the other side of the circle, across from him. While I distract him, you creep in, avoiding the hole, and free Lily. Once she's loose, take her and run. I'll subdue the earl."

"He's likely armed," Kara protested.

"I am twice his size," Niall said. "And Taggart can come in from behind him, if I need assistance. You grab the antidote."

She didn't look happy with the idea, but she eyed the blue bottle and nodded.

"Grier, you stay here. The rest of us have fifteen minutes to—quietly!—move into position. You can start to move toward Lily when I have his attention. Try to keep one of the stones between you and him." He grabbed Kara's hand and kissed it, and then they moved off in opposite directions.

Niall moved slowly and carefully. He listened, but heard nothing to betray the others. He got into position, with the stone circle between him and Balstone, and waited for the remaining minutes to pass. At last, he stepped out of the cover of the wood.

The girl noticed him first. Her eyes went wide. Niall placed a finger to his lips and pointed in the direction Will would come from. *Will is coming,* he mouthed silently.

Balstone took longer. The earl was digging with fervor, occasionally exclaiming over something. As he drew nearer, Niall could see he was digging up golden coins and stacking them beside him. Niall crept on, going to the northernmost stone, before he spoke. "Helping yourself, I see."

The earl froze, then casually sat up, sweeping the piles of coins into the sack. "Damn you, in any case, Sedwick," he said calmly. "This is all your fault. Why did you have to be in such a hellfire hurry to open the priory?"

Niall shrugged. "The place needed work. I was eager to get at it. And Balburn's hospitality is notoriously thin. It didn't bother me, but I couldn't have Kara stay there with your sister sniping at her."

"Damned Elfred. She hoards everything, even courtesy."

"What? Blaming me? Blaming your sister? What of you? If only you had found this place sooner, you might have completed your plan and moved it all to your own site."

Balstone only blinked at him.

"I did see the shallow, square pit beyond the midden heap. I didn't understand the significance at first, but now I see what you had in mind."

"Weeks. That was all I needed. Perhaps a month, or a tad longer. I could have moved it all over, piece by piece. But you had to move in, start inspecting everything, hire more and more people. When you wouldn't sell the land right out, I knew it was only a matter of time until you found it. Unless I stopped you."

"You nearly did, with that rock fall."

"Damned fiscal. I'd have got you if he hadn't pushed you out of the way."

"It was your nephew who found this place, in any case."

Balstone sighed. "That was Elfred's doing, I know. She set that dissolute boy of hers to watching Finley, but it must have been me he saw sneaking back here. He helped himself to the best of the treasures, too." Glancing down, he frowned. "Such treachery befouls this ancient lady's memory." He turned to glance behind him. "But he didn't bring you from the dig site after me, did he? I thought he must have followed me in that way. But he circled around and brought you through the orchard?"

Alarmed, Niall hoped Kara and Taggart were listening closely. If Balstone had been expecting them to approach from behind, there might be traps set in that direction, too. He let nothing show, however. He stepped forward, hoping to keep the earl's focus on him.

It didn't work. Balstone scanned the site, then laughed. "I see you, nephew," he called out. He reached into the grave, pulling out a spear, then took a few steps to bring Will fully into his view.

"Stop there." He brandished the weapon, past three feet long, with a wicked, barbed head. "This is Saxon made," he said quite calmly, as if delivering a lecture. "My father bought it after tracing our family lineage back to a Saxon warlord." He hefted the weapon. "Having met Finley, with his height and breadth and strength, I can understand that you might underestimate me, but I did have years of my father's tutelage. He started training me with this and other ancient weapons quite young, as part of my education. I'm quite skilled with it." His tone hardened. "And I will send it right through you, nephew, if you take another step."

Will rose from a crouch. He'd made it nearly halfway to the girl. "I'm taking Lily," he declared.

"And so you may, once I have collected everything and gone," Balstone told him. "You just sit right there. On the ground!" He gestured toward Niall. "You too. Stay where I can see you."

Will took a defiant step closer to Lily.

Balstone moved with clean efficiency, pulling back and sending the spear flying before Niall even registered his intent. A half moment later, Will shouted in pain and horror.

Niall spun around. He shuddered to see the spear had pierced Will's boot and gone right through his foot and into the ground.

"Do not attempt to remove it!" the earl shouted, growing more agitated. "Those barbs were specifically designed to wreak havoc on flesh on the way back out. Just stay right there. Sedwick can free you after I've gone." He pointed at Niall. "Stay there. Or the next blade will pierce your heart."

Niall raised his hands in acknowledgement, and Balstone shifted his attention again to the grave. He bent down toward it, and Niall tensed as he realized Taggart was rising out of his hidden position and had begun to creep forward out of the wood behind him.

Deliberately, Niall turned back to Will, who stood, stoically suffering and whispering apologies to Lily.

"When you free him," Balstone said, distracted, "I'd push the shaft through instead of pulling the spearhead out, or else you run the risk of permanently crippling him."

They both jumped as a loud *boom* sounded.

Balstone turned, and Niall stepped to the middle of the circle for a better view.

"Holy shite," he heard Taggart exclaim. "The wee arse has a cemetery gun!" The constable had been knocked down and to the side. Sitting up, he brushed frantically at a multitude of holes in his trousers. His boots were also afflicted. Niall saw the moment when shock faded and pain set in. "What have ye done, ye gobshite!" he shouted. "Ye've loaded it with rock salt?"

"I feel almost relieved for you, that you were smart enough to bring reinforcements," Balstone said to Niall over his shoulder. Suddenly, there was a blade in his hand, short but deadly sharp.

But Taggart had hiked up a leg. A long shard stuck out of the flesh just above the top of his boot. Hissing in pain, he yanked it out. "That stings like—" He stopped as a great, dark gush of blood welled out of the wound and ran down into his boot. He clapped a hand over it, but blood leaked out between his fingers. "Well, hell."

Balstone, however, was not watching. He raised his head and cast about. "You might as well come out, Miss Levett," he said loudly. "I know you are not the sort to stay at home and let the men handle all the scrapping. Two of your allies are down. Your betrothed will be next if you don't show yourself."

Niall's heart jumped as she stood and stepped up into the high grass on the mound. From one of her hidden pockets, she pulled a fold of clean linen. Reaching Taggart, she knelt down and moved his hand aside to press it against the freely bleeding wound. "Hold it tight and don't let up." She stood and silently faced Balstone.

"I've heard of your pretty little pocket pistol," he said with a smirk. "Take several steps forward and place it on the ground."

When she had complied, he motioned her back, then moved to pick it up and tuck it away. He spent a long moment watching her. "Damn me if you are not a pretty one." She did not reply. Balstone still stared. "I hear you are an artist, too."

Kara nodded. Niall took the opportunity to step to the next tall stone and duck in behind it.

"Can you sketch?" the earl asked.

"I can."

"Come forward and see."

Niall shifted his position so that he could see through a curve in the stone, but was still blocked from the earl's view.

Kara advanced slowly. Balstone pointed down into the grave. "Look at her. She's beautiful, isn't she? She must have been important. Will took the most obvious treasures, but even what is left speaks to her power and prestige. A hoard of coins. Look, can you see the gold circlet around her head? And those jars? They likely contained perfumed oils, grain, wine. They are themselves works of art. We can learn so much even from such simple objects." He sighed in frustration. "She should have been the making of me. I would have handled her with reverence and respect. Moved her so carefully. When I announced my discovery, she and I would both have become known the world over."

"You both still will," she said.

He scowled. "Yes. Listen, I want you to promise to sketch her faithfully, just as you see her now. Look closely. Set it all in your mind. And do the same in each phase as they move forward with the study of her. She deserves as much." He studied her. "Will you do it?"

"I will. I will make a hundred drawings, should you wish it. Every detail. I'll send them out with the story—the story of *your* find—to every journal and paper. *If* you give me what I need to make Harold well."

"Yes. Well. The boy. I never meant for him to be affected."

"No. You merely meant for my betrothed to sicken and die," she said blandly.

"He's strong and healthy. It likely would only have slowed him down for a bit. That's all I really wanted." He glanced toward the spot where Niall had been and realized he was no longer there. With a growl, Balstone snatched Kara by the arm and yanked her close to him.

"I told you to stay put, Sedwick!" his veneer of calm was fading. "Show yourself!" Niall stiffened as he thrust his blade to Kara's throat. "Or find yourself without a fiancée!"

Kara looked perfectly calm, but an angry red flush spread over the earl's face. "Damn you to hell, Sedwick. Must you thwart me at every step? I should cut her throat just as recompense for your consistent annoyance."

Niall knew Kara's background. He knew her training must have included this exact scenario. He suspected she could free herself in a moment, with just the right distraction.

He meant to give it to her. But before he could, another blade appeared, this one at Balstone's throat. A fierce, familiar face appeared behind the earl's.

Gyda.

"Drop it," she snarled.

Balstone didn't hesitate. He slammed his head back into Gyda's face. Her nose *crunched*. Blood flew everywhere. Stunned, she wasn't ready when the earl kicked back, striking her knee and sending her stumbling. Gyda's foot stuck in a chain curled beneath the wooden frame, and she went down.

Niall and Kara acted at the same instant.

He stooped, pulled his knife from his boot, and stepped out from behind the stone with the blade held high and ready to throw. "Let her go, Balstone."

But Kara was already moving. She reached up to grab the earl's wrist. With both hands she forced his arm straight while she cocked one shoulder high and slipped under his arm. Twisting his wrist, she knocked the knife free. Already bent low, she took it up in a flash and stepped away.

When Balstone straightened, he faced them both, each armed with a blade. But he came up with Kara's pistol. He held it steady, fury showing on his face as he leveled it first at Kara, then at Niall.

"Which of you first?" he asked. The gun turned back to Kara. "You, I think."

He meant it.

Niall threw his knife, but even as he did, he knew it was too late. He'd seen the earl's finger tighten on the trigger. He had no time to think, to shout. He just threw himself in front of Kara, just as she'd once done for him.

Pain bloomed in his shoulder, but relief was the primary emotion he felt. She was safe.

Then he landed on the same shoulder, and surely it must have exploded. The agony was swift and overwhelming. Darkness swallowed him.

He wasn't out long. When he awoke, Kara hovered over him. Taggart crowded close behind her. "Balstone?" he croaked.

Kara jerked her head, and he turned to see the earl lying at the edge of the grave. Niall's blade had lodged in his neck and blood leaked down into the shallow pit.

"Taggart?" Niall asked. Kara was pressing down on his shoulder with all of her weight. It hurt like hell.

"Yes?" Taggart limped closer, and Niall saw he had tied his neckcloth around his leg.

"What the hell is a cemetery gun?"

Chapter Twenty-One

NIALL WOKE UP with a start, sitting up in a panic. The motion tweaked his shoulder and sent pain streaking down his arm, but he welcomed it. He'd been dreaming again. Reliving that terrible moment. But Kara was safe.

His gaze automatically went to the bed set up across from his. Balgate had arrived the day after their ordeal, just as a fever had taken hold of Niall. With Harold, Niall, Taggart, and Darrow all in need of care, Kara's physician had turned the ducal bedchamber into a makeshift hospital ward.

Will had been taken into custody, where Niall assumed he was receiving adequate care for his injured foot. Lily had returned to her brother, at least until Will's future was sorted.

Niall looked across the room to check on Harold, but the boy's bed was empty. His stomach dropped a thousand feet. "Harold?" he rasped.

"The boy is fine," Darrow said from his bed. "He's much improved today. Kara has taken him out to the garden to read to him."

Relief flooded Niall, along with a strong desire to join them. Balgate had assured them of the boy's recovery. Turner's description of the boy's symptoms had brought the doctor straight from London. He'd had his suspicions, but the vial they'd taken from the gravesite had confirmed them. "Prussian blue," he'd said. "The poison is a component used in rat poison. The Prussian blue will bind and remove it from his body, but we must be careful of the dosage."

Kara had wept with relief. Niall had very nearly joined her, but he settled for wringing the doctor's hand.

Now, Niall noticed the object Taggart was showing to Darrow. "Is that—"

"The cemetery gun. Yes. I had the constables bring it over for Darrow to examine."

"I've heard of them, but never seen one," the fiscal said, examining the oddly shaped firearm. He swiveled it on its base. "I knew cemetery keepers have used them to deter resurrection men and body thieves, but they were outlawed years ago. It can use multiple tripwires, you say?"

"Yes, but Balstone only needed one," Taggart said, ruefully rubbing his leg. "How are you feeling, Sedwick?"

"Better," Niall said with an exploratory stretch. "And exceedingly glad—"

"*That it wasn't your hammering arm!*" the other two finished for him simultaneously.

Niall rolled his eyes. "Any word on Elfred Grier?" He'd been in and out of nightmare-laced sleep for days and had trouble recalling what was real and what his mind had conjured.

"Yes. She's blaming everything on her brother." Darrow shot him a look. "Easy to do, since you conveniently killed him for her."

"I don't regret it," Niall said. "Did you expect me to? The man was going to shoot Kara. He was nothing but thirst and ambition, with no soul." He glanced around at the table beside his bed and at the other bedsides. "Where is the bell?"

Both of the other men looked sheepish. "Mrs. Pollock marched in here and snatched it up. She said we were driving the maids batty with our demands."

Niall snorted. "Well, I don't need a bell." He drew a deep breath.

"*Turner!*" he bellowed.

Hasty footsteps sounded in the passage. "Your Grace?" The butler's startled expression eased as he entered. "You must be feeling better."

"Indeed. Come and help me up? I want to walk. You can keep an eye on me."

"Dr. Balgate doesn't want you going down the stairs yet. He says you must keep your shoulder as still as possible."

"Fine, then walk with me down the corridor. We have plans to make." Niall gripped Turner's arm and smiled up at him. "Secret plans."

⁂

Several weeks later

"OH, KARA!" KATE Dalwiddie said breathlessly. She was gazing up at the curved, painted wall of the staircase. "Tallenford Priory is every bit as magnificent as I've imagined. And that parlor! You've created something truly beautiful."

"Thank you. It's the only public room I've managed to complete, but I am happy with the result." Kara had had the walls replastered and painted an airy sage green. Creamy ivory curtains and furniture in the French style helped to make it welcoming. "We'll have our tea in there, if you are ready."

They had a lovely time. Mrs. Pollock had outdone herself with the teacakes and sandwiches. Kate was full of gossip about the villagers, some of whom Kara was gradually coming to know.

"We've quite a few visitors about just now. The Sheep's Head is filled to the roof."

"Have they come because of the notoriety and scandal? To see where Finley's murder happened?" Kara asked with distaste.

"Some, no doubt. But there are other attractions." Kate shrugged.

"And, of course, everyone is talking about Elfred Grier. Her trial will start soon."

"Darrow says that she's insisting it was her brother who killed Finley." Kara was not convinced. "But she cannot escape the charge of kidnapping, not with both the victim and her own son testifying against her."

"Did you hear that they've found the banker? Mr. Dunn was brought back from where he was hiding, somewhere along the Devonshire coast. He will speak at the trial as well. That will add a blackmail and bribery charge against her."

"I will be glad when it is all over," Kara said with a sigh.

"Well, you certainly have pleasanter things to occupy you," Kate said. "I hear you have a visitor?"

"Oh, yes. Lord Stayme could not be kept away when he heard Niall had been injured and Harold was ill. I was hoping to introduce you, in fact, but we will have to walk out to the Viewing House. Harold insisted on taking the viscount out there for a picnic today."

"How lovely. A walk will be just the thing after indulging in Mrs. Pollock's pastries."

They set out through the walled garden, where the new gardener's efforts were beginning to show. The path to the Viewing House had also been seen to, smoothed out and mowed, so the walk was very pleasant indeed. The day was warm, the sky clear and the breeze just right. Kara sighed in contentment, turning her face up to the sun, until she realized her friend had fallen behind. "Kate?"

"Coming! Oh, look! What a lovely bunch of Scottish primrose!" Kate turned around, a few of the purple flowers with their yellow centers in hand. "Shall I tuck them into your hair? They look as if they were grown specially to go with the lilac color of your gown." She eyed Kara with approval. "You do look particularly lovely today."

"Thank you. The dress is Niall's favorite. I had another with this sort of crossed front, but the colors were starker. He asked if I could have one done in lighter colors." She smoothed the skirts. "I confess, I do feel a little like springtime in the lilac and green."

Kate smiled. "Then we will complete the look." She placed a few blooms in Kara's coiffure, then stepped back to judge the effect. To Kara's surprise, her friend teared up a little. "You look like you bloomed right here in Scotland." She took Kara's arm. "Come, let's go join the fun."

Eventually, they stepped out of the wood onto the riverside shore. Kara's attention was caught by the spillway across the river. "It looks like someone has blocked the way through the rocks."

"Fishermen, perhaps?"

"You could be right." Kara turned toward the Viewing House, but after a few steps, she stopped short. "Good heavens. There is a *crowd* up there! What on earth are those boys up to?"

Kate stared. "Let's go find out!"

They quickened their pace and climbed the trail onto the cliff. A woman stood in the path, just outside the gazebo.

"Eleanor?" Kara gasped. "What on earth are you doing here?"

"Well, I've come to see you, haven't I, darling?" Her oldest friend kissed her cheek, then stood back to eye her critically. "Yes. You will do very well."

Kara's attention was caught by movement on the river. "What is that?"

A flotilla of lanterns came drifting downstream. Shaped like flowers, they were in colors of purple, cream, and green. They caught up in the wide bend of the river and circled slowly, looking spectacular.

"I believe that was your cook's notion," Eleanor said. "Come inside, then."

She moved into the Viewing House. Kara followed. Stopping inside, she gazed about in puzzled awe. The columns and railings had been draped in greenery and blooms. Music drifted from the other side of the structure. The wide, empty space was very nearly crowded with—

She stopped short.

Faces looked back at her. The faces of her friends and family. "Joseph?" she said faintly as her cousin nodded and waved. "Jenny?" She reached out to touch the hand of the maid from the White Hart. "Emilia? Beth?" The women beamed at her as she was gripped from the other side by—"Josie!" And was that Beryl over in the corner, next to Will, with his bandaged foot extended, and Lily hovering over him?

Kara stopped before a dark-haired woman. "Mrs. Cole?" she said, dumbfounded.

The woman nodded. "His Grace said a promise was a promise."

Kara gazed around. "I don't understand?"

Lord Stayme stepped up to her side and shot her a scornful look. "If you haven't figured it out by now, then you are not as quick as I thought you were, girl." The viscount gestured toward the far edge of the gazebo, where it looked over the view of the river and the rolling hills.

Niall stood there watching her with hopeful solemnity. Beside him stood Harold, stiff in a new suit. Niall's childhood friend, Rob, stood next in line. On Niall's other side, Gyda, resplendent in a split purple gown with trousers of the same hue underneath, beckoned her. Eleanor was just slipping in to stand beside her.

"You didn't!" Kara said to Niall across the room.

"He did," Stayme grumbled. "Now, let's get on with it." He offered his arm, and Kara automatically took it, her mind numb from shock. Her gaze widened as Inspector Wooten from Scotland Yard gave her a little wave from the midst of the crowd. Mr. Arthur Towland, magistrate of the Marylebone police court, stood next to him.

All at once, everyone quieted. A line of people stepped back, leaving a path clear to Niall. The viscount took a step, pulling her with him, but Kara abruptly halted.

Niall looked alarmed, but she merely shot him a cheeky look and bent to whisper in Stayme's ear. The viscount looked surprised, but then oddly pleased. He let her go and stepped into the crowd. He came back in a moment, leading a stunned Turner.

Sighing in relief, Kara took his arm as well as Stayme's.

"Are you sure, miss?" Turner whispered.

Kara shot him a wry smile. "I have always been sure of how much you mean to me, Turner."

The older man blinked rapidly, then straightened.

Kara set her shoulders. "Now then." And with a viscount on one side and her butler on the other, she walked down the aisle to meet her love.

The music changed suddenly, and Kara paused. She looked over to see that the musicians were The Bardic Tradition, the music group made up of members of the Order of Druidic Bards. They were playing the song they'd written just for her.

Tears welled, but she blinked them away before she arrived at Niall's side.

"You scared me," he scolded as the two men gave her over to him.

"You deserved it," she said with a meaningful glance around them.

"You don't mind, do you?" he asked softly. "I couldn't bear the thought of months of planning and waiting. Terrible of me, I know, after making you batter my walls and linger while you waited for me to sort myself out, but I had no wish to delay another moment. I am bonded to you, Kara Levett, mind and body, heart and soul, and I want to shout it out to the world."

"I have wanted nothing more than to wed you." She took his hands. "But I hope you are not harboring the notion that marriage will end our ... misadventures."

Niall laughed, and they both glanced at the unlikely gathering that watched over them. "No. I fear you are right. Our life will be a whirlwind, wild and chaotic. But look at what it has brought us.

Friendship, laughter, a melding of minds, and passion of every kind." He brought her hands to his lips. "The rewards of our love are so very much greater than the risks. So, marry me now? And let's move forward into the tumult together?"

"Yes, please," she whispered, with tears in her eyes.

And so, they did.

About the Author

USA Today Bestselling author Deb Marlowe grew up with her nose in a book. Luckily, she'd read enough romances to recognize the hero she met at a college Halloween party – even though he wore a tuxedo t-shirt instead of breeches and boots. They married, settled in North Carolina and raised two handsome, funny and genuinely intelligent boys.

The author of over twenty-five historical romances, Deb is a Golden Heart Winner, a Rita Finalist and her books have won or been a finalist in the Golden Quill, the Holt Medallion, the Maggie, the Write Touch Reader Awards and the Daphne du Maurier Award.

A proud geek, history buff and story addict, she loves to talk with readers! Find her discussing books, period dramas and her infamous Men in Boots on Facebook, Twitter and Instagram. Watch her making historical recipes in her modern kitchen at Deb Marlowe's Regency Kitchen, a set of completely amateur videos on her website. While there, find out Behind the Book details and interesting Historical Tidbits and enter her monthly contest at deb@debmarlowe.com.

Printed in Great Britain
by Amazon